A GOVERNESS TO PROTECT

Love's Addiction
Book Two

Marie Higgins

Dragonblade Publishing, Inc. is an imprint of Kathryn Le Veque Novels, Inc.
P.O. Box 23
Moreno Valley, CA 92556
ceo@dragonbladepublishing.com

Produced in the United States of America

First Edition March 2023
Print Edition

ARE YOU SIGNED UP FOR DRAGONBLADE'S BLOG?

You'll get the latest news and information on exclusive giveaways, exclusive excerpts, coming releases, sales, free books, cover reveals and more.

Check out our complete list of authors, too!

No spam, no junk. That's a promise!

Sign Up Here

www.dragonbladepublishing.com

Dearest Reader;

Thank you for your support of a small press. At Dragonblade Publishing, we strive to bring you the highest quality Historical Romance from some of the best authors in the business. Without your support, there is no 'us', so we sincerely hope you adore these stories and find some new favorite authors along the way.

Happy Reading!

CEO, Dragonblade Publishing

Additional Dragonblade books by Author Marie Higgins

Love's Addiction Series
A Wallflower to Love (Book 1)
A Governess to Protect (Book 2)

Maxey Langley has been tasked with finding the man who is responsible for killing her employer and stealing the earl's family ring. Against her will, she and another servant search for Lord Wentworth's younger brother Ignatius Burke, who has been estranged from the family. As the Wentworths' governess, what kind of skills does she have to find a murder suspect? None at all.

Nash Burke has lived as an opera singer for the past several years, keeping as far away from his family as possible. But when a beautiful governess comes looking for him and intends to inform the magistrate, charming the governess into thinking he is someone else is the only way to make her leave. Instead, the tables turn on him and she is the one stealing his heart.

PROLOGUE

MAXEY LITTLETON SAT on the couch with her comforting arms wrapped around the Wentworth children, Grace and Joshua. The two- and three-year-old siblings were frightened beyond belief, not because their father had been killed, but from watching their hysterical mother as the police inspector asked her questions.

If Maxey was a child, she would also be scared. The middle-aged lawman continued to prod Lady Wentworth with questions that the poor woman couldn't answer. Several times Maxey wanted to instruct the inspector to leave, but that wasn't her duty. She was to care for the children during this treacherous time.

"Lady Wentworth," the man with the double chins said in an irritating voice as he paced the floor in the parlor. "You must know something. Men like your husband are not likely to be strangled in their bedchambers unless it's one of your staff or…"

The man's voice trailed off, but Maxey immediately knew what he would say next. She held her tongue, not wanting to speak out of turn, especially in front of Lady Wentworth.

"Inspector Freeman," Carolyn said in a tight voice as she rose from the cushioned chair. "I beg you to remove those thoughts from your head. My staff has been very devoted to Lord Wentworth and me. They would *not* think of strangling him. And if you presume to think I had anything to do with this—"

"My lady," the inspector interrupted. "Forgive me, but everyone is a suspect until we figure this out."

The thirty-year-old woman folded her arms, staring at the lawman. "As I have told you before, I was not even in the house, and if you need witnesses to my whereabouts last night, I will get them." She blinked rapidly, but the tears continued to fill her eyes. "I loved my husband dearly."

"Forgive me for upsetting you, my lady, but I need to know where *all* of your servants were last night between midnight and three in the morning."

Carolyn turned her forlorn gaze to Maxey, and her heart nearly shattered to see such anguish on her employer's face. Maxey had been working for the Wentworth family as the governess for fourteen months now, after the death of her own father. She understood grief, and at times, she still mourned her father's passing, wishing he was alive so that she could talk to him and tell him she loved him one last time. Her mother hadn't been in their lives for many years, and for all Maxey knew, the woman was dead too.

Maxey had been home last night. After putting the children down for the night, she'd retired as well. But the children's rooms were on the opposite side of the house as the lord and lady's bedchamber. Maxey knew what servants were supposed to do in the house, but once she went to bed and fell asleep, she couldn't be responsible for everyone's itinerary.

Carolyn expelled a deep breath as her attention moved back to the police inspector. "Please, allow me time to speak to my servants. I assure you, I'll have your information by the end of the day."

He nodded. "If not, you shall expect another visit from me tomorrow."

He walked toward the door, motioning with his hand to the other two men who stood in the room, waiting for him.

Once the men left, Maxey let go of the clinging children and rushed to Carolyn, who threw her arms around Maxey's shoulders and sobbed. Maxey and her employer had become close friends, and she prayed nothing would change that.

She gently rubbed the other woman's back, silently letting Carolyn know she would comfort her in any way. With a death in the family, they would all be in mourning for a year.

Carolyn pulled away and wiped her tears. "Take the children to the nursery to play, and then come back. I have something to speak to you about."

Lady Wentworth hugged her children before Maxey took them by the hand and walked up the stairs toward the nursery. Each child showed signs of fatigue, which accompanied the moment of losing a loved one.

"Miss Maxey?" Joshua asked in a tight voice. "I don't wish to play. I want to sleep."

"Me too," Grace concurred, rubbing her eyes.

"I know how you feel." Instead of taking them to the nursery, Maxey took them to their rooms and tucked them into their beds. She kissed them on the forehead before leaving to meet her employer back inside the parlor.

Carolyn sat in her favorite chair near the hearth, staring at the fire. A tea service was on the table but hadn't been touched by Lady Wentworth. Maxey suspected Carolyn had no desire to eat or drink.

She moved back to the couch and sat, clutching her hands in her lap. She was certain Carolyn would ask her about the servants and their whereabouts. Maxey would be honest, but sadly, since she had fallen asleep, she didn't know what the others were doing between midnight and three o'clock in the morning.

The grandfather clock in the corridor clicked the passing minutes. Maxey didn't want to disturb her employer's thoughts, nor did she want to sit in silence.

She cleared her throat lightly. "My lady, what can I do to help?"

Carolyn brushed away a tear rolling down her cheek and

turned toward Maxey. "I think I know who killed my husband."

The words startled Maxey, and she hitched a breath. Why hadn't Carolyn informed the police inspector when he was here?

"You do?"

Carolyn nodded. "I do suspect one person who was friends with Lord Wentworth."

"Then I should fetch the inspector—"

"Not yet." Carolyn took a deep breath. "Not until I have evidence against him."

"Who is it?"

"I believe it was Lord Wentworth's brother, Ignatius Burke."

Maxey shook her head. She had never met the man, let alone heard about him. Why hadn't Lord and Lady Wentworth mentioned this name before?

"What makes you think it's him?"

Carolyn left the chair and moved toward the hearth, stopping in front as she stared at the flames licking the rock wall. "Ignatius has always envied my husband's title, but he was cast out from the family ten years ago. When William's father died, and he inherited the title and lands, Iggy tried to get William to welcome him back into the family. William refused."

Maxey wanted to ask what had caused the family to disinherit Ignatius Burke, but it wasn't her place.

"Does Mr. Burke hate his older brother enough to kill him?"

Carolyn shrugged and faced Maxey. "I don't know. I hope not, but… Well, there's something else."

"What?"

"William's father's ring is missing from the jewelry box. There is only one person who could have taken it."

"Ignatius Burke?"

Another tear slid from Carolyn's eye as she nodded. "That ring belongs to Joshua now that William is dead."

Maxey stood and walked toward her employer. Her chest tightened from the stress that Carolyn had suffered. "What can I do to help?"

"I need you to find Ignatius Burke for me before the police inspector finds him."

Confusion filled Maxey, and she shook her head. "Why? Just tell Inspector Freeman of your suspicions."

"Because I know the police inspector. He will arrest Iggy without any proof. Although Iggy has been disinherited from his family, William wouldn't want his brother arrested if he were innocent."

"How do you expect me to find the proof?"

"He will have William's ruby ring with the Wentworth crest."

Maxey's stomach churned with indecision. She wanted to help Carolyn, but a police inspector she was not.

"What about the children?" Maxey asked, wringing her hands against her middle. "Who will watch over them while I'm gone?"

"My sister is coming to stay with me for a month to help me adjust. I'll ask her to bring her governess."

"I...don't know. What if I cannot find Ignatius Burke? And what if Inspector Freeman suspects me, since I'm not with the children?"

Carolyn touched Maxey's shoulder. "Let me take care of the inspector. I'll give you all the information I have on my brother-in-law. Also, take Sally with you. She is a devoted maid and will do anything to help find William's killer."

Knowing Sally was coming along eased Maxey's nerves slightly. But she had never done anything like this before.

A thought popped into her head, and she wanted to chuckle but refrained. Her favorite cousin, Alexandria Templeton, loved to write mystery stories. Wouldn't her cousin love to write about this one? If only Maxey knew the story would end happily, but therein lay the issue. She feared this would be very dangerous.

CHAPTER ONE

Lake District, 1857

NOT DARING TO move or make a sound, Maxey Littleton stood in a cluster of trees and watched as a brown, furry rat crept toward her. As the rodent moved closer, she wished she could blend into the tree she had flattened her back against. If that blasted creature came any closer, she feared she would scream. That was not good, especially if her main purpose was to stay hidden.

Her heart pounded faster, loud enough to alert the deaf, she was certain. She breathed as calmly as possible, waiting for the rat's next move. Her mission tonight was not about the threat gradually getting closer. Instead, she needed to concentrate on a different type of rat. To be more precise, this particular rodent was robust and handsome and currently entertained himself at the soirée across the street.

She glared at the vermin on the ground as it took another step her way. Beady eyes fixed upon her with menacing intent. With one quick motion, it jumped and landed on her gown. Hissing, she shook the silk material. The beast flew through the air, landed yards away, then turned and scurried off.

Standing next to Maxey, Sally Jones, the Wentworth maid, erupted into a fit of soft giggles. Maxey elbowed her, scowling.

"Hush your voice," Maxey told her friend. "You would have squealed in horror if the rat had touched you instead."

Sally squared her shoulders and lifted her chin proudly. "Not at all. I'm not afraid of rats and would not have acted like a complete ninny."

Although Maxey had gotten to know the maid better in the last two weeks, and they had become friends, there were times she was tempted to slap the woman's face. It didn't matter if Maxey showed her knowledge with everything she did and said—Sally certainly didn't.

Nevertheless, Maxey would hold her temper and keep her irritated words from spilling forth. She felt they were so close to catching Ignatius Burke, which meant they could both return to their employer.

"The rat is gone, so we must focus on our goal." Maxey peered around the tree where she was hiding and toward the two-story manor across the street to see if they were exposed. Shadows played in the corridor as laughter floated from the opened windows. She waited for the right moment for her and Sally to sneak inside. Ignatius Burke was in there, and Maxey would do everything in her power to speak to him and discover if he had Lord Wentworth's ruby ring.

Sally stepped closer to Maxey and touched her arm. "I just want you to know how brave I think you are."

Brave? Maxey didn't feel brave. She sought justice and would do everything necessary to achieve it. Plus, she was eager to step back into her role as a governess. Playing the inspector was not for her. And she really didn't enjoy being back in the Lake District. There were too many memories of when she was younger before her mother left and her father died. The sooner Maxey could resume her role as governess, the better it was for her sanity.

She smiled at the maid. "You are the one who is brave for agreeing to come with me."

A mischievous grin stretched across Sally's lovely face. "Don't let Lady Wentworth know, but the reason I'm doing this is to take a much-needed holiday from my work. If she ever found out, she would rethink my employment status. I love working for her, but I wouldn't mind a break once in a while."

"I will not tell her. I'm happy that you are enjoying your holiday. However, I cannot wait to get back to those adorable children. I miss my job."

Maxey nodded and looked back toward the manor. A tall man exited from the main doors and stepped to the edge of the wide front steps. He glanced across the lawn. As he walked closer to one of the hanging lamps, his lithe movements caught her attention. From what she could see, he was strikingly handsome. The light sharpened his black hair and emphasized his perfectly chiseled face.

Maxey's breathing grew faster. Finally, the other rat she was waiting for had made an appearance.

She pressed herself against the tree, trying to calm her breathing. When she thought about catching the murder suspect, a grin tugged at her mouth, and determination surged through her. She planned on sneaking into the party and making it so she could speak personally with him. He couldn't know her true identity, and she wouldn't confess to being the Wentworths' governess.

She dared another peek around the tree. Her object of interest scanned the yard again, his hands linked behind him as he gently rocked back and forth on his black boots. After a few moments, he turned and strode back through the opened doors with a movement as smooth as silk. Although she had seen this man in the painting Carolyn showed Maxey of William's family, Ignatius Burke appeared more handsome than the painting, if that were possible.

At that moment, a masked couple raucously stumbled over the first two steps of the manor before meeting the doorman. The masked man, wearing an ostentatious red and orange costume with too many feathers, handed the servant a card. Once the doorman scanned the contents, he motioned for the couple to enter.

Maxey growled and turned to Sally. "The front door is no longer an option."

"Indeed." Sally nodded. "We will need an invitation."

Maxey fisted her black-gloved hands and groaned. How could she enter the party now? She couldn't have come this far only to have her plans fail. She would not give up.

She studied the perimeter of the estate. Large, manicured hedges outlined most of the property. Immediately, she had an idea, and she looked at her companion.

"I know what we will do," Maxey said decisively. "Since we don't have an invitation to get in the front door, we shall try the back way into the soirée instead."

Sally sighed and shook her head, motioning with her head toward the estate. "We cannot possibly do that. Those hedges are too tall to climb, especially in our gowns. And the bushes are so thick. I don't see a way through at all."

Maxey patted the waist of her silver evening gown trimmed with white silk to ensure her mask was still latched to the ribbon around her middle. It was fancier than anything she owned, and it would break her heart to soil Lady Wentworth's gown, even if it was for a good cause. She would do anything to get inside, and Sally would do well to follow her lead if she wanted them to return to their normal positions at the Wentworth estate.

Squaring her shoulders, Maxey met Sally's heated stare. "Make haste, Sally. Idleness is something we can ill afford right now."

Sally gasped. "You're not suggesting—"

"Indeed I am. We may have to squeeze through the hedges."

"Impossible."

Maxey scowled and pushed past her friend. If Sally wasn't serious about assisting, Maxey would do this alone. One way or another, she would make that murder suspect pay for stealing from his own brother, God rest his soul.

If she had to break a few rules just to find justice for Lord

Wentworth, she would do it.

"This is not right, and you well know it," Sally muttered.

"All I know is that we are close to catching our thief, and I'm not going to allow anything to stop me." Maxey lifted Lady Wentworth's gown to her ankles and stepped quickly toward the hedges.

Sally grumbled, "We will get caught and tossed out of the party."

Maxey shook her head. "We will be wearing masks, or have you forgotten? Nobody will know who we are. Not even Ignatius Burke, since he has never met us."

When they reached the hedges, Sally's breaths came out ragged. Perhaps Maxey should slow the pace. But time slipped by too quickly, and shadows grew thicker and deeper as the evening progressed.

Maxey bent low and studied the hedges as she slowly moved, hoping to find a break in the branches for them to enter through. Although maybe Sally wouldn't fit. Maxey glanced over her shoulder and eyed her friend's full figure. They had to try. Going onto the estate this way might be their only chance.

With each step Maxey took, her heartbeat quickened. To-night would be the ideal time to get to know the Wentworths' wayward brother. She even had the perfect topic of conversation: the opera. For seven whole days, she had attended the same performance. How could she not? Ignatius's singing had amazed her and left her breathless. She had tried numerous times to introduce herself to him, but he wasn't receiving visitors.

A light flashed between the hedges and caught her attention. There was a hole where the branches appeared to have been snapped. Her hopes lifted, and she smiled. *Perfect.* It might be a tight fit, but they could squeeze through.

She came to a sudden stop. Sally bumped into her from be-hind and let out a small squeal.

"Shh…" Maxey turned and placed her hand over the maid's mouth. "I found a way to get inside."

Sally's eyes widened. When Maxey pointed to the spot in the greenery, her partner scowled and shook her head. "My large body cannot wedge through that tiny opening," she mumbled against Maxey's palm.

"Yes, you can. We shall both fit." Maxey dropped her hand from Sally's mouth and stepped closer to the hedge. "I'll go first."

Bunching up the skirt of her gown and holding it close to her body, Maxey maneuvered sideways through the bushes. Branches yanked hair from her tight bun and swept dangerously close to her eyes. When she reached the other side of the hedges, relief gushed through her.

Quickly, she brushed her gown and smoothed her hair. Thankfully, deep shadows guarded her entry. Close to the house, a few couples strolled in the moonlight, their throaty giggles rising in the night. The couple seemed more interested in each other than searching the yard for intruders.

Grunts and groans from Sally brought Maxey's attention back to her companion. "For heaven's sake. Be quiet." Maxey held some of the branches back to allow her partner through.

The poor woman had scratches on her face, and more of her hair hung loose than had remained in the knot on the back of her head from this morning. Just as Sally stepped onto the grass, she tripped on a fallen branch and stumbled to her knees.

When she looked up at Maxey from the undignified position, she held in a groan. No doubt Maxey would hear a mouthful soon, but the first order of business was to fix Sally's hair before someone noticed. Hopefully, the mask would hide the scratches on her face.

"Have you completely lost your senses?" Sally muttered as she scooted out of the hedges completely. "Good grief, woman. Will you stop at nothing to find the man?"

Maxey crouched to her companion's level and frowned. "No. I'm here for a purpose, and I will do everything possible to accomplish what I came to do."

Sally folded her arms across her large bosom and huffed.

Ignoring the icy stare, Maxey pulled out her mask from the thick ribbon circling her waist.

"Quickly, get in disguise, Sally. We don't want to appear out of place."

As Sally searched for her mask in the crouched position, a large, very masculine hand appeared in front of Maxey, reaching out to help.

"May I offer assistance?"

"Yes, thank y—"

She sucked in a breath and fell back on her buttocks, staring up at the dark-haired man with a charming smile. Even though shadows played across his face, she would know him anywhere, since she had stared at his magnificent profile while watching him at the opera these past seven days.

The very man she'd sneaked into the party to find, the murder suspect, Ignatius Burke, stood in front of her...offering his hand.

With her pulse beating frantically in her ears, she scrambled for something intelligent to say. Now she must slip into character.

She cleared her throat, preparing the role she had worked on for two weeks of trying to find him. To Ignatius Burke, she would be an aristocrat and not a servant.

"Thank you, kind sir, but I fear my friend and I have lost our—" She scanned the area around her partner, who still sat on the ground staring with wide eyes at Ignatius. Sally's mask lay on the ground.

"Oh there it is, Sally." Maxey cheered as she picked up the mask and handed it to the maid.

"Um...yes." Sally took the mask and settled it over her eyes.

It tilted haphazardly on her face, and Maxey bit her lower lip to hold back an embarrassed groan.

Ignatius chuckled, his deep voice sending ripples of warmth over Maxey. She shifted on the ground, preparing to stand, and he took her hand, helping her up. As she had not yet put on her mask, she decided to introduce herself, since there wasn't anyone around to make proper introductions.

"My name is Miss Maxey Harring, and this is Miss Sally Smithers."

The Wentworth brother bowed. "Good evening, ladies. I am Nash."

"Nash?" Maxey asked warily. Was he the same man she searched for? He looked very similar to the man in the Wentworth painting. She curtsied and smiled. "It's a pleasure to make your acquaintance."

"No, the pleasure is all mine." His smile widened. "Have you been at this party long?"

Maxey shrugged. "Long enough to lose a mask."

He laughed and shook his head. "I admire your quick humor."

Her mind spun with possibilities. Ignatius must have changed his name. After all, if one was a murder suspect, one wouldn't introduce himself as that person.

"You are most kind, Mr...." She arched an eyebrow. "Nash? Just Nash?"

He nodded. "That is my stage name, and we are at a soirée for the opera, are we not?"

"Indeed."

He held out his hand to Sally to help her stand but kept his focus on Maxey. "Will you permit me to escort you and your companion inside for a drink? I'm certain you both are in need of refreshment after such a grueling search for those ever-missing masks."

She chuckled. "Indeed. Those pesky things tend to disappear quite often."

Sally took his hand, stood, and brushed her other hand over her attire to remove the broken twigs and leaves. Maxey swept her hand over her own gown and hair. Hopefully, she looked better than she felt.

So far, things had not gone her way, and it frustrated her. She needed to right the wrong, or else how could she stay in character? Having him know about her identity was not a good thing to do right now.

Nash offered his arm to Maxey. "Shall we?"

"Indeed she shall." She slipped her hand around his elbow, and immediately his body heat radiated into her palm. Delightful shivers danced over her, and she silently cursed her reaction to the attractive man.

After they entered the side door leading into a parlor, a man dressed in servant's clothing greeted them. The man's skin tone looked as if he was in the sun most of his life, like Nash. With a nod from Nash, the manservant moved to the liquor tray and poured drinks. Sounds of the party drifted through a set of double doors on the far wall, but they were the only occupants of the room.

What were the odds that Nash had already consumed his share of alcohol? With the easygoing atmosphere, he would undoubtedly tell Maxey what she needed to know.

Staying in his gentlemanly character, Nash escorted her to the sofa. As she and Sally sat, he moved to his manservant and whispered something in his ear. Maxey wished she could hear what he said, especially why Nash had a gleam in his eyes as he looked her way.

In the light, Nash was more handsome than she could have imagined. With hair slightly longer than it was in the painting, Nash radiated masculinity. His broad shoulders and chest fit comfortably into his pearl-white silk shirt, gold cravat, and vest. Deep blue trousers molded very nicely to his long legs, and his black boots had been elegantly shined to perfection.

From the information Carolyn had given Maxey, Nash was a rogue and left a trail of broken hearts in his wake, which was how they'd found him. He was definitely a notorious scoundrel who could make any woman swoon.

Maxey sighed. Tonight would be difficult because of her silly infatuation with his singing voice and appearance. Try as she might, she could not deny the sudden attraction, but it was a while since she'd found any man this intense and handsome.

As he spoke to his manservant, Nash gazed across the room and again met her eyes. A humorous smile touched his scrumptiously shaped lips while he ran his finger over his black-as-midnight, well-groomed mustache. He whispered something to the servant before crossing the room, coming toward her.

Maxey held herself still, trying to stay in control. His towering frame stopped next to where she sat on the sofa. Deep chocolate eyes held her prisoner.

So far, Nash had proven to be a gentleman, very placid and charming. Still, she was leery that this might not be the right man. A glint sparkled in his soft eyes, promising Maxey his company would be a pure delight. Sadly, she couldn't keep company with him unless he was Ignatius Burke.

He handed a drink to Maxey, one to Sally, and took one for himself. When the manservant left the room, Nash sat on the two-seater chair across from her. He ran his fingers over the stem of the glass, his eyes twinkling as he looked at her, almost as if he held some kind of secret.

She sipped her wine, hoping he didn't suspect she had secrets of her own.

"I must confess," Nash began after a few awkward moments of silence, "I recognize you from the opera."

Maxey nearly choked on her drink. "You do?"

"Indeed. It surprised me to see the same face night after night in the balcony box. Usually, one performance is enough for most people."

Maxey laughed, remembering to uphold her aristocratic character. "I am not like most people, Mr. Nash. If there is something I enjoy, I strive to maintain the pleasure for as long as I can."

"As do I." He smiled. "But please, just call me Nash. As long as I may call you Maxey?"

Her belly fluttered, and she silently scolded his weakness over her. "Of course."

He sipped his wine before lowering the glass. "May I ask you a question?"

"Certainly."

"In all the times I saw you sitting in the balcony box, not once did a man escort you. Do you not have a beau or husband?"

"No, I am not married or have a beau."

His dark brows rose. "But how can that be? Because of your beauty, men should be lined up at your door."

Her face heated as she silently cursed her innocence. Pretending to be an investigator, she should have more experience. Why hadn't Carolyn thought of that before sending Maxey out into the real world? But now, she must learn to control her blush. Although she was very innocent, she didn't want Nash to think she had just come from a convent. She'd had nobody to teach her how to be a woman and flirt with men, so she must make rules up as she went along.

Thankfully, she'd convinced Sally they should take on these roles. After all, Ignatius might not share himself or his feelings with servants.

Ignatius was clever, but Maxey viewed herself as a perfect adversary. Nobody disappeared without leaving some clue behind, and he had taken more than just his brother's ruby ring this time. Ignatius Burke was a ladies' man who stole women's hearts, which made it easier to find his trail.

Maxey smiled. "Men are not lined up at my door, especially when I refuse to encourage them. If a man does not interest me, I let him know immediately." She sipped her drink. "I would rather not waste his time if I can help it."

He relaxed in his chair, crossing one leg over the other. The material stretched indecently across his muscles. It was highly unprofessional to be this attracted to him. It didn't matter if he looked like Greek gods had sculpted him. She must get over this infatuation with him fast. That would be the only way to concentrate on her goal.

She glanced at her companion, whose eyelids drooped. Maxey dared not elbow Sally in the arm and make a scene, but it disappointed Maxey to think the maid could not be more conscientious. True, they hadn't slept much these past two weeks, but now that they had found their man, both of them should be alert.

Maxey tried to give Nash a relaxed smile, even though the soured mood didn't call for it. She would certainly reprimand Sally after this was over.

"Nash? What made you decide to perform in an operetta group?"

"My love of singing leads my heart right now."

"I think you have the most fascinating voice. I also enjoy watching you perform. Your acting abilities are better than I have ever seen. You delve into your character, and your deep emotion captures the audience."

It wasn't difficult to flatter the man, only because she truly felt this way. Nash Burke, the opera singer, was magnificent.

"What a kind thing to say." He smiled and sipped his drink. "I led a boring life before I joined, so when the opportunity presented itself, I climbed aboard and rode off into the sunset."

"Was your family not upset with your decision?"

He shrugged. "They were, but alas, I followed my heart."

"Not many men do that, you know." She took another drink of her wine.

"I'm very much aware, and I have lost some family members because of it. But it was what I had to do."

"How old were you when you left home?" she asked.

"I had not yet reached my eighteenth year."

Her breathing quickened. So far, his life fit well with what Carolyn had told Maxey, since William's younger brother was disinherited when he was eighteen.

"Then who raised you?" Now, if she could just get him to confess his real name…

He hesitated, and she thought a line of anger crossed his brow, but his expression softened again. "My father's brother, but for only a few months. I joined the military not long after I left home." He shrugged. "It seemed the thing to do at the time."

She frowned. "I am truly sorry about your family. I'm certain if they had heard you sing, they would have been very proud of you."

"I thank you, Maxey. I, too, wish they could hear me sing."

The comforting timbre of his voice relaxed her while he talked. So far, their conversation had gone smoothly, and she hadn't experienced that uncomfortable, giddy feeling since she first looked at him. As long as he kept his distance, she would be able to keep from falling apart like a love-struck girl experiencing improper feelings for the first time.

Keep things nice and simple, and everything will go splendidly.

A slight noise caused her to glance at her companion. Sally was slumped in the corner of the sofa, her head lolling back as gentle snores fluttered from her open mouth.

Embarrassment burned Maxey's face. She reached to shake her friend awake, but Nash sprang from his chair, knelt by Maxey's side, and grasped her hands.

"No," he commanded softly. "Let her rest."

Maxey forced down the lump of panic in her throat. What could possibly be wrong with Sally to make her nod off like that?

"But she fell asleep. I must wake her."

He grinned. "I would not count on your companion waking anytime soon." He patted Maxey's hand. "You see, my servant put a small amount of sleeping draught in your companion's drink. She will be out for a few hours."

A gasp tore from Maxey as her heartbeat took on a fierce rhythm. She swallowed the knot of fear lodged in her throat. "Why…why would your servant do something like that?"

"My manservant is very suspicious of overprotective companions." Nash rose and pulled Maxey with him.

She held her breath as her mind scrambled to think of what to do next. Did Nash suspect her treachery already? She thought she had covered her tracks. If so, then why did he drug Sally? His manservant wouldn't have done it without Nash's approval.

Anger poured through her, and she fisted her hands. It was important to remain strong and stay in control. She could not lose her temper now. *Think, Maxey!* But no matter what, she needed to gain his trust and get him to confess.

Nash stepped forward, closed the space between them, and wrapped her in his arms. The room seemed smaller, and her wobbly legs were unsure of their strength.

His improper intentions frightened her to death. If the man was to blame for drugging Sally's drink, what did he have in store for her? And if he was indeed his brother's killer, would she be next?

No matter what, Maxey must do something to gain control over her innocence. She *must* make him believe she knew what she was doing.

CHAPTER TWO

NASH HAD ONE thing on his mind, and it didn't include waking Maxey's companion. Maxey was more beautiful and charming than he'd imagined, and he didn't want to waste a minute of his time or hers. She had told him earlier she informed men when their attentions were not wanted, and so far, she had yet to convey a negative response to him.

That was a good sign.

He stroked her face, which was still warm from embarrassment over her companion's untimely slumber, and trailed his thumb over her bottom lip. Fascinated, he admired its gentle curve, loving the luscious raspberry color that contrasted with her creamy, smooth skin. High cheekbones, a straight nose, and a delicate, curved chin made her face nearly perfect. Her hair was a lovely blondish-brown, almost like wheat. But it was her eyes that held him prisoner. Bluish-gray flecks of sunshine.

Her beauty could hide her charade up to a point. She had a secret, and determination pushed him to find out why she asked so many questions and why she was so innocent. Yet she had come to this party. Invited guests were in *no way* innocent. And many of them were doing not-so-proper things at this very moment.

He wondered why she took such intense interest in him. His manservant had told him about this woman who came to the opera every night and sneaked around backstage while asking questions about Nash. When he saw her and her companion crawling through the hedges, Nash became more curious by the second.

"Maxey, would you accompany me outside for a walk in the gardens?"

As he studied her hesitant expression, her tongue slipped from her mouth and moistened her tempting lips. The urge to kiss her became strong, but he refrained for now. There would be time for that soon. He would see to pleasing her later.

She hooked her arm around his elbow, and he escorted her through the side door onto a small patio that overlooked a flower garden. A thick patch of trees bordered the secluded area, keeping their walk very intimate. As they strolled, her body shivered against him, her breath escaping in uneven spurts. He smiled, loving the power he had over women. He had always thought himself experienced in the art of seduction. Rarely did a woman refuse him. This one would fall as easily, he was certain.

"So, Nash, where will your operetta group travel next?"

Her voice shook, and he tried not to grin. Certainly, he made her nervous. He loved knowing that she was falling fast for his charms.

"Since it is the end of the season, we will take a short break for a few months. I plan to stay in the Lake District during that time." He looked down into her face. "Does that please you?"

One of her perfectly shaped eyebrows rose. "Why would you wonder if it pleases me?"

He chuckled deep in his throat. "Well, I hope it does, because we will have more time to get to know one another. Is that not why you are here with me now?"

Her lips twitched as if she was trying to keep herself from smiling. "I think you are jumping to conclusions."

"Maxey? Are you not interested in me?"

She shrugged. "I have not decided."

The moon gave enough illumination to show him her amazing eyes. He moved in front of her, circling his arms around her slender waist, pulling her body against his. A gasp sprang from her throat, but she obeyed his gentle prompt and rested her hands on his chest.

"You mentioned earlier that life is too short. If I find something I enjoy, I, like you, want to savor the moment. You, my dear Maxey, are one of the pleasures I seek."

"How can that be? You have only known me for a short time."

"But I have sung to you for a whole week. I have memorized every line of your face." He traced his fingertip along the side of her jaw. "And every curve of your delicate figure." He dropped his hand to her shoulder and caressed it. "How can you say I don't know you when, in my mind, I have already touched you? In my dreams, I have kissed your sweet lips and held you tightly as your uncontrolled breath brushed the skin on my neck."

Her breathing grew faster, almost as if she was preparing to run. Oddly enough, she seemed more relaxed in his arms. Seduction was within his grasp.

He lowered his head and swept his lips across her cheek. "And I know you have been thinking of me. Why else would you come every night to see the opera? Why would you look at me the way you do with your fascinating, angelic eyes?"

Her eyes closed, and he nearly cheered aloud. *Almost there.* Brushing his lips across hers, he hesitated, teased, and prolonged the sweet pleasure—if only for a moment. But he couldn't wait any longer. He had to kiss her.

Nash stifled a victorious groan as he settled his mouth over hers. When she turned her face and his lips grazed her skin, he realized his victory was short-lived.

"Oh, you are good." She chuckled low.

He looked into her glowing red face and arched an eyebrow. "Pardon me?"

Her smile widened. "Yes, you are very good indeed."

"I thank you for saying that, but I have not given you enough by which to judge me."

"No, I refer to your attempt at seduction, not your kiss." She withdrew from his embrace and walked to a potted plant near the edge of the patio, glancing over her shoulder. "Your words are perfect, your timing precise, and your teasing kiss could not have been better. But I decide when I will let a man take liberties, and now is not that time."

This beautiful creature amazed him. No other woman was able to see through his charade. He inhaled deeply. What other things could she see in him? Perhaps he should be careful around her. His suspicions made him want her that much more.

Perhaps she was a temptress who came to put a spell over him. That could be the reason he felt this way.

In an attempt to set her at ease and lower her guard, he gave her his best charming smile. "I assume, then, you are an expert at being seduced?"

"No, but I saw through your performance, which is somewhat surprising, given how impressed I have been with your acting ability."

Leaning against the waist-high rock wall separating the patios, he relaxed and folded his arms. "You think I jest?"

"You are not being honest with me."

Her silver evening gown of shimmering silk fitted tightly, enhancing her generous curves. Rows of glittering beads adorned the bodice and long sleeves. The sophisticated ensemble made her eyes sparkle greater than before.

"Maxey, you have placed a spell over me, and I find myself waiting...no, anticipating the very moment I have you in my arms, passionately kissing you."

After the words left his mouth, he was surprised to find they were not lies. This woman affected him differently than most, and it intrigued him. Could it be because he suspected her charade? He had never met a more adventurous and secretive woman.

In the sensually charged silence, her gaze traced his face and traveled down his body briefly before she met his eyes again. The corners of her lips lifted in a mocking grin.

"Why don't I believe you?" she asked.

Fascinated, he kept his smile steady. This woman was brilliant, almost too brilliant. How could she read him so well?

"What is it that you desire, my sweet Maxey?"

"I want to know what you want."

"But I have already declared my intentions."

She shook her head. "But I have refused to believe you."

He pulled away from the rock wall and stepped to her side. "Then how, my sweet temptress, am I supposed to make you accept the truth? What can I do to convince you of my loyalty?" He caressed the side of her face, letting his thumb trace her lips again. "Because I cannot go much longer without wanting to hold you, touch you, and kiss your sensuous mouth."

"Tell me, Nash." She placed her palm on the golden lapel of his vest. "When, during all of your performances, did you get the chance to look at me?" Her eyebrows rose. "In those seven days, the sole time I saw you even glance my way was tonight, and not until the very end."

He lifted her slender fingers away from his chest, slowly pulling off her glove before bringing her fingers to his mouth and brushing light kisses along their tips. "Oh, but I noticed you. How could I not when you made the balcony booth light up like heaven?"

She chuckled. "I believe you have memorized these words and used them numerous times on other women you pursued."

"You insult me." He kissed her palm, letting his mouth linger perhaps a moment longer than he should have.

"And you insult me if you think I'm going to fall into your arms and be swept off my feet." She snatched her hand away. "I am not some simpering female waiting to swoon at any moment."

He studied her with greater interest. No other woman had ever presented such a challenge. Maxey was more intelligent than most women he'd tried to charm, and his pride stung over her refusal. He wasn't certain he appreciated that.

"You are an amazing woman, Maxey, and you have captured my interest." Before pulling back, he sighed heavily. "But tell me what I can do. Since you have no desire to be seduced tonight, there will be no flowery words or tender touches, but I want you to stay a little longer, if that is all right with you."

With a smile, he realized he wanted this. Had he ever sat and talked to a woman? What could he say to a female who actually used her mind? "Promise you will stay?"

"Do I have a choice?"

"Of course, my sweet lady. I will not keep you if you wish to leave."

She hesitated as she glanced inside the opened doors toward Sally. Maxey's expression held a flicker of distrust for a moment, but when she met his eyes and nodded, the lines in her forehead softened.

"I would really like to get to know the real Nash—not the performer, singer, or the seducer, but the man inside this body." She tapped lightly on his chest.

"As you wish. I will watch my suggestive words, and for the remainder of the evening, I will speak about the most boring subject ever…my life."

This time, the smile she gave him brightened her face and put a twinkle in her blue-gray eyes. He could get trapped in her stare if he didn't watch it.

"Thank you," she replied. "Your acceptance has made my night."

Nash knew it would be harder to break this incredible woman, but soon she would make *his* night very memorable.

MAXEY TOOK A deep breath to calm down. She had the upper

hand. At least for now. But it worried her because Nash was good. Almost too good. The sensations her body experienced from his touch were nearly impossible to control. This man knew how to get his way. Thankfully, she knew how to argue.

Her wild cousin, Charlotte—Alexandria's older sister—had educated Maxey with stories of her escapades with men. Charlotte once showed Maxey how to flirt. Charlotte explained how a woman felt when a man touched them. Maxey didn't really want to know—didn't want to be reminded of her mother's past mistakes—but had listened anyway, since it would help her charade with Nash. How else could she pretend to be a woman of experience?

With a practiced smile, she followed him through the wide double doors into the parlor, then to the fireplace. Sally hadn't moved from her slumped position on the couch and looked as though she purposely tried to catch flies with her opened mouth. Maxey frowned. What would possess Nash to have his manservant drug her?

Shrugging away the concern, Maxey reminded herself to be watchful. If she wanted to prove to her employer she could be trusted and find Lord Wentworth's missing ruby ring, she dared not act like a worrisome female.

Nash's sensuous smile took her breath away. Resistance to his charm was almost futile. Already a few times, she had wanted to lose herself in his arms and allow his mouth possession of hers, but she was barely able to control her emotions as it was. Kissing him would complicate matters. It was essential to stay focused on her objective. She couldn't allow passion to rule her feelings.

Not like it had ruled her mother's life.

Maxey vowed she would never become the woman her mother had. Temptation and yearning for a man's touch would not weaken Maxey.

Silently, she said a prayer of thanks that Nash had decided to play things her way for now. Perhaps now she would get some answers.

"Would you like another drink?" he offered.

"Surely you jest. After what your servant did to my companion, I'm skeptical about accepting any more refreshments from you."

When he took the poker and bent to stir the fire, his supple movements stretched the fabric of his clothes, which strained across his muscular frame. He was very well put together, and she couldn't stop the improper thoughts from flooding her mind. She grumbled under her breath and bunched her hands into fists.

He stood and faced her. "So, my sweet, what do you want to know about me?"

Her red face betrayed her stoic act, and she willed herself to gain control. If only she could find a way to control her blush.

"Nash, I find it fascinating you left your family when you were eighteen. Do you mind sharing with me what you did during those years before you left home?"

He led her back to the opposite end of the sofa where Sally slept. Nash patted the cushion next to him. Reluctantly, Maxey sat.

Nash relaxed and crossed one leg over the other knee. "I have a brother and two sisters. My father is titled, and so is my brother, but I will never have the privilege."

"Were you close to your family?"

He shrugged. "I suppose I was when I was young, but when I reached my fifteenth year, my uncle and father quarreled, and at that point, my father became controlling. My uncle hasn't spoken to my father since that time. But I believe my father is the one who drove me away, just as he did my uncle. My uncle owns a large piece of land in Devonshire, which was where I stayed for several months before joining the military."

She arched a brow. This, she hadn't heard. But then, why would Carolyn tell Maxey about William's brother? "In Devonshire? I have a cousin who lives there. I wonder if she knows your uncle."

"If she grew up in Devonshire, then I'm certain she knows or has heard of him."

Maxey didn't dare tell Nash that she was very young when her family lived in Devonshire. Then Father moved them to the Lake District, but once the scandal with her mother spread like wildfire, he moved them to Wales. Maxey wouldn't remember anyone in Devonshire, anyway.

"Is your uncle wealthy?"

Nash shrugged. "It depends on what you consider wealthy. My uncle lives like a king, yet the only wealth he can claim is the land."

"Only the land? No family jewels?" Perhaps she shouldn't have brought it up, but she needed to steer the conversation in that direction.

Nash shook his head. "My father was the older brother, and after their quarrel, my uncle left with nothing that connects him to the title."

Her heartbeat picked up, and she sucked in a breath. It sounded as if Lord Wentworth's brother could indeed be a suspect. If he were given nothing at their parting, it would make sense for him to want to steal the ring with the family crest.

Maybe Nash was the thief and murder suspect after all. If only she knew if he had the ring.

"Were you given anything connecting you to your family before you were cut off?"

"Nothing but the clothes on my back and my horse. I waited for my father to take the horse away from me, but thankfully, he never did. But now, the one thing of importance I care about is my singing voice. To me, that is worth far more than any family jewels."

A groan of defeat that she dared not release hung in her throat. She would not admit failure. No matter what it took, she would get him to confess.

"I agree. I have never heard a man with such a beautiful voice."

He folded his arms and stared at her. "Now, we will talk

about you."

Maxey straightened. "There is not much to tell. My life does not compare to yours. Besides, you haven't answered all my questions."

By the narrowing of his eyes, she received the impression that he didn't want to continue the conversation. She had to do something in order to discover if he was the man she was searching for.

There was no way around it. She had to use her womanly wiles on him, even as unskilled as she was at this. She must remember what her cousin had taught her about charming men. Could she charm him without being affected herself? Her mother was a wanton woman, so maybe the daughter had this talent, also.

After much hesitation, she touched his knee and leaned closer. "Please, Nash, tell me more about your life and estate."

His chest shook with silent laughter. "But I am not a storyteller, Maxey."

"Just for a few minutes longer? Please?" She lowered her eyelashes. "Besides, I cannot return home until my companion awakens."

She pouted, hoping it would work. This gesture always seemed to help other women get the upper hand over a man, or so her cousin had told her.

He laughed out loud this time. "Now who is putting on a performance?"

"I'm just trying to get my way."

He ran his finger and thumb across his mustache, drawing her attention to the gentle curves of his lips. A mouth that might be heaven to kiss.

She silently scolded herself. *Stop it! You must stay strong.*

"I assume you always get your way." His voice lowered.

"Usually."

"Has anyone ever refused you?"

She shrugged. "On rare occasions."

As Nash continued to rub his mustache, his gaze moved over her face and swept down her neck. His close inspection made her squirm. As he ceased toying with his facial hair, he peered into her eyes and smiled.

"I, too, rarely lose, but it seems after meeting you tonight, that is all I have done." Closing the gap between them, he leaned closer and touched her chin. "I have a deal to make with you that will proclaim us both winners this evening."

"And what is that?" Her voice shook, and she prayed she could regain the control she had just lost.

"You give me what I want, and in exchange, I shall give you what you want."

Did he mean what her wayward mind thought? Her face burned, and her throat turned dry. Anticipation rushed through her. Her chance to charm him into submission had finally come. She had to, but she had to remain professional about it and not let the emotions get the best of her.

"What do you have in mind?" she asked in a voice she almost didn't recognize as her own.

Her heart hammered out of control as she tried her best to appear calm.

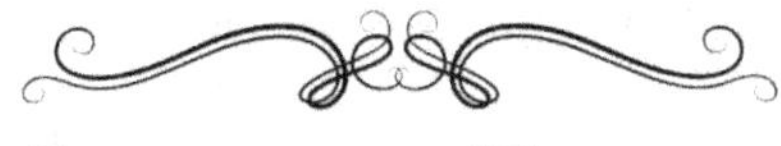

CHAPTER THREE

DESPITE HER BOLD attempt, Nash detected an underlying innocence about Maxey. She couldn't hide her timid nature, no matter how hard she tried. He had been with plenty of experienced women, and Maxey was certainly not in that category. So now he wondered what game she played with him.

He teetered between doubt and amusement, knowing he shouldn't laugh at her expression. He cupped her face, enjoying the way she snuggled against his hand.

"You are very beautiful." He inched her face closer to his. "And it makes me wonder if you use your beauty to get what you want."

"I fear I don't know what you mean."

"I will explain myself." His lips hovered closer to hers. "But first, I want a quick sample."

When his mouth touched hers, a small sigh breezed through her lips, but she didn't pull away. Her shoulders stiffened, yet her lips moved with his. He took his time, savoring her tender flesh, nibbling on her top lip and then the bottom.

This woman tested his strong control and drove him to the limits of his endurance. The newfound feeling exhilarated him—and confused him.

She caressed his neck, and he slanted his head to deepen the kiss. Maxey moaned, and his heart soared with triumph. Finally, she was under his spell.

Her kiss seemed quite inexperienced, which told him his suspicions were correct: she wasn't the type of woman he was used to consorting with. Was it her bold personality that made her so courageous? He would love to find out and perhaps be the one to teach her about passion, but at a different time. He couldn't cross that bridge until he received some answers.

Ending the kiss, he placed a few smaller pecks on her lips before pulling away.

Her eyes opened half-mast as she looked at him. "Is that what you wanted?" she asked, passion still laced in her voice.

He detected a hopeful note and grinned. "Not exactly." He paused for a moment before scowling. "I want to know why you have been following me. Why did you sneak into this party without an invitation? And why is it so important to know personal things about my past?"

Her eyes flew open, and she jumped back as if he was on fire and couldn't stand to be so near.

"Are you accusing me of something, sir?"

"You are not whom you pretend to be, Maxey. I may not know your secret, but what I do know makes me suspicious."

"And what is it that you think you know about me?"

"You are not Maxey Harring, a noblewoman, as you have proclaimed, but Miss Maxey Littleton, a servant."

Her face lost color. Just as he had suspected, she was lying to him. He wasn't the only one playing a charade tonight. Disappointment washed over him. He had hoped he was wrong about her.

She shook her head and, in an apparent attempt to regain her composure, smoothed her palms down her gown as she took a breath.

"Once again, Nash, I think you are talking nonsense. What have I done to make you doubt me?"

He lifted himself off the sofa, strode to the liquor tray, and poured a drink. "Gossip spreads quickly through the operetta."

He faced her with a drink in his hand. "From what I have heard from my informant, it seems a pretty little governess has been asking questions about me, seeking answers even my closest friends from the opera do not know. A few days ago, one of my friends, Peter, discovered something interesting about you, and since then, I have been suspicious of your persistent actions."

After taking a sip of his drink and setting it on the counter, he walked to the sofa and stood in front of her. Bending, he took a lock of her blondish-brown hair and twisted the loose ringlet around his finger tenderly.

Her body stiffened, and her lips narrowed into a thin, taut line. Nash puffed his chest in victory and straightened to full height.

"Now," he said, staring down at her. "Are you going to tell me the truth before I embarrass you further by releasing more information about your falsehood?"

Despite her square shoulders, she wore a strained smile. "Nash, I have no idea what you are talking about."

"Very well. I shall proceed." Nash cleared his throat. "You were born and raised in Devonshire, even though you told me your cousins lived there." She gaped at him, and he chuckled. "I have to admit, you are a good performer, better than most of the women I work with."

She sat still, keeping her mouth pursed.

"Peter followed you one day, and he listened to your conversation with your friend, Sally, while you were sipping tea in a café. Apparently, both of you work for Lord and Lady Wentworth. However, that doesn't tell me why you found me in the Lake District and why you are asking me such personal questions about my life. All I can assume is that my brother sent you to find me, which doesn't make sense, because he doesn't want anything to do with me and has enough money to hire a real investigator."

He knelt beside her, taking her stiff hand in his. "Now, the question running through my head is, why would a governess and a maid want to search for an outcast like me?"

Trailing his finger down her arm, he kept his attention on her face, waiting for a verbal response, but still, she remained quiet. A quiver danced across her skin, but other than that, she was certainly out of character.

"Have I slept with your sister? Perhaps I insulted Sally's brother and he wants to challenge me to a duel. Maybe your mother is in love with me and sent you to track me down." Her lips tipped up at the corners from his humor. "Or maybe my singing is legendary in Wales, and someone you know is a jealous opera singer and accuses me of stealing his part."

Her smile stretched, but she didn't speak.

"Tell me, Maxey. Why are you so curious about me?"

Rolling her eyes, she pushed him back so hard he wobbled on his heels before falling back on his bottom.

She stood and, through narrowed eyes, challenged his stare. "Nash, your imagination has run away, and I fear it has left you addled." She maintained her fake noble decorum. "I assure you, I am who I say."

Legs splayed across the floor, he looked up at her from his humiliating position, trying his best to remain in control of the conversation. "And I assure you, Miss Maxey, that you are not."

"You would believe your servant over a noblewoman?"

He chuckled and scrambled to stand. "I have known my manservant for many years. I befriended him in the military, and he saved my life several times." He paused, reflecting briefly on the past. "I trust Peter with my life, and when he tells me something about a woman who is hunting me, yes, I believe him."

"He must have been misinformed, because what possible reason would I have to pursue you, especially if you think I'm a mere governess?"

He gently massaged her shoulders, letting his hands travel down the length of her arms. When he imprisoned her wrists in a viselike grip, she let out a soft cry.

Enough of her stories! It was time for the truth. Sweet-talking her obviously wasn't working, so he must change tactics.

He pulled her resistant body up against his. "I grow weary of dancing around the subject, Maxey. You have five minutes to confess to me, or I assure you, you will not be happy with the consequences."

She kept her stubborn chin tilted. The way she remained unwavering made him proud, but he would get some answers one way or another.

"I do not appreciate these threats, sir." Her voice trembled.

"It is not a threat. It is a promise." He swept his gaze over her face and rested it on her trembling lips. "I think I shall personally return you to my brother and show him what a failure you have been. If I can conduct better detective work than you, it is obvious that Lord Wentworth should have paid for a professional instead of sending his servants."

Seeing her beautiful mouth set in a grimace, he almost ceased the cruel tongue-lashing. He didn't want to hurt her, but harsh treatment might be the key to unleashing her temper and getting the truth.

He continued his verbal assault. "I feel certain that my brother will be very disappointed in you. I have no idea what information about me you seek, but you seem to have come up empty-handed."

When a look of defeat crossed her features, his stomach twisted. Where was that stubborn streak in her he so admired? Within moments, anger lines appeared around her eyes and lips. She straightened and shoved her hands against him, breaking free from his grasp.

"I'm *not* a failure." She huffed in a flurry of anger. "I've done the job I sought out to do because I've found Lord Wentworth's brother, who also happens to be a murder suspect."

Her words confused him. He sauntered to the liquor tray and poured himself another drink, wishing it was something stronger. What was she talking about? Why would a governess accuse him of being a murder suspect?

"So, you are chasing someone who has killed another person?" he asked in a much calmer tone.

After taking a long swallow, he turned to meet her stare. In the past, he had enjoyed the ability to know what women thought, but Maxey Littleton was certainly proving to be different. He liked that almost too much.

"Yes, and I am to retrieve the piece of jewelry you stole."

Confusion surged to his head stronger than before, creating a dull throbbing in his skull. It was a while since he'd met such a challenging woman.

He arched his eyebrows. "You believe I'm a murderer *and* a thief?"

"Indeed I do. The man I came looking for," she continued, "took his brother's ring with the family crest before strangling him in his sleep." She wagged her finger at him. "Shame on you, Nash. You must know that you're a wanted man now."

A different emotion welled within his chest. Anger and revenge threatened to suffocate him, but he kept his eyes narrowed on her as the words sank in. His chest tightened.

"My brother…is dead?"

"Of course. After strangling a man, do you honestly expect him to live?"

"And you think *I* killed him?"

She nodded. "Is that not what I have said a few times already?"

Bile boiled in his stomach and threatened to come up at any moment. "When did he die?"

"Two weeks ago."

It had been several years since Nash talked to William, and the crushing blow that someone would think he killed his own brother was almost more than he could stand. And that they were also accusing him of stealing the family ring was absurd. He was raised the second son of an earl and knew the importance of lineage and heirlooms. He also knew that when one was disowned from their family, they gave up all rights of receiving anything.

Nash forced himself to laugh even though it was not in humor. "You think I killed my brother and stole his ring? That is the most ridiculous thing I have ever heard."

"Because of the information I've gathered on you," she continued as though he hadn't said anything, "I have no doubt you are Ignatius Burke, even if you use the name Nash."

"Nash is a shortened version of Ignatius."

"Forgive me for not knowing," she answered sternly.

He sought support from the counter behind him and leaned against the edge. Despite his uneasiness, he feigned calmness. "What led you to think I was guilty?"

"I was informed that Ignatius was trying to get back into his brother's good graces but was denied. The day William was found dead, his wife realized the family ring was missing."

"How did you find me?"

"Sally and I followed your trail and asked about a man fitting your description. We asked the older gentry because they would have remembered you before you were cast out of the family." She paused briefly, closing the space between them until she was a foot away. "But it was when we talked to the not-so-proper connections when we found our answers. Do you have any idea how many harlots were willing to talk about you?"

Inexperience showed in her, making him question once again why she and Sally had stepped out of their boundaries and decided to play the part of investigators. Obviously, she believed him to be the culprit, and he doubted he could say anything to persuade her otherwise. Suspicion of her real intent niggled at him. Her acting rivaled his own, and he wasn't certain what to believe. Was she really as innocent as she seemed?

He chuckled. "You think you have all the answers, but I assure you, I didn't kill my brother."

"And I'm just as confident that you have more secrets than you care to admit."

"Just because one has secrets does not make one a criminal."

As she tilted her head, her attention roamed across his face before trailing down his body. A spark of desire flared in her eyes. Without warning, heat stirred within his chest, and he recalled their kiss. Although she infuriated him, he also wanted her back in his arms so that they could continue the passion inside them that needed more examination.

"I don't believe I'm wrong," she replied.

"How will you know? You insist you are right, and I say you are not. We seem to be at an impasse."

"The truth will be determined when I contact the constable to have your personal items checked for the missing family ring."

Worry plucked at Nash's mind, but he maintained his stoic expression and finished his drink. After placing the empty glass on the liquor tray, he studied her face. "What fate will grace this unfortunate criminal?"

"I'm sorry to say, but when we find the ring, you will be arrested, and chances of hanging will be in your future."

"And what if I can prove my innocence?"

She shrugged. "Then you will have many of us fooled."

Nash laughed, covering his growing unease. "Oh, Maxey." He caressed her cheek. "If I were not so enamored with you, I would be insulted."

Her smile softened. "And if I didn't know what a great performer you were, I would believe in your innocence. But I know you are the man responsible for your brother's death, and I plan on contacting the constable first thing in the morning to report your whereabouts. He will then arrest you."

Panic constricted his chest as the walls of deception closed in around him.

MAXEY HAD NEVER been so confident in her life. Although Nash's excellent performing skills were evident, she still sensed deep in her heart that Nash was not an honest man. He had his brother's ring. She could see it in his eyes. Of course, if he had the ring, that meant he killed his brother. Guilt and fear were his present emotions, no matter how hard he tried to mask them.

Perhaps she shouldn't have informed him of her plans, but when he accused her of being a poor investigator, her temper made its debut. Now that she had spouted the truth, how could she keep him from running? She must find a way. Carolyn had faith in Maxey's abilities, and she couldn't let her employer down.

Then again, what if Nash decided not to let her go because she knew too much? She could probably handle this situation, but she needed her partner's help to stay focused on her goal. Nash's sensual nature was too strong, and Maxey had almost succumbed several times already. She prayed Sally would awaken soon.

Dropping his hand, he stepped back, his shoulders as stiff as the muscles in his expression. "Tomorrow? Do you think you'll be able to contact the constable so quickly? I assure you, he is a busy man, and he might not believe your story."

"And why would he doubt me?" She scowled, not liking the way this conversation was headed. "Is it because I'm a woman or because I'm a servant?"

He shrugged. "I suppose he might have time for you because you are a lovely woman, but he will undoubtedly lean toward listening to my story before arresting me because I was raised in an aristocratic family. He is also an admirer of the opera, and goes often. I believe he won't be as quick to judge me as you are. Along with that, I can tell you that Constable Lawrence isn't in the Lake District. I saw him in London three weeks ago. He was visiting family."

Maxey felt she was losing again, and what he'd hinted about her lineage was quite rude. His words hurt more than she'd expected.

She couldn't be certain that Constable Lawrence was in this area, but she must not let Nash see that she had doubts or that he had hurt her. "I'm certain once the constable hears that I have talked to you, he will quickly add you to the top of his suspect list. Killing a lord by strangulation or any form will put one on that list."

Nash's eyes widened as genuine panic crossed his face for the first time tonight. She *was* correct in assuming Nash was the criminal, no matter how much he denied it. Excitement shot through her, and she wanted to jump up and down, clapping her hands. Instead, she would stay composed and not show her feelings.

He took long strides across the carpet as he swiped fingers through his thick black hair. Back and forth, he paced like a caged animal.

He cursed, but his voice trailed off, and she couldn't hear the last part. But her father used to swear, and she knew what Nash had said.

His actions erased all doubt from her mind, placing victory within reach. Yet his temper frightened her. The opera singer she had conversed with for the past hour was nothing like the irate man he had suddenly become. Even when he threatened her before, he hadn't appeared this menacing.

She swallowed a knot of fear and forced herself to stay strong. What other choice did she have? She glanced at her friend, praying Sally would soon regain consciousness and be the supporting partner Maxey expected.

Nash abruptly stopped in front of her. Maxey quickly forgot about Sally and focused on him.

"Who else knows of your suspicions?" he snapped.

"Lady Wentworth, of course." She pointed to Sally. "And the maid."

"Carolyn believes I killed her husband?" He grasped her arms.

She hitched a breath, but not from Nash's closeness this time. The steely look in his deep brown eyes made her shudder. "Yes. Carolyn was the one who suspected you and gave me information about you in order to find you."

Confusion filled his expression. "Of all people, I thought

Carolyn would be the one to believe in me."

Maxey's chest tightened. The hurt from his sister-in-law's betrayal was evident in his eyes and especially in his tight voice. He must have been close to Carolyn at one time. For a moment, Maxey doubted her belief in his guilt. But if he had the ring, it would prove everything.

"Tell me exactly what she said as to why I'm a suspect."

"She says you envied your brother's title and lands. She said that the ruby ring with the family crest was missing. It should go to their son, Joshua, but she thinks you stole it. I wanted her to tell the police inspector instead of having her servants search for you, but she didn't want that. No matter how ill-qualified I am to track down a criminal, Lady Wentworth wanted us to find you. She instructed us to bring you and the ring back to the estate so that she could talk to you before getting the police inspector involved."

His shoulders relaxed briefly, and the grip on her arms lessened. He inhaled deeply before releasing his breath slowly.

"Then perhaps Carolyn wants me to prove to her I didn't steal the ring. That is why she wouldn't inform the police inspector of my whereabouts." He shrugged. "That gives me a little hope."

"Nash," Maxey said calmly, "just come back to the estate with me, and you can tell Lady Wentworth why she shouldn't suspect you. The poor woman is distraught, and I'm sure that having you there to share in her grief will help her considerably."

At this point, she was weary of trying to convince him to come back to the Wentworth estate. Their arguing was going in circles. She just wanted to be done with all this and leave the Lake District forever. Her childhood home wasn't far from here, and she didn't want to think about all the sad memories that place brought. The home was still in her brother's name, and she wondered if he still resided there.

A heavy sigh escaped from between Nash's teeth, and he loosened his hold. Lines in his face relaxed, nearly disappearing.

The drastic changes in his mood confused her. Was this just another one of his exceptional performances from being in the opera? What was he hiding, and could she gain his trust enough to expose his deep, dark secrets?

"Nash. Although I think you're a wonderful singer, your days of glory are going to end. Taking your brother's ring was wrong, and you must be punished."

When a smile touched his tempting mouth, uncertainty overwhelmed her. Why would he appear happy so soon after his little fit of temper?

His hard chest moved noticeably with each deep breath. "Maxey, my sweet, I am sorry to tell you, but you have been misinformed." He shook his head. "I also don't believe Carolyn thinks I'm guilty."

Irritation rose inside her, and she folded her arms. "Nash, this has got to stop. Of course Lady Wentworth thinks you guilty. Why else would she send her servants to find you?"

"Exactly." He nodded. "She sent her servants instead of the police investigator because she doesn't want me arrested. Why would she not want me arrested if she thought I was guilty?"

Maxey bunched her hands into fists. Confusion swam in her head, and she hated doubting her own thoughts.

"Maxey," he continued as he gently stroked her chin, "you think you have captured my brother's killer and thief, but I am not that person. I didn't steal my brother's ring, and I certainly didn't kill him."

Tingles warmed her skin from where his fingers touched, and she pushed aside the feeling. Emotions had no part in getting to the bottom of this case.

"Then why would Lady Wentworth have us find you?" She stared into his intoxicating chocolate eyes, wishing they weren't so dreamy.

"If my suspicions are correct, it is because she wants to know about my uncle."

She arched a brow, finding his excuse as false as his plea of innocence. Did he assume she would believe anything he said? Not this time—and certainly not with this woman! Gullibility was not her weakness any longer.

"Nash, I still don't understand. Did you not tell me your father and uncle quarreled and parted ways? Then, if your uncle holds no claims to the Wentworth estate, why would Lady Wentworth care at all about the man?"

He nodded slowly. "Because Uncle Matthew still wanted Father's title and lands. I believe that Carolyn suspects my uncle of killing my brother instead. Although I lived with Uncle Matthew for only a few months, I did learn one thing: he tells so many lies that I doubt he would know the truth if it slapped him in the face. I also know that since my father and Uncle Matthew parted ways, he has been slowly building up his wealth and power. He is a very influential man in Devonshire."

She wanted to laugh. At the same time, she almost pitied him for making up such a tale and trying to show his uncle in a different light.

"Do you have proof that your uncle killed your brother for the title? Or perhaps you are accusing him of just stealing the family ring."

Nash sighed heavily. "My sweet Maxey. Although you say you are not an investigator, you certainly act like one. Your mind is positioned on the guilty, not the innocent."

"What is that supposed to mean?"

"That means you believe everything you are told to be the truth. You believe that just because Carolyn sent you and Sally to find me, I am my brother's killer. You aren't even allowing any possibility for doubt." Nash folded his arms across his muscular chest.

A dull throb knocked against the inside of her skull as doubt filled her mind again. Hoping to bring a little relief, she massaged the pain. Nash had a point. Then again, what if he came from a family of professional sweet talkers? She hadn't known Lord Wentworth that well, and although he was a like mind, she never saw him trying to charm anyone but his wife.

Nash cupped her chin again, forcing her to meet his warm eyes. "Tell me what I can do to make you believe me."

Like before, his nearness created greater confusion while his gentle touch clouded her mind. "If you're not guilty, then why did you panic when I told you about Constable Lawrence coming to arrest you?"

Nash turned away from her, strode to the fire, and, with the poker, separated the broken logs. "I confess that I had a moment of fear. If Carolyn suspected me, then of course everyone else would. However, now I believe differently."

He returned the poker and moved away from the hearth. Before, whenever Nash's gaze drifted over Maxey, trickles of delight had danced on her skin, but this time he tilted his head and studied her with a judgmental stare that made her want to squirm.

Anger sparked inside her once again. How dare he make her feel this way. He *was* guilty. His actions proved it. She also needed to gain his trust. How else could she convince him to come back to the estate with her?

Slowly, she let the frustration inside her leave her body. "Nash, I have decided I will allow you to prove you are inno-cent."

His dark brows rose. "Indeed?"

Through her lie, she tried to keep a serious expression. She wasn't ready to believe him. Still, too many holes lay uncovered in his story, especially about his uncle. "Yes."

"Show me."

She inhaled sharply. "How am I required to show you? You do not make sense, Nash."

During Nash's silence, Maxey's fierce heartbeat knocked harder with every second that passed. Although she wanted to believe, there was still that matter of proving her worth to Lady Wentworth. With so many doubts lingering in Maxey's head, she had no other choice but to string Nash along. For now, she would pretend to believe his far-fetched story until she held the tangible proof of his guilt. That was when she could contact the police inspector herself.

Nash smoothed his finger over his mustache yet again, drawing her attention to his lips, the very same heavenly pair she had kissed not too long ago. She scolded her wayward thoughts. The heat in the room must be what was melting her brain.

"Come with me to find my uncle," Nash said. "When we find him with my brother's ring, we shall know he killed for the title. After all, the ring proves who is the rightful heir."

She chuckled. "That will not work. Lady Wentworth is expecting me to return to the estate soon."

"Does she know you have found me?"

"Of course not. Before tonight, I had only *suspected* you were Ignatius Burke."

Nash stepped closer, and his masculine, spicy scent enveloped her. He circled her waist with his arms and pulled her to his solid chest.

She rested her hands on the lapels of his gold vest and stared up into his beautiful brown eyes. It was going to be hard to pretend to believe him—to let him touch her in such a personal way and allow his affection. But she had to. How else could he start to have faith in her?

"My sweet Maxey, if you want me to prove my innocence, do this one thing for me. That is all I ask." His expression relaxed as his eyes pleaded with her. "One more day is all I need to prove to you that my uncle is the killer. Not me."

Curse his irresistible, hypnotic eyes. She didn't know how any woman could resist him, because she definitely couldn't when he gazed at her like this. But she must. Determination flowed through her, and she vowed she would be strong. Of course, that meant she couldn't look at him or allow the moment to turn passionate.

Pretending this way would prove to be harder than she had expected.

CHAPTER FOUR

NASH TIGHTENED HIS arms around Maxey, and the quick rhythm of her heart pounded against his chest. When uncertainty flickered in her eyes, he held his breath and waited for her answer. A smile touched her lips, and he breathed a sigh of relief.

He couldn't allow her to take him back to his brother's estate. There was still the chance that Carolyn wouldn't believe him, and Nash wasn't about to go to prison for a murder he did not commit.

"Nash, you're a hard man to resist, and although I'm going against my better judgment, I'll agree to give you one more day."

Relief rushed through him. With her help to prove his uncle's deceitfulness, maybe Nash could bring an end to his sister-in-law's suffering. Not knowing who killed her husband must be the hardest thing she had gone through.

"I thank you, sweet Maxey," he murmured, then lowered his lips to seal the bargain.

She closed her eyes and let her head fall back, allowing his lips to pay homage to hers as he kept the kiss gentle. She slid her hands up his neck and threaded her fingers through the hair at his nape, as if not wanting him to pull away.

Her jasmine scent enclosed him in a flowery haven. Without being able to stop it, he released a soft moan and pulled her closer. Her passion surprised him, but he welcomed the cooperation. In the days ahead, he would need it to prove his innocence.

He broke the kiss and buried his face in the sweet curve of her neck, trying to calm his irregular breathing. "Curse you, woman. You certainly know how to twist emotions inside of me," he whispered against her silky throat.

She drew back from him, her forehead creased. "Why do you say that?"

"Because you are so hard to resist even as much as I try to fight it."

A brilliant smile touched her mouth. "Then we are evenly matched, because I have the same confusing emotions flitting through me."

He chuckled, gathered her close again, and bent his head to kiss her again, but a thundering knock on the door startled him.

"Nash, I must speak to you," his servant said urgently.

Nash placed a quick kiss on Maxey's lips before stepping to the door and opening it.

His servant hurried in and closed the door. "Forgive my intrusion, but several minutes ago, three men presented forged invitations and tried to enter the party."

Unease crept into Nash's heart, tightening his chest. "Are you certain?"

"Yes."

"Did they ask for anyone in particular?"

"They wanted to meet the main performers, and mentioned your name in particular."

"Did anyone at the party recognize them?"

"The few guests remaining in the dining room denied their acquaintance."

"Peter." Nash placed a hand on his friend's shoulder. "What are your suspicions?"

The slender man with blond hair shrugged. "I think they are here to harm you...or worse. They are not gentlemen. They appear as if they were hired to take someone out."

Cursing under his breath, Nash pushed his fingers through his hair. With William dead, Uncle Matthew would come looking for Nash. And once he was dead, Joshua was next. Nash would not let his uncle harm one hair on Joshua's tiny head.

"Where are they now?" Nash asked.

"Out front by the trees."

Nash released a heavy sigh. "I need to leave without drawing attention to myself. But how?"

"We will disguise you."

Nash chuckled, even if humor was not his first emotion. The only clothes he had were the ones on his back. There was nothing to use as a disguise. If they were at the opera house, there would be many outfits to change into.

"Peter, I don't have a costume here." He motioned down his body. "This is all I have."

Frowning, Peter glanced across the room and then stopped on something over Nash's shoulder. He jerked his thumb in that direction. "I have the perfect attire for your escape."

Nash swung around to see what his friend had in mind. The maid remained slumped on the couch with her head tilted back as soft snores fluttered her lips. Nash groaned and shook his head.

"Surely you jest," he mumbled as he and Peter hurried to the couch.

Maxey rushed to stand by his side and clasped his arm. "What is going on?"

"Remember when I told you about my powerful uncle?"

"Yes."

"I do not know how, but it looks as if he has found me. I believe some of his men are outside the house waiting for the right moment to seize me."

She arched a brow. "But why?"

"To make certain that he is the last remaining Burke heir."

Gasping, she lifted a hand to her throat. "Surely you jest."

"Miss," Peter said, "those men appear very dangerous. They are lurking by the front trees as we speak."

Maxey switched her attention from Peter back to Nash. "And you think they came to *kill* you?"

Nash rolled his eyes heavenward as irritation bubbled inside him. "Have you not been listening to one word I said this evening? It does not matter. To go over it again would be a waste of my time." Nash turned to Sally asleep on the couch. "Maxey, help me undress the maid."

"What?" Maxey's voice rose in panic. "If you think I'm going to—"

"Maxey," Nash interrupted, "I am not going to argue with you. But don't fear. I will not take advantage of the poor unconscious woman. I just need to borrow her clothing so I can leave without being noticed. Thankfully, she is tall, and I think I can fit into her dress."

He prayed this disguise would work. He couldn't have his uncle find him now.

"Nash, I must protest this insanity." Maxey leaned over and placed her hand on his fingers while they plucked the buttons of Sally's dress apart. "What if those men enter after you leave and see my friend lying here without her clothes? They will certainly realize something is amiss."

Nash exchanged grins with Peter. When Nash met her stare again, he chuckled. "My dear, sweet woman. Those men will not suspect a thing. Half the women at this function tonight are wearing less than this."

Maxey blinked, and her mouth fell open. It took a few moments before she gasped and lines of anger appeared on her face.

"Nash Burke! Are you suggesting this place is…is…a house of ill repute?"

He wanted to laugh over her innocence, but he refrained. "No, Maxey, but neither is it the social event of the season. You see, the people who came to this party expected to end up in a room sharing a bed with a willing partner for an unforgettable night of pleasure."

"*Oh,*" she shrieked, slapping his arm. "I can't believe I'm in an establishment such as this."

"Must I remind you"—he returned his focus to Sally and yanked down her skirt—"you two snuck into this party without an invitation. I'm certain you would have known what to expect if you were properly invited." He glanced over his shoulder at her. The tightness of her mouth and red face let him know how upset she was. "Are you going to assist me or not?"

He realized the news wasn't to Maxey's liking, but he couldn't dwell upon that now. He would do anything to get out of this party alive, and the more time they wasted arguing, the quicker his uncle's men would find Nash and kill him.

She finally moved beside him and helped undress Sally, leaving the maid in her shift, pantaloons, and stockings. Maxey grabbed the woolen throw off the back of the couch and placed it over the other woman.

Quickly, Nash pulled Sally's clothes over his own. Maxey watched with a blank expression. Once he'd draped the black scarf over his hair, he donned Sally's bonnet, using the black netting to cover his facial hair.

"I think you'll have to shave," Maxey snapped. "Those men outside will have to be blind not to notice your mustache."

Pretending to cough, he covered his mouth. "Not if I do this."

She scowled. "You still don't look very feminine."

Nash arched an eyebrow. "And you think Sally does?" He glanced at his friend, who nodded. In an attempt to hide his lack of womanly assets, Nash gathered Maxey's black lace shawl around his shoulders. "Is this better?"

Maxed folded her arms, scowling. "Yes, but Nash? I have one more question. What will happen to Sally when you leave? I mean, she will need clothing so that we can leave tonight."

Hesitating, he realized he could not leave Maxey here. If he left her alone, she would run to Constable Lawrence. Nash couldn't allow that. Not until he had the proof that showed his uncle was the murderer. "Not to worry, dear Maxey. Peter will see that your friend is returned to your place of lodging."

"And will Peter make certain I return to the inn, as well?"

He grinned. "No."

She gasped. "What an inconsiderate thing to say, *Mr. Burke*."

"Maxey, you won't be leaving with Sally. You are coming with me."

"*What?*" She shook her head quickly. "I am certainly not leaving this party with you."

"You won't be. You will be leaving with someone dressed as your companion." He grabbed her hand and held tightly. "Come. We have no more time to waste."

⇒⟫⟪⟸

SITTING RAMROD STRAIGHT, Maxey folded her arms across her chest, ready to spit nails. Nash was nothing but an inconsiderate fop! How dare he force her to go with him? Why, it was practically kidnapping. And poor Sally. The woman would not be forgiving when she awoke and found Maxey gone. Hopefully the maid would understand that Maxey couldn't do anything about the situation.

Would Lady Wentworth understand? Probably not, since Maxey had inadvertently placed another person in harm's way just to prove she had found Ignatius Burke.

She cringed. Carolyn would definitely never forgive her.

After Nash practically dragged Maxey into the coach, he asked where she was staying, and she wouldn't tell him. There was no way she wanted her reputation ruined by taking him to the inn. Instead, she gave him the address of the house she knew was still vacant and had never hoped to see again.

She blinked back tears. Had she made a mistake by having Nash take her to the place that held nothing but bad memories?

He swung his head and peeked out the back window of the darkened coach. His body jerked with every bumpy movement, and although she sat beside him, she tried not to let her body bump against his. She didn't even want their clothes to touch. How could she get rid of him once they arrived at her house?

She halted her thoughts. Did she really want to get rid of him? No, he remained a suspect. Staying by his side was essential. Carolyn expected Maxey to bring Nash back to the estate, and Maxey feared what would happen to her position as a governess if that didn't occur.

Now she had other worries. What was she going to do with him for the next little while with them sitting so close? She must forget about how his kiss made her weak. Instead, the plan was to remain strong and remember that he was still her suspect.

Nash sank back in the seat and removed the ridiculous bonnet. When his knee bumped Maxey's leg, she scooted toward the wall of the coach without looking at him.

"I want to thank you," he said after much silence, "for not causing a scene when we left."

"What else could I do?" She huffed. "I wanted to kick and scream and cause attention, but I didn't dare."

He scooted closer and slid his arm along the back of the seat, resting it near her shoulders. She threw him a glare.

"Indeed, you could have called for help and drawn attention to yourself. Instead, you walked to the coach with dignity. You made me proud to be your lady's companion."

She swung her head away, hoping he didn't see the grin pulling at the corners of her mouth. Even as much as she despised him right now, his appearance made her chuckle, especially with his comment.

He captured her chin with his fingers, turning her face back to him. "Although you are trying to remain upset with me, I know you are glad you helped."

"No, I'm not," she said gently. "I'm quite put out with you for leaving Sally behind."

He smiled. "Nonetheless, you are happy you helped." His thumb slid across her lower lip. "You want to believe in my innocence. Am I correct?"

She held her breath. He needed to trust her again, which meant she had to put aside her anger. "Yes. I want to believe you."

"Then peek out the window behind us and you will see a rider following."

She turned, parted the curtains on the window, and glanced out. True to Nash's word, a man on horseback followed at a distance.

She swung her head and met his stare. "Peter said there were three men. Where are the other two?"

"They must think I am still back at the house."

"Then why is this one following us?"

"To make certain I did not escape with you. Because I believe these men are being paid well by my uncle, they are not going to take any chances. It is like I said before—my uncle is a cunning man."

She sighed and faced forward as she relaxed against his side. "What is next?" Tilting her head, she raised her gaze to his. "What will happen when we reach my house?"

"I do not know. We shall have to see how long he stays and watches us."

"I pray he gives up easily."

"He will not."

Dropping her focus to the shawl he still wore, she played with the fringe. "I hope Sally doesn't hate me for leaving her."

"She probably will hold a grudge against me, not you."

"You had better be correct. Don't forget, Sally and I work together every day."

"Then yes, she might hate you."

She scowled and slapped his leg. He grabbed hold of her hand, and suddenly, their closeness and the semi-darkened coach created a heady mood. A quick rhythm started in her heart as he stared deeply into her eyes. Dare she allow his touch? She knew how quickly her body melted. However, this might be the way to gain his trust again.

"How long before we reach your house?" His voice came out deep, sensual.

She swallowed the cottony dryness in her throat. "In about ten or fifteen minutes. I live just over the bridge."

"Are you tired?"

"Not really. Are you?" she said, hoping that he would fall asleep soon and leave her with some peace.

"How can sleep lure me to its lair when the beautiful woman sitting beside me is more enticing?"

As always, his words stirred flutters in her chest. "Nash, you're doing it again."

"Doing what?"

"Trying to make me swoon."

"And what is wrong with that? Besides," he continued without waiting for her answer, "what else have we to do for ten minutes?"

Oh, the rotten man! Did he think of nothing else besides passion and desire? "We can talk."

He gently rubbed the side of her face, trailing his fingers down her neck. "We have talked enough tonight. Now it is time for something else."

He dropped his mouth to hers and pecked, encouraging her lips to open, but she remained uncooperative. As much as she wanted to welcome the passion budding inside her, she couldn't. She wouldn't!

He held her face and tilted his mouth over hers, but she still did not open up for him. "Maxey, please."

She kissed him with her closed mouth, then pulled away and moved to the seat across from him. "Nash, I don't want to be seduced."

He let out a sigh, running his fingers through his wavy hair. Silence lasted in the conveyance for a few minutes while his gaze swept over her. His lips were tight, his eyes narrowed.

"Why?" he asked.

She couldn't tell him the real reason. If he knew what kind of mother she had, he would certainly believe his advances were welcomed. "Because I'm not ready."

"Maxey? Have you ever *been* with a man?"

She rolled her eyes. "What an imprudent thing to ask. Of course I've been with a man. Am I not with you now?"

Chuckling, he shook his head. "No, my dear. I mean in the Biblical sense."

She held her breath. What an improper question! How dare he assume… How dare he even mention such a thing? She should scream at him, slap his face—or something. Women didn't go around telling men of their exploits. That was what men did. There was no way she could answer something so personally. Absolutely not!

Yet gaining his trust remained first and foremost on her mind. Curses! Once again, she couldn't be herself around him and needed to act like a different person. She must talk to him about this, no matter how ill-mannered and appalling it was.

CHAPTER FIVE

NASH FOCUSED ON Maxey, waiting for her answer. Inwardly, he prayed she wasn't innocent. He didn't seduce those types of women. Strangely, though, he wanted to make an exception in her case.

From the way her attention dropped to her lap and her unsteady fingers twisted the material of her dress, he sensed her fright of being alone with him. Twin spots of pink highlighted her cheeks courtesy of veiled moonlight filtering through the shadows of the coach's curtained window, indicating her attraction to him—and her innocence.

"What an improper topic of conversation. Of course I'm a… Um, you know… I have never been touched." She lifted her chin in defiance. "And I shall remain that way until I'm married."

He held up his hands in mock surrender. "Fine. I will not touch you again."

After he made the promise, emptiness invaded his chest and arms. He didn't want to release her to another man so soon. Although he should never touch her, something about her kept his interest, and he yearned for more. He had never tried this hard with any other woman. Most females fell easily for his charms, and as he had expected, they only wanted him because of his wealth and fame with the opera. However, Maxey was different, and he liked the challenge.

"Is your wedding day forthcoming?" he asked.

She shook her head. "I have yet to meet the man with whom I would like to share the rest of my life."

"Forgive me for inquiring on such a delicate subject, which is obviously uncomfortable for you to talk about."

"I'm not uncomfortable. We can discuss this if you would like."

He wanted to grin, but kept his expression solemn. *Brave woman.* "Maybe after my uncle is caught and proven guilty, you will be free to start looking for the right man to fill your life?"

"Perhaps."

Silence stretched for another few annoying minutes, driving Nash to distraction. Maxey made it evident with her creased forehead and sulky, pursed lips that conversing with her would do no good.

Obviously, she didn't want his touch. The thought appalled him, but he must allow her to make the first move from this point forward. His ego wasn't used to rejection.

He turned and focused his attention out of the slit through the curtains. The rider was farther back than before, but keeping up with their tracks.

Nash slumped in the corner of the seat and closed his eyes. Why couldn't he tempt the beauty sitting across from him?

Shaking his head, he tried to push her from his mind, but the harder he tried, the more he remembered her softness against his frame as he held her tight, and especially the way her mouth fit perfectly with his. Her sweet taste was like nectar from the gods.

Growling softly, he adjusted himself on the seat. How could he get these images of her to leave his mind? Especially when her jasmine scent lingered in the air, teasing him, tempting his every thought.

He blew out a gust of air and looked at her. Wide, luminous eyes rested upon him, but she quickly turned her head. She couldn't hide the glimpse of interest he detected in her expression. Why did she fight her feelings? It was obvious that she was just as attracted to him as he was to her, so why couldn't she admit it?

In a way, she had confessed her feelings. She had told him that his singing hypnotized her at the opera. Suddenly, an idea rooted in his mind, making him straighten in his seat. Maybe he would change his charming tactics a bit.

He moistened his throat and prepared to sing one of the Italian arias performed in the opera. To begin, he hummed the tune. Maxey slowly turned her head in his direction, her expression guarded, but she remained silent. When he started singing, he kept the volume low, even though he knew their follower would not be able to hear. He detected a hint of question in her wide eyes, but she didn't speak.

As he sang the aria, he held her eyes prisoner. He put all of his feelings into the song as he tried caressing her with each word. His mind drifted to the place where men couldn't hunt him, where he could be free…and where one special woman wanted to love the real Nash Burke. Once again, music soothed his soul.

Soon, her expression softened into a smile, and her body relaxed, eyelids drooping, the lines of her forehead smoothing out. The song came to a low finish. She dabbed the tip of her finger at the corner of her eye, removing a tear.

"What was that song about?" she asked. "I've heard you sing it several times, and although it's very beautiful, I don't understand Italian as much as I would like."

"As you know from the opera, my character is leaving for war. He is promising his true love he will return to renew their relationship. He swears he will marry her upon his return."

"The song is very powerful. When you sing, you project deep emotion." She brushed her fingers against another tear sliding down her face. "Are you really just an excellent performer, or did you have a childhood love to whom you could relate?"

He laughed softly. "In my youth, I had many infatuations, but they meant nothing."

"Then how do you sing with such conviction?"

He moved from his seat and sat next to her, laying his arm across her shoulders again. "My character is not only going to war, but he is leaving his family and home. That is something I have known, and I still feel the heartache. Although it was my choice to leave, I still miss my family, and I have not stopped mourning my parents' deaths."

"Forgive me." She placed her hand on his chest. "I should have realized."

With tender care, he took her hand and kissed her fingertips. "Would you like me to sing you another song?"

Her smile widened. "If you don't mind."

Keeping her hand in his, he began singing. Immediately, moisture collected in her eyes. Because she had been to the opera every day for a week, he was certain she knew this song well. Emotion gathered in his chest, causing it to ache. She remained quiet as he sang, and just as before, he put feeling into his words. Tears trickled down her cheeks, but this time she didn't stop them.

When he finished, his heart swelled. "I take it you remember that song," he whispered.

"That was the last song you sang to your true love before your character died. Every night when I sat in my box seat and watched you sing, I cried at that point." She hiccupped. "I don't think I was the only one. Everyone in the audience was affected."

Using his thumb, he swiped a tear from her skin. "You must have a very passionate nature to cry so easily."

"No, just when I go to sentimental operas."

"I will try not to make you cry ever again."

She smiled. "If you continue to sing to me like that, I fear you will break your promise."

He wanted her more now than before. It wasn't very often he witnessed a woman so affected by his performance, especially one that made him want to curl up like a kitten and have her stroke him with a loving touch.

"I am afraid you have tempted me to break another promise

given to you. Because I want to kiss you so much right now, I ache." He placed a brief kiss on her tender lips. "Seeing you like this has made me insane with wanting. Your presence has controlled my every thought and action, and I feel as if I could sing to you forever."

He kissed her again. This time she welcomed his mouth on hers. He silently cheered with victory, yet the emotion was a different kind of triumph than before. Instead of just seducing her for the thrill of conquering, his feelings ran deeper, and he couldn't explain why. All he knew was that he wanted her to know the real Nash Burke.

As he began to thoroughly enjoy their passionate moment, the coach jerked to a stop, bringing him back to awareness. In silence, he cursed his wandering thoughts. He must be insane to feel this way about a woman who didn't trust him and around whom he had a difficult time trusting himself.

Maxey pulled away and looked out the window. She let out a heavy sigh. "We are home."

ONCE MAXEY STEPPED down from the coach, she looked upon the small cottage she had once considered a haven. For a time, she thought her family was happy here. For a time, she was youthful with happy dreams of the future.

Until her mother ruined everything.

Thankfully, the cottage didn't appear abandoned. It was late in the evening, and knowing her brother's wicked lifestyle, she doubted he was home. She and Nash wouldn't stay for very long, only because she didn't know how to explain him to her brother. Then again, she would be surprised if there was food in cupboards at all, and even if there was, eating it might make them sick.

The darkness made the cottage appear run-down. The once-white paint was now a chipped, dingy gray. The shutters hung off the windows as though a hurricane had passed through this part of town. And the lawn was nothing but weeds.

Pushing back the memories from a life worth forgetting, she hustled straight into her house. The furniture hadn't been replaced since she left, and looked very rickety. A few cobwebs hung in the corners of the walls. She shuddered. Indeed, they would not stay here long. Spiders frightened her. Obviously, her brother didn't know how to clean.

Not caring if Nash was behind her, she hurried into her bedroom and slammed the door. Her face still burned from the heated kiss with Nash, especially how much she had enjoyed being with him and having him sing to her.

A wave of shame washed over her from head to toe. Why had she allowed Nash to kiss her the way he had? His romantic voice had hypnotized her. She would have allowed him to do anything—anything at all.

Good grief, something was wrong with her. She was *not* her mother!

A lamp still sat on her vanity, and she tested it to see if it would light. Within seconds, the room brightened. Frowning, she stared at her reflection in the mirror. She was a fool for coming back to this house.

She glanced at the items still on the vanity and noticed her hairbrush. She picked it up, blew off the dust, and cleaned it as well as possible. Out of anger and frustration, she pulled it through her curls in wild abandonment, cringing at each punishing stroke. Pain she well deserved.

How could she have allowed passion to control her thoughts? As much as she didn't want to be anything like her mother, it seemed that after meeting Nash, she longed for that feeling he inspired inside her that flowed through her faster than she could ever imagine. The mere thought of succumbing to his advances frightened her to death.

She tossed the brush aside and stared at the mess she had

made. Heat still consumed her, and her lips were puffy from Nash's scorching kiss. Why had being in his arms made her feel like a real woman?

Gritting her teeth, she balled her hands. Heaven help her, but she wanted to feel his arms around her again. That would go against everything she had tried to accomplish these past several years. Could she become a strong, independent woman if she allowed a man to control her emotions?

Heavens no!

A loud bang echoed from the main room in the front of the house, as if Nash had hit a wall. Then a curse rent the air. She jumped, hoping he hadn't broken anything.

"Why does he not leave me alone?" Nash snapped from the next room.

Letting out a deep sigh, she pushed her fingers through her mess of tangled hair, trying to make it look halfway decent. She flattened the unruly locks away from her face, but the strands of blondish-brown hair bounced back, giving her appearance an untamed look.

In defeat, she sighed. Too late to repair the damage now. She must talk to him, even looking like she had just awakened from a sleepless night.

Maxey walked out of her bedroom and into the main room. Nash stood in front of the window, peering between the draperies. He hadn't lit the lamps, aiding the ghostly moonlight as the pale streams coming through the windows gave the house an eerie feeling. He had removed Sally's attire and was back to wearing the clothes from earlier. Heavens, he looked incredibly handsome.

"I'm assuming that man is still out there?" she asked.

Nash glanced her way, and by the small light coming from her room, she noticed the moment his angry look changed to one of desire. A breath released from his opened mouth, and an out-of-control rhythm pounded in her chest. His mesmerizing gaze made her want to run and launch straight into his arms.

That, she could never do again.

Could his response be due to her tangled mess of hair? She should have left it alone. Her father had always told her proper ladies kept their hair styled, but brazen women left it unbound. Was she brazen like her mother? Could that be why she had been so difficult and unruly as a young girl? She prayed it wasn't.

Nash moved away from the window and to her side with the grace and elegance of a panther. His eyes never left her face as he drank in her features. He lifted a lock that had fallen over her shoulder and rubbed it between his finger and thumb.

"Nash," she whispered, thinking to stop him, but her voice trailed off as she met his smoldering gaze.

"You are beautiful. I have never seen hair so lovely."

She forced a small laugh. "It's just hair."

"Why did you take it out of the coil?"

"To be honest, I usually don't style it as grand as I did tonight. If you remember correctly, I was playing a role."

He arched an eyebrow. "Am I now looking at the real Maxey Littleton?"

"No. I'm usually not adorned in such a fancy gown. My tastes are toward a more plain and modest attire, befitting my role as a governess."

"Then change." His eyes slowly moved over her. "I want to see the real you."

Her breathing quickened. The idea tempted her, but she couldn't do it. "No, Nash. We cannot stay here long. As you have noticed, my brother hasn't taken care of the place since I left."

"Sadly, we cannot leave." His face hardened as he glanced toward the window. "My pursuer is outside watching the house."

"Do you truly believe your uncle sent him to kill you?" she asked, still not certain if Nash was telling her the truth.

"If he's not here to kill me, then it must be your beauty he is infatuated with." He winked.

Her heart skipped a beat. "You must stop teasing me like that. I am not pretty at all."

"Then why does your beauty take my breath away?"

Feeling suddenly uncomfortable with his compliment, she walked past him and into the kitchen. Changing the subject was needed at this moment. "I wonder if there is anything to eat."

"If you have tea, that will be wonderful."

Maxey nodded. "But I would have to fetch some water from the well out back, and we would have to fire up the stove or start a fire in the hearth."

"If you want to start a fire in the stove," Nash said, "I'll sneak out back to the well. My clothes are darker than yours, and the man watching the house won't notice me."

Her poor nerves were already shattered, and as Nash crept out back to fetch the water, Maxey's hands trembled while she stoked fire into the stove. She honestly didn't know if meeting Nash Burke was the worst thing in her life...or the best. She wished her emotions were not so scattered.

Soon, the back door to the kitchen opened, and Nash hurried inside, carrying a bucket of water. He placed the bucket on the counter next to her.

"Did he see you?" she asked.

"No. I was very quiet, and I stayed in the shadows."

"Thankfully, the trees in the back give us plenty of shade."

"Indeed." He turned and glanced around the room. "Where are your dishes?"

She pointed to one of the cabinets. "If we have any left, they would be in there."

As she heated the water, Nash searched for two cups. To her surprise, he found two that were chipped, but they would still function as teacups.

At the stove, she prepared the drinks in the dark—just the moon shining through the curtains gave her light. Footsteps from the passionate man in her house clicked on the wooden floor, but she refused to turn. When the soft noise ceased, his masculine scent settled around her. Heated chills trickled over her skin.

Hot breath fanned the side of her neck, and she closed her

eyes to fight for control, but her soul weakened. He had a strange power over her. She was sorely tempted to stop fighting and relax against his rugged frame.

He touched her hips and slid his hands around her waist, pulling her against him. Nash dropped his face to her neck, and she allowed his lips to brush against her flesh, where he blessed the area with feathery kisses. Goosebumps trickled over her, and she gritted her teeth to keep from sighing heavily.

"I don't know what you have done to me, Maxey, but I cannot keep myself away from you, despite my promise." He kissed the gentle curve of her neck. "I have tried not to touch you, but you are irresistible."

She placed her hands over his to peel them away, but once she covered them, she found herself holding on to him instead. There was no way she could let him go now. "You must be completely foxed, Nash. I haven't done anything to warrant your attention."

"Yes, I am certainly intoxicated. What other explanation could there be? You have drugged me senseless, and I'm in your power." He buried his face deeper in her neck and took another breath. "You smell heavenly. I can imagine walking on clouds with you."

"Nash," she sighed when no other words came to mind.

"I want you, Maxey. Heaven help me, but I want you desperately."

He kissed her neck again, and she relaxed against him, resting the back of her head on his shoulder, allowing his experienced lips to partake of her skin. His gentle kisses touched the place between her ear and shoulder, and chills multiplied over her body.

Moving to her ear, he whispered kisses until suckling gently on the lobe, causing more havoc to her system. She turned her head to break the contact but instead found his seeking mouth.

Although their position felt awkward, she wouldn't move out of his arms for anything. The way he held and kissed her made her body want to remain there forever.

Just as her mind resolved to allow him to seduce her, someone banged at the front door. The sound startled her back to reality. Panicked, she jumped and turned in his arms, clutching his shirt.

"Nash? Who could that be?" she whispered.

He shook his head. "It is the devil himself!"

Maxey's heartbeat took on a different rhythm as panic filled her. If Nash's fear was correct, and this unknown person worked for his uncle, they were going to die.

CHAPTER SIX

A TOMBLIKE SILENCE hung thick in the air. Nash didn't dare breathe, yet his chest continued to heave from the passionate kiss he'd shared with Maxey. He had forgotten about the rider who followed them tonight, and Nash suspected his uncle's man was the person at the door. Who else would venture into the late-evening hour?

"It's the man who works for my uncle," he whispered.

"He wouldn't come to the door, especially if the lights are out." She glanced up at him. "Would he?"

"The lamp in your room is still on, and I'm certain he could see that, along with the smoke from the stove's chimney. If my uncle sent him, he will not rest until he has finished the assignment."

Maxey shivered against him. He tightened her in his embrace. The poor woman was frightened out of her wits.

All because of him.

The person at the door pounded again. Maxey gasped and clutched his hands. "What should we do?"

"You must see who is here." Keeping her hands in his, he walked toward the door.

"Nash, don't leave me."

"Do not worry. I shall not let him harm you."

Before seeing to her visitor, Maxey lit the lamp in the hallway, smoothed her trembling hands down her dress, and walked to the door. She reached for the door handle, but before she grasped the brass knob, the rude intruder knocked again, making her jump higher than before.

Her hand flew up to her throat. "Who…is it?"

"I am looking for Miss Littleton."

The stranger's voice was too confident, and Nash silently cursed. Maxey swung her head toward him, pleading with wide eyes.

He nodded. "I am here. Do not worry," he whispered. Strength appeared in her eyes and gave him hope that she could handle the situation.

"I'm Miss Littleton," she called back, her voice much stronger now.

"May I speak with you?"

"Who are you?"

"I am a friend of Mr. Ignatius Burke."

"Then you'll forgive me if I don't let you in. It's very late, and I'm not properly chaperoned."

"Where is your companion? I saw her come home with you."

She glanced at Nash again. His breath caught in his throat. Why hadn't he thought of that?

Maxey pulled her shoulders back straighter and lifted her chin. "She has taken to her room with a headache and is asleep, so please return tomorrow, and we shall speak in the light of day."

Nash grinned. He had to commend her for her quick wit.

Hostile stillness lasted for only a few moments. "Please, Miss Littleton," the voice started again. "I have come a long way to talk to you. It is most important. At least open the door so I may speak with you face to face. I need not enter."

She looked at Nash again. He released a soft growl as he massaged his temple. He didn't want her to allow the man inside. But Nash didn't want the stranger to become suspicious, either. There was no other way. Maxey must open the door.

"Do as he wishes, but don't let him inside," Nash whispered.

"Turn down the lamp. I will go around front and grab him from behind."

Turning down the lamp, she shook her head, but he ignored her protest. He couldn't stand to see her wide eyes begging in that manner. His twisting heart couldn't take it. After giving her a wink, he turned and hurried toward the back door.

"I can speak to you for a moment," she called out as she slowly unlocked the door.

Quietly, Nash opened the back door and crept outside. The moon hung high in the sky, lighting his way around the house perfectly. Shadows danced everywhere as the wind rustled the trees.

Swift and sure, he took cautious steps, trying his best not to make any noise. The voices had disappeared, and he hoped Maxey could handle the stranger without problems. If that man laid one finger on her, Nash would be tempted to snap the intruder's neck with his bare hands.

Once he turned the corner of the cottage, the stranger's voice rang through the night air. Nash stopped and flattened himself against the wall. The small, pudgy stranger doffed his hat, and his bald head shone in the moonlight. Within a few hours, the sun would peek over the horizon and turn the man's head a pinkish color.

"I am sorry to upset you, Miss Littleton, but it was most important I see you now."

"You still have not told me your name."

"My deepest apologies. My name is Mr. Eduardo Gleason. I work for Mr. Burke, Ignatius's uncle."

She nodded. "I have never met those men, so what is of such great importance that you must disturb a lady at this late hour?"

Nash felt relieved. Maxey held her own with the stranger. He knew firsthand how stubborn she could be even through her fear.

"I have reason to believe that Ignatius is the opera singer, and I know you were at the party for the opera tonight."

She cocked her brow. "It seems you know more than I do,

Mr. Gleason. Although my companion and I were at the party, I never met anyone by the name of Ignatius Burke. So it seems your visit here was all for naught."

He nodded. "I understand, Miss Littleton. However, my search has led me to believe that Ignatius goes by the name Nash."

She huffed. "Suffice to say, your search led you to the wrong man."

"So, Ignatius Burke is not the opera singer?"

"If he is, I never met him tonight."

"Are you certain the performer is not lying, Miss Littleton? Perhaps we should let his uncle know so he can look at him."

"If you think it's necessary, then do what you wish. However, the man I visited with this evening at the party was not the man you are after. So please, be on your way. It's very late, and having you on my doorstep is improper. I would hate for you to waste more of Mr. Matthew Burke's precious time on someone who doesn't know his nephew."

In a flash, the bulky stranger scowled and stiffened. "How did you know my employer's full name? I did not tell you."

Panic flowed through Nash, but he kept still and waited. If that man touched her even one time…

"I'm certain you did tell me," she answered with a quiver in her voice. "How else would I know?"

"No, Miss Littleton. I don't give out my employer's first name."

"Then how would I know it?"

He lunged forward and grabbed her arm. "Because I think you have been talking to his nephew, Ignatius."

The moment she cried out, Nash sprang into action. He tripped over a bush but righted himself before sprinting toward the man standing on the porch.

"Please, sir," she begged, "you're hurting me."

"Tell me where I can find Ignatius Burke," he demanded.

"I…don't know."

Gleason raised his arm to hit her, and she flinched. Nash grabbed the man by the shoulders before whipping him around. When Gleason's gaze met Nash, he gaped. Nash didn't give him much time to recover from surprise before plowing his fist into the stranger's face, hitting his nose dead center. A sickening crunch echoed through the night before blood poured from the wounded man's nose, causing him to crumple to the ground in a motionless heap.

"Is…he dead?" Maxey whispered shakily.

Nash knelt beside Gleason and touched the side of his neck to feel for a pulse. A slight beat pounded against Nash's finger. "He's alive."

She sobbed and quickly covered her mouth. Nash stepped toward her and took her trembling hands in his, giving them a gentle squeeze. "Are you all right?"

"I am now," she answered breathlessly.

She moved closer, and he wrapped his arms around her waist, holding her loosely. His shoulder braced her head as she took deep breaths.

"What will we do if he awakens?" she asked.

"My first thought is to find the local constable, but since I know he is out of town, that attempt will be pointless."

Her body quaked, and he rubbed her back and arms. Several silent minutes later, she relaxed and lifted her head to look at him.

"I know what we can do," she said. "We'll put this man in the wagon out back, and you can drive him to an empty field—or perhaps lay him by a busy road, and then someone will spot him."

Nash arched a brow. "I suppose that is the best option right now. Not to worry, my sweet Maxey. I will take care of him, and then I will leave you alone."

After he said the words, pain sucked the breath from his chest. Although he really didn't want to leave, staying with her was not safe, either. The longer he remained by her side, the more danger he put her in.

She narrowed her eyes. "What do you mean you will leave me alone?"

"I have dragged you into my problems, which is not right. You do not need to be on the run as I am."

"But Nash, I'm the one who came looking for you."

He smiled and caressed her chin. "Indeed you did. However, this situation is more dangerous than we have realized, and I will not imperil you any longer." He kissed her forehead and reluctantly stepped away. "Go into the house and lock the doors. I will find someplace to leave him."

She glanced into the house, then back at him as if undecided. Her forehead creased as she nibbled on her bottom lip. "Will you return and...say goodbye?"

He nodded. "I promise. Now go."

When she stepped into the house and shut the door, the ache in his chest grew. He would walk out of her life soon. Although he didn't know her that well, the few hours they'd spent together were most entertaining. Would he ever see her again? Perhaps if his uncle weren't trying to kill him, Nash and Maxey could get to know each other more intimately. That woman had so much passion, and it was hard to walk away.

Unfortunately, that was what he must do.

He heaved a sigh and leaned his head against the door. Too many things to think about, but he had made the correct decision, no matter how much his heart argued.

Nash had killed many men in his life, but only for his country and amid battle. Never in cold blood. He would have killed tonight just to protect Maxey. If Gleason had been more forceful with her, Nash would have strangled him without any qualms.

After wrapping the unconscious man in one of Maxey's horse blankets, Nash placed him in a rickety wagon and drove to the next town. He carefully laid Gleason in the tall weeds beside the road. Thankfully, guilt didn't nag on Nash's conscience until he thought about Maxey.

He shouldn't have told her the truth from the very beginning.

However, that wouldn't change her distrust for him. She still believed he killed his brother. No matter what, he needed to prove his innocence.

Bringing her with him probably wasn't the wisest choice, but he hadn't wanted this night to end. And now he must leave her, but the clenching pain in his chest and throat told him how difficult it would be. When had she become so important to him? Or was it that he had high hopes she might be the woman who would finally get to know the real Nash—the man who was raised in a noble family and was the second son to an earl?

As he drove the wagon back to Maxey's house, he cursed fate. This evening had been utter chaos since he met the very beautiful and enchanting woman, yet his life had never been more exciting and challenging. But he had inadvertently placed her in harm's way. For that, he would never forgive himself.

Somewhere out there, his uncle still searched for him, and if Uncle Matthew discovered what Maxey knew and where she lived—and Nash was certain this would happen—Matthew wouldn't be as patient as his henchman. Nash could not allow his uncle or his men to harm her in any way.

Growling in frustration, Nash stretched the kinks out of his neck and rolled his shoulders in an attempt to alleviate the tenseness. Although he didn't want Maxey hurt, leaving her alone to deal with his uncle was out of the question. Maxey didn't deserve a life on the run, but if his uncle ever found her…

Nash shuddered. Indeed, that would not do! He must protect her at all costs. Until Uncle Matthew was caught and imprisoned, Nash and Maxey were not safe.

To protect the woman who had become so important to him, Nash must bring her with him.

The proof of Uncle Matthew's crime would come out once they found the ring. That man had more reason to kill William than Nash did. Power and money were all that Matthew Burke cared about, and now he was after the Wentworth title.

With the decision firmly rooted in his mind, Nash lodged the wagon in Maxey's barn and stalled the old horse. She might not agree with his plans, but he would force her if necessary for her own good. His heart skipped with anticipation. He wouldn't be saying goodbye to her after all.

He must convince her that this was the right way for both of them.

Not only would he be protecting her, but once the true story came out, perhaps Carolyn would welcome him back into the Wentworth family. Nash missed his niece and nephew and wanted to get to know them as well.

As he approached the house, the light from the kitchen window drew his attention. Maxey sat at the table, the parted curtains doing very little to hide her from view. She stared at the teacup in front of her. The lamp burned high, illuminating her profile and making her more beautiful than he could ever imagine. Her long hair waved down her back and shoulders, and she wore a full-sleeve white wrap over her nightdress.

He groaned. Her attire was not good at all. No matter how his body tried to convince him otherwise, he had to control his attraction to her. Restraint was the key to their successful journey. He had to keep his wits about him to defeat Matthew.

Instead of tapping on the window and scaring her half to death, he moved to the front door and knocked. "Maxey? It is Nash."

Within seconds, she opened the door and let him in. "How did everything go?"

He closed the door and locked it. "Nobody spotted me. The man is resting near the road as we speak. Somebody will come across him soon."

She frowned. "Oh, Nash. I'm so sorry I got you into this muddle."

Unshed tears swam in her big eyes. He cupped her chin. "It is not your fault."

"How can you say that? If I hadn't tried to find you, your uncle would not be after you, and that man on his payroll would be conscious—with a whole nose instead of a broken one."

Nash gathered her in his arms. "Men like that do not deserve your sympathy. Men like Matthew Burke make other lives miserable for their own pleasure. If I had not harmed him now, I would have hurt him in the near future to protect myself from being the victim."

She nodded. "I know. I just feel so terrible."

"As do I, but Maxey, he attacked you. All that passed through my head at that moment was to stop him." He stroked her cheek. "Do not worry about it any longer. I have come up with a way to stop my uncle."

Her eyes widened. "How?"

"I'm certain he would have kept William's family ring at his grand estate."

"In Devonshire?"

"Yes, in Devonshire."

"That is quite a journey by land."

"Indeed it is, which is why I need to obtain passage by ship."

Maxey frowned. "When will you leave?"

"I'm hoping I can set sail by tomorrow evening."

Her body stiffened. "Why so quickly?"

"Because I want my uncle stopped immediately. This will all be solved once I find the ring he took from William that claims the Wentworth title and lands."

Her expression wavered before her gaze rested on his chest. "Will you come back and see me when it's over?"

His heart soared, and he wanted to smother her with kisses. It thrilled him that she cared.

"No, my sweet Maxey." He paused, waiting for her reaction, but when her lips had a slight tremble, he couldn't take any more. He kissed her forehead. "I will not come back to see you because you will be with me."

Her head snapped up. "Pardon me? What did you just say?"

"You are coming with me to Devonshire."

She forced a laugh. "Are you insane? I cannot do that. What

about my position as Lady Wentworth's governess? And Sally… I must explain what happened to the poor maid before she hates me forever. Besides, I hate to sail. I—I'm afraid of the water."

"You will have to get used to the idea, because I am not leaving you." He faced her toward her bedroom and gave her a slight push in that direction. "Now get dressed and pack a few things. Time is of the essence."

She swung back around to face him, her hair flying over her shoulder. By the fire flashing in her eyes, he knew he would be fighting her all the way. He looked forward to the challenge.

"Nash Burke! I'm doing no such thing. You have dictated to me all evening, and I won't have any more of it. If you're in a hurry to leave, you better go by yourself."

"Maxey," he said in a warning tone.

"Will you not allow me any time to set my affairs in order? I need to speak with Lady Wentworth and make certain Sally is safely at home."

Smiling, he walked to her and slipped his arms around her waist. Why did she have to feel so good pressed up against him?

"The maid will be safe, I assure you." He touched her stubborn chin. "You have exactly thirty minutes to ready yourself, and if you are not packed, I will take you to Devonshire wearing your nightclothes. It is your choice what you wear." Taking a step back, he scanned her body and grinned. "But personally, I rather like you in this."

"Oh," she shouted, stamping her foot. "I don't live here, which means I don't have many clothes at this residence."

He shrugged. "Then I shall buy you more dresses. Now hurry."

Growling, she spun in a half-circle and marched into her room, slamming the door behind her.

He listened for a lock and thankfully did not hear the metallic click. He chuckled. Yes, this journey would be exciting one way or another.

He walked into the kitchen and picked up Maxey's cooling

cup of tea from the table before gulping it down. After she packed, he planned on returning to his townhouse to gather his belongings and the money he had saved.

Leaning his hip against the table, he scanned the kitchen and front room. Maxey had mentioned a brother, and the only sign that a man lived here was the untidy room. Nash strode into the front room to the worn cushioned chair beside the fireplace, and on the floor was a permanently dirt-stained throw rug just inside the front door. Pictures on the walls were of mountains.

He snooped through the rest of the house, which consisted of one more room besides her bedroom. The door to the unknown room remained shut, so he turned the handle and opened it. The faint smell of tobacco hung in the air, and the scent of dust tickled his nose, making him sneeze.

He assumed the tobacco smell came from Maxey's brother. But she hadn't mentioned a father. By the inch-thick layer of dust on the old wooden drawers, he surmised the occupant had been absent from the home for a while. Perhaps this was her father's room and not the brother's.

Once he closed the door softly, Nash stepped to Maxey's door and listened. For somebody who was supposed to be packing, she certainly wasn't making any noise.

"Maxey? Are you almost ready?"

From the other side of the door, she growled. He smiled, loving her feisty mood.

"No, I'm not ready. It's only been about five minutes."

"You are so quiet in there. I wondered if you were done."

"I know you'll be disappointed to hear this, but I don't make a lot of noise when I'm dressing."

He chuckled. "Do you need any help?"

"No. I have been doing just fine for several years, thank you."

He ran his finger alongside the doorframe. "Maxey?"

"What is it now?"

He steadied his voice to a serious tone. "How long ago did your father die?"

Again, silence stretched on the other side of the door, but he waited patiently for her answer, hoping it didn't upset her too much to talk about it.

"Two years," came the faint reply.

"I am sorry. How did he die?"

"He contracted some lung ailment, which slowly ate away at his body."

"Where is your mother?"

Silence stretched again, but Nash waited.

"She ran out on the family and left with another man when I turned ten. I haven't seen her since."

Sadness tightened his chest. He had never known such a thing. But then, he was raised differently. To have a mother leave the family was probably the worst thing a child could experience.

He flattened his hand on the door, mentally reaching out to her for comfort. "My apologies. I did not realize."

"Of course you didn't. Nobody did. I mean, mothers aren't supposed to leave their families and seek a new life with other men, are they? She took away my childhood and made me wait on a sickly father and lazy brother."

"Oh, Maxey…"

"Do not pity me, Nash." Her voice turned harsh. "The situation shaped me into who I am today."

"Indeed, you are very independent."

"I certainly am."

"I will not speak of the matter again." He pulled away from the door, returned to the front room, and sat on the sofa.

Maxey was such a strong woman. It explained why she was so stubborn and spoke her mind. He smiled. He wouldn't have her any other way.

On the small table next to him sat a framed mini-portrait of an older man. It must be her father. Same smile, same oval-shaped face, and identical eyes. The man's smile warmed Nash's heart.

Strange to think their lives were similar. She grew up without a mother, and he was shunned by his father. His mother and Uncle Matthew's housekeeper had raised him.

Mrs. Jackson! Excited, he bolted off the chair. He had forgotten about her. Even though he hadn't lived with his uncle for very long, Mrs. Jackson was the one responsible for keeping him fed. Mrs. Jackson would know where Uncle Matthew had hidden the ring. The old woman would be an enormous help in fighting the many lies his uncle had spread. Of course, Nash would have to do some serious searching to find her, because after he left to join the military, they lost touch. Trying to find her might delay going to his uncle's estate, but it was worth the chance. Mrs. Jackson had family in Devonshire, so he was certain she was still around.

A movement from out the window caught his attention. He dove to the floor and crouched, wanting to stay hidden in case another one of his uncle's men had come snooping around.

Nash rose enough to barely peek over the bottom of the windowsill. Blackness filled the yard. Not even the moon helped his vision, but he concentrated on the shadows, the trees, and wind-blown leaves drifting over the ground.

Searching the grounds surrounding Maxey's house, he studied every inch, hoping to discover what he had seen. After a few moments, there was another movement. Long, wavy, blondish-brown hair streamed in the breeze as Maxey darted behind a tree. He groaned and fisted his hand.

The little tart was running from him. He should have guessed Maxey's intentions wouldn't be good once he told her of their travel plans.

Springing into action, he dashed out the door and chased after her. When she spotted him, she screamed and ran faster, but he caught up quickly. He grabbed her arm, pulling her to a stop. She tripped and fell. He followed her down, covering her with his body.

"Blast you, Nash!" She hit his chest with her fists. "Get off me, you big brute."

He took hold of her hands and pinned them to the ground above her head. Her chest heaved in a quick rhythm against his. Glancing down at her clothes, he noticed the man's black shirt. He also remembered seeing the black trousers that molded to her legs only moments ago.

"You fool," he snapped. "What do you think to accomplish by running?"

"I—I—I feel that Lady Wentworth needs to know where I'm going. She will be worried if I disappear without a word, and after the death of her husband, I cannot put her through any more turmoil."

Nash shook his head irritably. "Have you forgotten so soon? My uncle is after us. If you inform my sister-in-law where we are going, she might tell my uncle's men if they come looking for you at the Wentworth estate. My uncle cannot know where we are going. Nobody can."

She met his stare as confusion crossed her lovely features, and he waited for her answer.

"I—I—I never thought of that."

"Please trust me, Maxey. I will prove my innocence, and especially that my uncle killed William. You just need to give me more time."

He swept his gaze over the lines creasing her face. With her wild hair framing her head, she looked very tempting. He liked seeing her this way, except without the look of hatred blazing in her eyes.

"Maxey? May I ask you a question?"

She shrugged.

"Do you believe me at all? Or is all of this for naught?"

"Why do you ask?"

"Because if you believed me, you would not have run. You would *want* to come with me to help clear my name and find the proof at my uncle's estate."

She blinked, her face growing red. "I do want to believe you, Nash. Truly, I do."

Her words told a different story than her expression, and he could read her well. Disappointment crushed his chest. She really *didn't* believe him.

It hurt, and he wasn't prepared for the stab of pain like a knife through his chest. But for some reason, she wanted him to think she believed.

What game was she playing with him now?

CHAPTER SEVEN

I T SHOCKED MAXEY that Nash didn't bind or gag her. Not only wouldn't he let her out of his sight, but she wasn't allowed to go as much as three inches away. No matter what, she could not admit defeat. Instead, she would make him believe that traveling to Devonshire with him was an excellent idea, even though she really didn't want to go. After all, what other way could she discover the truth? And, since she didn't believe him, she needed to find the true story. He was hiding something. She just knew it.

With a groan, she realized going with him surpassed her call of duty as a governess, and she wished Lady Wentworth hadn't given her this task. She wasn't an investigator but a governess. She doubted other servants went to such great lengths to help their employer.

Maxey tried to convince herself this was a good thing. After all, if Nash were telling the truth, they would discover Lord Wentworth's killer, and she could return to her position at the estate.

Nash had taken her back into town and to his townhouse. He pulled her inside just as the sun rose, announcing a new day. With her eyes drooping with fatigue, she stepped into the hallway and gasped. For being an opera singer, this man lived in luxury. She sincerely hoped his money came from his opera career, not his uncle's fortune.

She panicked as she followed him through the small corridor and upstairs. A few servants stood back and watched. They didn't appear at all shocked. With Nash's fingers grasped around her wrist, he brought her into a room and shut the door. Closed curtains hung over the windows, so he lit the lamp nearest the door, illuminating his glorious chambers.

Never in her life had she been in a man's bedroom, except for her father's, of course. She sucked in a breath and took in everything around her. Walls covered in moss-green damask, the bedroom filled with Hepplewhite furniture, close to that which adorned some of the rooms at the Wentworth estate. A small marble-topped table stood beside an Empire sofa decorated with gold-painted seashells. In the corner of the room sat his bed. His very large bed. All in white with its twisted posts and damask hangings.

"I suggest you relax, my sweet Maxey. We are staying here until we obtain passage on the ship."

Clearing her throat, she forced herself to speak. "Nash, there is no way I'm going to stay in the same room as you. It's not proper at all, and you know it."

He laughed and walked across the room to the window. Parting the curtains only a tad, he peered outside. The morning sun shone through.

"In time, you will see it differently, I assure you. Do not think of it as indecent." His eyes met hers. "Merely remember that I am protecting you."

As he loosened his cravat, his grin stretched across his tempting mouth. Her heartbeat took on a different rhythm.

"What are you doing?" she said, breathless.

"I am making myself comfortable."

"Not like *that*, you're not."

"Yes, I am."

"Nash, I really must protest."

Ignoring her, he shrugged out of his overcoat and waistcoat, then loosened his shirt. With a gasp, she turned her head away so as not to see his naked chest, fearing it would be as muscular as she had imagined. Nothing could sway her, especially this sensual man who constantly tried to charm her.

A full-length mirror in the corner of the room caught her attention, and she couldn't tear herself away from studying his reflection as he undressed. Oh glory! The sight of his bare chest caused her throat to dry. Her fingertips itched to graze the black hair sprinkled over him, so she quickly balled her hands into fists to keep from acting out.

Her cheeks burned, so she squeezed her eyes closed, but his magnificent image remained branded in her mind. Suddenly, his masculine scent in the room surrounded her, quickening her breathing.

Folding her arms across her stomach, she concentrated on the anger she had lost in the last few minutes. How dare he not allow her to contact Sally or Lady Wentworth? At least the maid should know Maxey was in no immediate danger. Nash was such a demanding man, and she had to keep in mind he was still a murder suspect and thief.

True, she had told him she believed his story, but deep inside her, doubt niggled at her, reminding her of the obvious holes in his explanation. Unfortunately, she must pretend to trust him. Until she could expose the truth.

The low rumble of his chuckle made her disregard her thoughts, and she glanced back at the mirror. He had just finished pulling on another shirt. The material could be almost transparent if she concentrated hard enough. His laughter grew, and she lifted her eyes to meet his in the mirror.

"Did your innocent eyes catch something they should not have, my sweet?"

Embarrassment washed over her in a heated wave. Quickly, she turned away, but there was no way he could have missed her humiliation. The soft tap at his door made her forget her mortification. Saying a silent prayer, she hoped for someone to rescue her from this handsome brute. The blunt truth was that nobody could save her. She had to stay by his side until she could return him to Lady Wentworth.

Nash hurried to the door. "Who is it?" he asked as he rested his hand on the knob.

"It is I, Peter."

Maxey's hopes dropped. *He* certainly wouldn't help her.

Nash quickly let his servant inside, closed the door, and walked to his desk. "Did anyone follow you?"

"No."

"Good." From his money pouch, Nash pulled out a fistful of gold coins. "I need you to book two passages on the next ship sailing to Devonshire. I think the booths will be opening soon. If not, use my connections to get tickets posthaste."

"Of course, Nash." Peter took the money and slipped the heavy coins inside his coat pocket. "I will do it immediately."

"Peter?" Maxey called to him before he reached the door. "How is Sally? You remember, my friend at the party?"

He hesitated while his hand rested on the doorknob. "She is safe at the inn where you two are registered."

"Are you certain she is safe?"

"Do not worry. She is well." Peter grinned.

Maxey sighed. "Will you send her a note for me and tell her what has happened? I don't want her to worry."

Peter glanced at Nash for approval, but Nash shook his head. Without another word, Peter left.

Anger surged through her, and she marched to Nash, her arms planted on her hips. "Why did you tell him no? Sally is going to be distraught, fearing something awful has happened to me."

"I have already taken care of that. Peter informed your friend you are with me, but he did not tell her where we are going. I do not want her running to the police and informing them of our whereabouts. Who knows if they are on my powerful uncle's payroll or not?"

"Sometimes, you can be a cruel and heartless man, Nash."

He grinned. "No, but you keep believing that, and maybe it

will help you with your unwholesome thoughts toward me a minute ago when I caught you peeking in the mirror."

Her mouth dropped open. "How dare you—"

"My sweet Maxey." He stepped to her. "I am not blind. The proof is right here on your scarlet face." He brushed his fingers softly over that heated spot, but she slapped them away.

"Mr. Burke, I have decided not to be attracted to you any longer. If we are going to be in close quarters from now until we reach Devonshire, we must maintain some professionalism."

He shrugged. "That sounds terribly boring and will make for one tedious excursion."

She pursed her lips, knowing she would agree with him if she didn't keep remembering her business manner.

"I think you should get a little sleep," he said. "If we travel to the docks at night, it will help us stay hidden better."

She stifled a yawn. "I do feel tired. But I'm not about to un-dress in front of you. Would you kindly step outside?"

"No. I do not trust you by yourself, especially if there are windows that can be easily opened."

She arched a brow. Apparently, she wasn't trying hard enough to convince Nash that she trusted him. "But we are on the second floor. I'm not about to jump out of a second-story window. Besides, it won't be proper if you stay here while I undress."

"I am not going anywhere, and I promise not to peek as you did." Chuckling, he winked.

Once again, her face flamed. She glanced at the full-length mirror and realized that standing behind it would be her only protection. Unfortunately, the room did not have a dressing screen.

She marched to the bed, yanked open her bag, and grabbed the flannel nightdress on top. Stubbornly, she lifted her chin and moved behind the mirror. True to his word, Nash turned his back to give her more privacy.

This time, undressing was easier because she wore men's

attire, and soon she had wiggled into her nightdress and settled it over her body. After bunching up her clothes, she took them to the bed and stuffed the garments into the satchel.

Without asking his permission, she drew down the blankets and crawled into his bed, pulling the cover high up her neck. His masculine, spicy scent surrounded her, making her head light.

Nash glanced over his shoulder at her. A grin spread across his handsome face.

"Try to rest, Maxey. It is uncertain right now when we will leave."

She nodded as he settled in the heavily cushioned chair beside the bed.

"Sweet dreams, my dear Maxey." He reached over and turned off the lamp.

She squeezed her eyes closed, but images of his naked chest popped into her head. Silently, she groaned. Working side by side with him would be pure torture...and their adventure hadn't even begun.

NASH BOLTED STRAIGHT up in his chair, blinking away the sleep that crept upon him. A noise had awakened him, but as he searched the shadows in the darkened room and listened, he couldn't tell what brought him alert. On stiff legs, he moved to the window and peered through the slits of the heavy drapes. The afternoon's sun made him squint as he looked down at the street in front of the townhouse. Merchants peddled their wares while children played near their governess. Horses pulled wagons and conveyances, their hooves and the wheels crunching on the ground as they passed.

The noise he heard hadn't come from outside. It came from somewhere in this room.

Releasing a heavy breath, he rubbed his hand across his bare chest. The morning was warm, and after Maxey fell asleep, he had removed his shirt. Stretching his body from the cramped position he was in, he walked back to the chair.

As he sank into the cushions, he heard the noise again. His gaze snapped to the bed. A bright sliver of sunlight peeked through the curtains and shined a small amount of light on Maxey. She lay on her back. The sheets were gathered around her legs as she fitfully tossed to her side, letting out small moans. Judging from the tight crease on her forehead, her dream was not pleasant. He couldn't decide if he should wake her or let her sleep.

For a few moments, she lay still before rolling his way, flinging her arms over her head and pulling her lips into a pout. Still, she looked adorable. When she made another noise, her mouth opened, her breath coming in gusts as if she ran from someone. Warily, he moved closer and watched.

"No," she mumbled, "please, don't hurt him."

Who was she dreaming about? The worry etched in her brow revealed she cared deeply for the person in her mind.

"No, please." Her voice rose, and this time she lashed out at some invisible object in front of her. Her arm dropped to the bed, but her breathing came faster. "Watch out. Nash," she screamed, then bolted up.

He jumped to her side and crawled onto the bed, but she closed her eyes and sank back on the mattress. His heart beat with renewed life. Apparently he had become the object of her affections, at least while she slept.

Suddenly she tossed her head on the pillow as she clutched the bedsheets. "Let him go. Leave him alone." She sobbed. "Please, don't hurt him."

Nash slid underneath the blankets and gathered her in his arms. When her face rested against his bare chest, her heavy breathing subsided, and peacefulness settled about her. Like a kitten, she cuddled next to him, her arms wrapped around his waist. Sparks ignited inside him, and he didn't want to release her.

Perhaps she would be upset later, but right now, he needed this. He wanted her against him. If just for a moment, he had to feel as if she truly desired him.

Nash made himself comfortable, bringing her body fully against his as he rested his head on her pillow. Now she slept like a babe. He smiled, kissed her forehead, and then closed his eyes. The sun would start to descend very soon, and he anticipated seeing her reaction when she awoke in his arms.

After several minutes, sleep failed him. He blinked his eyes open and stared into the semidarkness, pondering his decision to take her with him to Devonshire. Had he forced her? And more importantly, was it really necessary?

He remembered the way his uncle acted before Nash left to join the military. The people in Devonshire treated Matthew with deference only because he demanded it. As a young boy, Nash thought his uncle was well liked and admired, but now, he realized the man pushed people to do his bidding or suffer the consequences.

Those feelings of panic returned as he realized his uncle now wanted him dead just to gain the Wentworth title. Nash had seen enough war and senseless killing. He'd left it all behind after sacrificing the home and family he loved. If Matthew wanted the title that badly, he could have it.

But it wasn't just Nash that needed to die for the title to be passed to Matthew. Poor, helpless Joshua also needed to die. The boy didn't deserve such a cruel fate.

Nash would stop his uncle at all costs. If necessary, he would kill his uncle himself. Of course, that wasn't what Nash wanted, but if it came down to it, he would do it to save Joshua's life.

Maxey stirred in his arms. He stared upon her angelic face while fear gnawed at his gut. Matthew would certainly use Maxey against Nash. The ruthless man would make her a hostage just to force Nash out of hiding. He vowed to keep her from his uncle's clutches.

Maxey definitely had to come with him. Nash couldn't stand

seeing her hurt in any way. Although she put up a brave front, she would never be able to withstand Matthew Burke's form of torture.

A deep sigh slipped through her slightly parted lips as she rubbed a soft cheek against his chest, snuggling closer. He kissed her forehead, letting his lips linger on her creamy skin before withdrawing. Leisurely, her eyelids lifted. She looked into his face and smiled.

Assuming she wasn't quite awake, he remained still and waited for her true reaction once she established her bearings. With a small, pleasure-filled sigh, she rested her face on his chest and rubbed her gentle lips across his skin. It was his turn to groan, but he kept quiet for fear awareness would finally come to her, and she would realize her mistake.

The covers stirred as she crossed her leg over his. Beneath the blanket, her hand swept over his abdomen, sending a heated shiver through him. Sweat beaded his forehead. Nash gritted his teeth to hold his desire in check, wishing she would awaken and end this unbearable pleasure.

He slid his hand up and down her full sleeve lightly, but she remained in a dream world. Another soft sigh slipped through her lips, making him smile. Dare he wake her? But then again, how much excruciating enjoyment could he take without wanting more?

He kissed her head again, and she peered into his eyes. Although she seemed aware, the dazed mist in her stare revealed her semiconscious state. Maxey's focus dropped and rested on his mouth. Silently, he cursed his weakness. He knew when a woman wanted to be kissed, and right now, she showed all the signs.

Refusing her unspoken wish was out of the question.

In a moment of weakness, he brushed his lips across hers, but when he tried to withdraw, she forged on, leaning up to meet his mouth. She combed her fingers through his hair and pecked at his lips. There was no stopping him now.

Cupping her face, he pushed her back onto the bed and used his lips to begin his seduction. He followed her lead, just enjoying the softness of her mouth. But that was apparently all she wanted, because she sighed again and turned her face, snuggling against his shoulder.

"You are safe now," she whispered. "I'll not let him hurt you again."

An unexplainable emotion cut through Nash's heart, confusing him greatly. If not for his feeling so troubled, her words would have elicited laughter. Although it touched him to think she cared, he didn't deserve it, especially since he knew he was taking her against her will. Unfortunately, it had to be done.

When sleep again settled over her, he pulled away and left her side, returning to his uncomfortable chair. His mind was too scrambled to sleep, especially when a strange emotion threatened to fill him. An emotion he had no name for.

MAXEY BLINKED HER eyes open and stretched her arms above her head. The descending sun's pink light from the window caused her to squint, and suddenly the objects in the room came into focus.

Nash's bedchamber.

With a groan, she covered her face with her hands. She was stuck. Even if she wanted to get out of this mess, she couldn't. Not until she collected some hard evidence against him. If she didn't, she would be sailing to Devonshire in the near future.

Slowly, she lowered her hands and glanced around the spacious area. Although his masculine scent continued to hang in the air, she didn't hear his deep breathing. She sat up as she surveyed the room. Nash was gone. Did that mean he had left and sailed without her? Doubtful, knowing Nash. Then again, she really didn't know him that well.

But while he was away, she would make herself useful.

She whipped off the covers and scampered out of bed. Not caring that she wore a nightdress, she hurried to the large oak dresser in the corner of the room. Resting her hands on the handle, she took a moment to listen for any noises outside the door. Luckily, the hallway remained quiet.

Careful not to make much noise, she slid open the first drawer. Piles of Nash's underclothes took up most of the space. Her heartbeat thudded rapidly as she realized she would have to touch his most personal garments to move them aside during her search.

The first drawer didn't hold any hidden secrets, so she moved to the second, then the third. The fourth drawer wouldn't budge, as if something was caught inside. She resisted tugging harder for fear of making too much noise.

Quickly, before Nash decided to return, she hurried to the nearest closet. His clothes hung neatly inside, and his strong, manly scent melted her insides. Why did he have to smell so wonderful?

She knelt and searched through the closet, but the blasted thing was too clean. He definitely didn't have anything hidden here.

Letting out a frustrated breath, she moved to the trunk sitting near the window. A lock hung open on the latch. Excitement grew in her chest as she opened the lid and peered inside.

Knickknacks and drawings littered the bottom. There wasn't enough time to study every item, but she skimmed through a few. Most of the sketches were of a little boy and a woman. Probably Nash and his mother. So far, none were of an older man, Nash's father.

Although the absence of his father in the drawings didn't prove anything, it made her wonder what had really happened to make Nash and his father part ways. What had Nash truly done to make himself an outcast?

The trinkets mixed with the sketches were not expensive, and the family's ruby ring, really what she'd hoped to find, was not amongst the items in the trunk. She sat back on her heels and glanced around the room. Where else could she search?

Voices and thudding footsteps in the hallway drew her attention. Her throat clutched with panic, and she hurried to the bed and jumped on the mattress before climbing beneath the covers and pulling them up to her chin.

She barely had time to breathe before the door opened and Nash walked in.

He met her gaze and smiled. "Good evening, Maxey. I trust you slept well?"

She shrugged. "As well as could be expected, I suppose."

"Have you been awake long?"

"Not long at all." It really wasn't a lie, but a pang of guilt stabbed at her for not being entirely truthful with him. Even though she knew he still held secrets, that didn't mean she should lie as well.

He glanced around the room before his focus rested on his trunk. When she realized she had left the lid open, she stiffened and subdued a groan.

He shook his head. "Tsk, tsk, Maxey." He walked to his trunk. "I suppose I should not be surprised you searched my room. After all, my clueless sister-in-law tried to turn a governess into an investigator."

Heat burned her face, and she wished she could control her embarrassment.

He closed the lid and turned to her. "Did you find anything of value? A stolen ruby ring with the Wentworth crest, perhaps?"

In defiance, she lifted her chin. "A good investigator never gives away her secrets or findings."

"Ah, so I have heard." He grinned as he moved to the bed and touched her cheek. "But, my sweet, your face cannot lie to me. Your blush tells me you did not find anything." Giving her a wink, he pulled away. "Now, you must dress quickly. Adorn yourself in your best traveling gown, because we will leave within the hour."

Fear grew inside her. "Leave? Already?"

"Indeed, it is time. I assume you want to help me discover the truth about who killed my brother, correct?"

Hesitantly, she nodded. What else could she do? She had already tried to reason why she should not go, and he ignored her plea.

"Splendid. Then don't dally. We do not want to miss our ship."

Fear slowly crept into her. Was she making the right choice? Could she sail alone with him, knowing how the attraction between them was so great that she felt helpless? And could she keep her emotions from becoming involved? She had to.

"Nash?"

"Yes?"

"I think you have overlooked one important matter."

With an arched brow, he cocked his head. "I do not think so, my sweet."

"Who is going to be… Um, what about…my chaperone?"

A grin sneaked across his handsome face as he sat on the edge of the bed. "My dear Maxey. Have you changed into a chameleon now? Why are you so proper when last night at the soirée you were—"

Her face burned again, and she held up a hand. "Nash, must you insist on bringing that up? You know my reasons."

"Then what are your reasons now?"

"Last night, I was with Sally. This time I'll be alone with you in public. It's not proper."

He reached across her lap and softly took her hand. "So you think we should have some kind of cover?"

She nodded. "It's my reputation that is at stake, after all."

"Perhaps we should travel as a married couple."

"That's utterly ridiculous." She yanked her hand away. "We will *not* become that close. Besides, I'm only going to act as your partner. After all, are we not sailing to find your brother's killer?"

"Indeed we are."

"Then pretending we are married is out of the question."

"You want us to act more like partners, then?"

"Precisely."

He scratched his chin. "I fear that will not work, so what would you say to acting like my distant niece?"

She tried not to grin, but the corners of her mouth twitched upward regardless. "I think people could see we are not."

"I will say you are my relative on my mother's side."

She shrugged. "That might work, I suppose."

He slapped his knees and stood. "Very well, niece Maxey. Hurry and dress, because the hour is slipping away. The sooner we climb aboard that vessel, the better for both of us."

Her hopes sank. Could she act accordingly? She didn't understand how her body melted every time he touched her. And heaven forbid they shared another kiss. *That*, she would not let him do again.

CHAPTER EIGHT

MAXEY STOOD BY the ship's railing, inhaling the salt air in hopes of calming her shifting stomach. She had warned Nash about her fear of sailing, but he'd insisted she go with him nonetheless.

Another wave of nausea tackled her belly, and she gnashed her teeth. He would just have to get used to her illness and the unruly temper that accompanied it.

Beside her, Nash's alert eyes kept watching the semi-crowded deck for anyone who seemed suspicious, something he'd been doing since they set sail yesterday. His cautious nature kept him attentive, and because of his disguise, he mingled with the crowd and didn't stand out. Maxey thought he looked more handsome now than when she first saw him on stage.

Since first boarding, Nash had dressed more like a farmer's son. His sideburns seemed slightly longer, and he'd reshaped the goatee around his tempting mouth. Could *this* be his true identity and not the opera singer? Just maybe his story was correct. She couldn't decide. She blamed her clouded judgment on her interest in him.

When another bout of seasickness hit her, she leaned against the railing and breathed deeply. She prayed she didn't humiliate herself in public again, as she had during those first few hours on the ship. Her head pounded from trying to restrain her stomach, but she welcomed the distraction.

Nash's hand grazed her arm, but she refused to meet his eyes.

"Maxey? Are you all right?"

"I will be in a moment," she mumbled between clenched teeth.

"Do you wish to return to the room?"

She shook her head. "The fresh air is helping."

"But you have been like this since we first sailed. Have you kept any food down at all?"

"A small amount." She breathed deeply, and the turbulent rolling in her stomach subsided. "It's this wind, stirring the waves and causing the ship to rock." She placed her cool hands on her face. "I'll be better in a moment."

He swept his fingers across a lock of her loosely bound hair. "I worry about you. I am not pleased with your pale coloring."

Meeting his stare, she shrugged. "The sea and I do not get along well."

"May I ask why you don't like to sail?"

"Being in the water has scared me since I was young. I don't like the unsettled feeling of walking on moving ground. I especially don't like the idea of falling overboard and plunging into the icy waters and sinking to my death."

He chuckled. "You will not fall overboard. I will not allow it."

"Perhaps you should have left me back with Sally."

"You know I could not. Keeping you by my side is the only way I can protect you."

"So you keep telling me," she mumbled.

He leaned on the rail, his attention on the lightly rolling sea. "I am beginning to think your bout with seasickness is purely for my benefit. More and more, you are proving how much you dislike my company."

She poked his shoulder. "I told you how I felt about sailing before we ever set foot aboard this ship." Folding her arms, she took a deep breath. "And I have never told you I dislike your company. Just because I don't choose to fall for your charm doesn't mean you won't make an entertaining traveling partner."

He snapped his head toward her. "You think I am constantly trying to bed you?"

She arched a brow. "You cannot lie to me, Nash. I read you well."

"Maxey." He shook his head and sighed deeply. "I am taking you with me for your own protection. I am aware this trip is not solely for pleasure."

She compelled a laugh. "I shall believe that when I see it."

Anger marred his forehead with deep lines. "Believe me when I say the only reason I brought you along is to keep you away from my uncle. If he ever got his hands on you…"

She turned her back to him. Keeping up this farce of believing him gnawed on her nerves. Then again, in the back of her mind, a niggling doubt squeezed through, and she wondered if he was truly innocent. If only he would show her some proof. All this confusion gave her a headache. With a deep breath, she realized the sooner they arrived in Devonshire, the better.

Nash pulled away from the rail and moved in front of her. "Maxey, we need to learn to trust each other. This trip will become very long if we cannot."

Silently, she scolded herself for not turning out a better per-formance. No matter what, he couldn't see the doubt in her eyes.

She patted his hand. "Of course I trust you, Nash. I wouldn't have come with you otherwise."

"Even if I practically kidnapped you?"

She forced another laugh. "I'm quite certain you didn't. I would have been able to get away from you sooner or later if I really wanted."

"I still worry about you." He touched her cheek.

"I shall be fine, just as soon as I am used to the turbulent waves. Until that time, I will be extremely moody." She flipped her hand through the air in a dismissive wave. "Please, Nash. If you don't mind, I wish to be alone right now."

"I wish you were not like this. Trying to talk to you is almost impossible."

"I know. It's the seasickness."

"Then I will seek out some real company. I hope you find something to entertain yourself for the days ahead." Grumbling, he turned and left her side.

Her heart dropped with each step he took away from her. Why didn't he understand? Her seasickness had nothing to do with him. Did all men think about themselves and no other? Apparently.

She promised herself that as soon as this bout with sickness passed, she would be the headstrong woman she knew she could be. Hopefully, that time would arrive shortly. Even she couldn't stand her own sour mood.

Although anger burned in her chest over Nash's refusal to understand, foolishness rooted her to the spot. She stood alone and was somewhat shocked at his threat of seeking other companionship. Loneliness crept over her, and she didn't like it one bit. Perhaps she was too hasty in asking Nash to leave.

Would he find another woman and spend time with her? The thought twisted her stomach. If he did, she didn't know how she could handle seeing him charm another woman.

Putting aside her raging emotions, she strolled across the deck to the other side of the ship. The Lake District was no longer visible, and she remained trapped in a world of churning water. A horrific thought of falling into the sea passed through her mind, making her stomach clench again. She had never learned to swim, and drowning wasn't her idea of the perfect way to die.

When her mother was in Maxey's life, the family went on a boat ride, and Maxey fell overboard. Although her mother bravely jumped into the cold water to save her, the nightmare of being unable to breathe stayed with Maxey for quite some time. Never again did she want to feel so helpless.

A gust of wind ruffled her hair and chilled her face. Pulling her shawl tighter around her shoulders, she wondered which was icier—the breeze coming off the ocean or the look in Nash's eyes when he walked away.

Several couples strolled across the deck. A few stood out among the others, with the same tanned skin that made Nash so beautiful. A couple of the men looked her way. Suddenly, doubt filled her. What if these strangers worked for his uncle? Her gaze shifted to another man. Could he be employed by Matthew Burke, too?

She chastised herself for letting Nash's paranoia consume her. He thought every well-dressed man was after him. She straightened her stance and snickered at Nash's wild imagination. Why, then, did she keep checking over her shoulder? Clearly, the distress of the situation had made her lose her mind.

If Nash were guilty, as she had first suspected, would he sail to Devonshire just to prove his innocence? Nothing made sense anymore, and she hated doubting herself.

She needed Lady Wentworth's advice now more than ever. Then again, Carolyn would have never approved of what Maxey was doing right now.

From the corner of her eye, a hooded, cloaked figure caught her attention. A middle-aged older woman stood across the deck, her stare fixed directly on Maxey. Most of the woman's face remained shadowed because of her hood. Chills of the unknown rushed through Maxey, and they had nothing to do with the weather. A few awkward minutes passed as they stared at each other. Maxey didn't think she knew the woman, yet she was too far away to tell for certain. However, the chills running up and down her spine made her uneasy.

Finally, the woman tightened her cloak under her chin, spun around, and hurried away.

How very strange. That was definitely something Maxey should check into, but not now. It was too chilly up on deck today. Besides, she doubted the woman worked for Matthew Burke, so perhaps Maxey shouldn't be concerned about her.

Another gust of cool air whipped off the sea, blowing her skirt around her ankles, freezing her legs. She turned to flee and head back to her cabin, but bumped into another passenger. When the man's hands steadied her shoulders, she glanced into his face. The stranger stood very tall and was very handsome, like Nash. The man's maturity showed in the streaks of silver that lightly tinted his black hair. Wrinkles decorated the olive skin around his eyes and mouth, and unlike Nash's whiskered face, this man was clean-shaven.

"Pardon me, *señorita*," he said in a thick Spanish accent. "Did I harm you?"

She gave a nervous laugh before stepping back. "No. Forgive me for not seeing you, but the sudden nippy air turned my thoughts to getting back to my cabin for warmth."

Despite his good looks, he still didn't hold a candle to Nash's perfection when he smiled. Why did these thoughts about her suspect continually forsake her vow to remain uninterested?

"Is this your first trip?" he asked.

"This is my first trip sailing this far from home. I have been on a smaller boat, but only for an hour, and not far from shore."

"Then you had better get used to these gusts of wind. Out here on the sea, one minute the sun will shine like a midsummer's day, and the next moment, clouds will fill the sky as if it is the middle of winter."

"Your warning is very much appreciated, sir. I certainly feel better now."

He chuckled. "You packed warmly, did you not?"

"I certainly hope so. I would hate to think I made this voyage only to be in my cabin, bundled in blankets. My stuffy room makes me more nauseated than out in the open."

He glanced around the deck. When he snapped his attention back to her, he smiled. "Are you here with your husband?"

Without meaning to, she snorted a laugh. The idea of her and Nash posing as a married couple was still very humorous. "Oh no. I'm not married."

"But you do have an escort, I presume?"

She shrugged. "Yes. He is my uncle and will escort me until

we reach Devonshire." She glanced across the deck, but she couldn't see Nash. Strange, because he had talked so much of protecting her, so where was he now? "I suppose my uncle decided to go below."

Like a true gentleman, the stranger stepped back, straightened, and offered his elbow. "Then permit me to guide you back to your room, *señorita*."

She wanted to distrust him. Obviously, this was something Nash would do. Gut feelings didn't lie, and hers told her to beware. Then again, if this man knew anything about Nash's uncle and the story Nash continued to tell her, perhaps he was worth getting to know—for the sole purpose of finding more information on Matthew Burke.

Not only that, but this was the perfect way to pass the time.

With the firm decision in mind to dig deeper into her new *amigo's* life, Maxey nodded to the stranger. "You must tell me your name first. I cannot allow you to take me to my cabin otherwise."

"My name is Raúl Zamora." He bowed slightly.

"It's a pleasure to meet you, Señor Zamora. I'm Miss Maxey Littleton." She slipped her hand into the crook of his arm. They walked side by side toward the stairs, heading for her cabin.

"I would prefer it if you called me Raúl."

She smiled. "Then you must call me Maxey."

He nodded.

"Are you traveling alone?" she inquired.

"*Sí.*"

"For what purpose, if you don't mind me asking? Business or pleasure?"

"I travel back and forth from Britain to my homeland, Spain. I am in the trading business."

"How fascinating." And it truly was. He would possibly know about Nash's uncle and have information for her.

"It is, and yet it is not. You see, Maxey, rarely do I have someone accompany me on my trips." He patted her hand. "So I always appreciate the opportunity to meet new people. It keeps me from going insane."

"I would like to get to know you. I find the trade business fascinating and would like to learn more."

"Then will you permit me to be your companion for the duration of the trip?"

She cocked her head and studied his profile with a grin. Nash would have a few words to say about that. But what if Raúl knew something about Nash's uncle? The only way she would know was by getting to know this man better.

"I will certainly have to think about it."

After realizing her journey to Devonshire wouldn't be as awful as she had first thought, her spirits rose. Hopefully, with Raúl as her new friend, he would keep her mind off her sinfully handsome and overpowering protector.

In the late hours of the night, when she lay awake in bed, memories of Nash's kisses would disrupt her thoughts again—just as they had done since she met the incredibly charming man.

She widened her smile. "Shall we meet back up on deck after dinner?" Had she been too forward? Would Raúl suspect she was working with Nash to get information?

"I thought of inviting you to have dinner with me instead."

Panic surged through her, and she breathed slowly to calm her fear. Strange, but she didn't feel right being alone with him. So why had she not felt this way with Nash?

"As much as the idea is enticing, it would not be proper, and I need my uncle to be my chaperone."

"Then bring him along."

She laughed. "You don't know him as well as I. Moving a mountain might be easier than convincing him."

He chuckled. "So, dinner is out of the question?"

"Yes, for now. Let me speak with him tonight. Perhaps he will be in better spirits this evening."

"That sounds wonderful." He leaned near her ear. "Until the time when I can get you alone, that is."

She pulled back. "You shock me with your forwardness, sir."

"You do not seem to mind it overmuch." He grinned, almost too smugly.

Are all men arrogant, or is that just their charm?

They stopped in front of her door. "Thank you, Raúl, for your escort."

"Perhaps I will see you up on the deck after dinner?"

"Only if the weather permits."

He bowed slightly. "Then until later, *señorita*." He took her hand and placed a chaste kiss on her knuckles before turning and walking away.

Her smile widened. Nash would probably hate Raúl immediately, and not because he felt any kind of jealousy. No, Nash would be suspicious of Raúl for fear he worked with Matthew Burke. She wouldn't let Nash know that, behind his back, she would do some investigative work herself.

Maxey opened her wrist purse, withdrew her key, and unlocked the room. Before closing the hard oak door, she lit the lamp on the desk and quickly searched every corner to ensure she was safe. Nash's fears kept her more worried than she'd been before. But being cautious was good. He had taught her that.

She stepped inside and closed the door. After removing her shawl, she flung the black lace garment to the bottom of the bed and flopped on the mattress. Immediately, her attention dropped to the blankets on the floor where Nash slept. He had insisted on sharing a room. Now she realized it was a good thing to tell Raúl that Nash was her uncle. She could only imagine what the other passengers would think if they knew the truth.

So far this trip, he'd acted the part of a gentleman and slept on the floor, giving her the semi-comfort of the lumpy mattress. But it worried her that he would eventually try to change that arrangement.

Keeping away from him had been easy, thanks to her unsettled stomach. Gradually, she felt a little better, and soon there could be no excuses. She would have to face her attraction for him, yet controlling her thoughts and actions was very important.

On the nightstand, she found the mints and popped one into her mouth. These helped slightly with her seasickness. Then she picked up the book she had brought to keep her entertained during the trip. Thankfully, Nash had thought to pack several novels while he readied for this voyage.

With a sigh, she lowered the book to her lap and frowned. Nash's distracting image crept onto each page. She had to admit that some of his actions were thoughtful, and he looked out for her welfare and comfort most of the time. However, his charm and sweetness could not be overlooked.

But she couldn't let him control her mind. She hated that her body still weakened from his sultry eyes.

She snapped to awareness and pounded her fist against the mattress. Curse those irresistible chocolate eyes for mesmerizing her whenever she thought of him.

When heavy footsteps sounded at her door, she jumped. The door flew open and hit the wall with a resounding crash. Nash stepped inside, his muscular frame filling the area perfectly. His eyes were narrowed, his forehead creased.

Her heart hammered wildly. What had she done now?

CHAPTER NINE

NASH'S CHEST HEAVED with quick breaths. Scanning the area, he searched for the man who had accompanied Maxey to their room. Really, there wasn't any place to hide in such cramped quarters, but he still checked every spot he could find to ease his worry. She sat on the bed with her feet on the blankets, a book in one hand, staring at him with wide eyes as the other hand reached for the mints on the nightstand.

No longer did she appear sick. The color had even returned to her face.

"Why did you make such a grand entrance?" she snapped.

She must have suspected his insecurities. He relaxed and calmly walked into the room, closing the door behind him.

"Maxey? Who was that man with you?" He kept his voice steady even while unwanted emotions jumped in his chest.

She cocked her head. "You saw me with a man?"

The corner of his mouth twitched up as he tried not to grin. "Do not play coy with me." He moved to the side of the bed and sat by her legs. "I saw him escorting you down the stairs a few minutes ago."

"His name is Raúl Zamora." She paused, but only for a moment, before she gave an irritated chuckle. "You saw me with another man and thought the worst, correct? Especially when we headed in the direction of the cabin."

"Maxey, I did not think such a thing."

"Yes, you did." She crossed her arms over her chest. "Which is why you made such an explosive entrance. You thought to catch us doing something improper."

"No, my sweet." He tried to keep his expression blank, hoping not to give away his true thoughts. "I worried you had taken up with a man you hardly knew." He caressed her shoulder. "Because of our situation, we cannot trust anyone."

She swatted away his hand. "No, because of *your* situation, *you* cannot trust anyone. I, on the other hand, am free to trust whom I may."

"But if by chance someone on the ship is watching me, they will know you are with me."

"Stop, Nash, please." She closed her eyes and kneaded her forehead. "Do you really think someone that evil is on the ship? You sneaked us out of my house without being spotted. We even left your townhouse in disguises." She met his stare. "I don't think anyone followed us, and I definitely don't think anyone on this ship is watching you."

An invisible knife of distrust sliced through Nash's chest again, and he cursed the feeling. Although her words tried to convince him otherwise, the tone of her voice led him to believe she still questioned his innocence.

Ever since meeting the very exciting Maxey Littleton, he'd experienced a wounding ache in the middle of his chest, and he knew he had to control it before it engulfed his whole soul. It saddened him to think she would not believe him—that he couldn't make her understand about his dangerous uncle.

He caressed a lock of her hair that had fallen across her brow. Silky, just as he remembered.

"It hurts that you do not believe me, Maxey, but I will not stop trying to protect you. I know the truth, although you refuse to believe it, so I will not relent. Only I know what despicable things my uncle will do, which is why I cannot turn my back on you, nor him."

Scowling, she shook her head. "I don't know why you think such things. I believe you, Nash. Why else would I be here with you now?"

She wasn't a good performer, but for some reason, she wanted him to think otherwise. He would continue to let her believe she had the upper hand.

"Because I practically forced you to come."

"Please, Nash, no more." She tried to move past him off the bed, but he circled her with his arms, holding her tight against him. Pain thickened in his chest, and he wished he could make the agony of caring for her disappear.

"Oh, Maxey." He kissed her forehead. "What can I do to make you trust me?"

She didn't answer. He didn't expect her to. But experiencing her softness pressed against him was his undoing. Fervor ignited in him, and he didn't want the powerful, exhilarating feeling to end.

He trailed his lips from her brow down the side of her face, just content to feel her soft skin. Even through her stiffness, her breaths puffed against his neck.

Threading his fingers through her hair, he loosened the ribbon holding it together and let it drop behind her on the bed. With her head tilted back, her stare rested on him, but no longer was it hard with anger. Heated desire filled her bluish-gray eyes now.

"Maxey," he whispered. "You are so beautiful." He placed a kiss on the tip of her perfectly shaped nose. "I do not know what would become of me if my uncle were to hurt you." He pecked at her lips briefly. "If Matthew ever got hold of you, I would search the ends of the earth to tear you away from him. I would never give up until I had you in my arms, protected."

"Nash, please." She gazed at him with so much tenderness.

"Please what?" he asked.

He waited for her to stop him, to halt this passionate moment as she had done before. She lowered her focus to his mouth and sighed. As if wanting him to kiss her, she closed her eyes. He could not deny her body's silent urging for his kisses.

When he covered her mouth, her sigh blended with his. She tasted strongly of the mints she had eaten. Timidly, she slid her hands around his waist, running her fingers along his muscles, which drove him mad.

Urgency consumed him, and he slanted his mouth, deepening the kiss. She gasped but responded the way he had hoped for, the way he had thought about since he held her in his bed during her dream.

Nash pushed her back on the bed. Tingling sensations danced over him. Her fingers moved to his chest, then climbed to his neck as she held his face to hers.

He never wanted this moment to end. But a knock came on the door and jerked him to awareness.

Still holding her in his arms, he cursed, hoping the intruder would pass. Her bosom rose and fell in a fast rhythm that matched his breathing. He inhaled her sweet jasmine scent. Closing his eyes, he rested his forehead against hers, enjoying their closeness for just a little longer.

The knock came upon the door again. "Mr. Black? Your meals are here."

Maxey pushed Nash up until he met her eyes. "Does he have the wrong room?"

"No."

"Then why did he call you Mr. Black?"

"Do you not remember? While I am on this ship, my name is Nash Black."

"Oh yes," she replied, still breathless.

Grudgingly, he pulled away and stood. Maxey picked up her ribbon and began to fix her hair.

He answered the door and then took the trays of food from the porter. "I thank you." Turning, he kicked the door closed with his boot. He placed the trays on the small table at the far wall before glancing at Maxey. She sat on the bed, her eyes downcast as she did her hair.

He sighed in frustration. It seemed impossible that, once again, something had thwarted his plans for holding Maxey and enjoying her closeness.

She had given him confusing, mixed signals. Did she indeed want his touch, his kiss? Did she enjoy them, or was she like the women who enjoyed teasing a man to insanity?

"What smells so tasty?" Maxey asked without meeting his eyes.

He lifted the cover to one of the plates. "Looks like fish and some elegant potato dish."

She climbed off the bed and came toward him. Her lips held the swollen proof of his ardent kisses. He wanted nothing more than to pull her back into his arms and finish what they had started. Unfortunately, the moment had passed, and he knew Maxey would never allow it to continue.

Without looking his way, she moved to the chair and sat. Poking the fork in the tender meat of the fish, she licked her lips. She brought the utensil to her mouth and slipped the food inside, closing her lips around it.

His chest ached from knowing that she was being so difficult. It would be easier for her if she admitted her true feelings and trust him.

"Are you going to eat?" she muttered with her mouth full of food as she nodded toward the empty chair.

"No, Maxey. I have suddenly lost my appetite." He walked to the door and rested his hand on the doorknob.

"Nash?"

He glanced at her, and hope flowed inside him. Would she invite him back to partake of her passion again?

"Promise me you won't kiss me in that manner again."

His dreams plummeted, dissolving in front of him.

"We shouldn't have done that." She dabbed her napkin to her mouth. "I shouldn't have let you, and I'll try really hard to resist you from here on out. I want to help you prove your innocence, but when you get too close to me, it's very distracting. If I'm to assist you in any way, I'll need to have my wits about me. So please, Nash, promise you'll not touch or kiss me like that again."

He folded his arms and casually leaned against the door. "Will you believe me? If I recall, you have doubted my word since we first met."

She lowered her attention to her plate. "If you promise as a gentleman, I'll trust your word."

He squeezed his eyes closed, clenching his fists. If he made that promise, he would stick to it. But blast it all, he wanted to hold her again and kiss those sweet lips. She'd nearly admitted her fascination for him, but her stubborn streak wouldn't let him win.

"Nash? Will you promise?"

He looked her way, but she still remained focused on her food. "No, Maxey, I will not."

She looked up and gasped. "You won't?"

"I cannot deny my attraction for you. I hunger for your smile, your touch, and especially your kind words. If one day you decide to allow my caresses, I will hold you and enjoy doing so." He shook his head. "And because of my weakness, I cannot make that promise. If I cannot touch you, steal a kiss from you, and feel you in my arms, I would rather someone kill me and put me out of my misery."

He walked out the door, slamming it behind him.

MAXEY STROLLED ON stiff legs beside Nash across the deck. The evening's cool wind teased the tendrils near her ears and nipped at her nose. She bundled the cloak tighter around her neck as she glanced across the sea. The sun had made its departure beyond the horizon, leaving shadows to dance across the water in a soothing motion.

Her bout with seasickness earlier must have disappeared,

because it hadn't disrupted her day since this morning. Then again, a lot had happened to keep her mind off her stomach.

Nash must be her cure.

Frowning, she silently scolded herself. She mustn't think that way about him, or she would become weaker.

Maxey kept herself from accidentally bumping into his arm, mainly because she didn't want him to accuse her of teasing him. And he would. He knew how she felt, and she certainly would never forget his words.

Why was he so attracted to her? Could it be because he wanted to seduce her, and she wouldn't allow it? Men were fickle when it came to women, and so far, Nash had proven to be just like every other man she knew.

Poor, pathetic creatures.

First things first, she needed to introduce him to Raúl Zamora. Once she'd had time to think about her new friend, she wondered if their meeting earlier today wasn't planned. The more she thought about it, she realized something didn't add up. He had obviously seen her with Nash, believing they were married. And why had he seen her at all, enough to become interested in her? Seasickness had kept her at the railing since they boarded the ship, so why would any man want a woman who continually embarrassed herself when she couldn't keep anything in her stomach?

For now, she would continue to act friendly, and in Nash's eyes, make him think she would ask Raúl questions about the location of Matthew. But inwardly, she would study the new Spaniard and see if perhaps he told the truth or lied.

She couldn't tell with men anymore. She had been lied to most of her life, which resulted in her distrustful nature. Her father had not told the truth about her mother—the worst lie of all.

For several years after Maxey's mother left her husband and children behind, Father led his children to believe their mother would return one day. Maxey waited day after day, week after week, until months turned into years. Each day, she got her hopes up that her mother would open the front door and announce that she was home for good. And as each sunset darkened the sky, Maxey's heart shattered.

On her father's deathbed, he finally confessed the truth. Her mother would not be returning, since she had married another man and started a new family. Her father even referred to Maxey's mother as a harlot.

After that point, Maxey became distrustful of men, and although they seemed sincere on the outside, on the inside, they kept secrets.

Nash proved her theory. Just as she would prove his guilt.

"Maxey?"

Her name in Nash's sensual voice jerked her out of her thoughts. "Yes?"

"You have been quiet this evening. Would you share with me what is on your mind?"

If he only knew.

"Not much. I've been thinking about asking my new friend, Raúl, to join us for our walk this evening."

She dared take a peek at his expression. Head cocked, he arched a dark eyebrow at her.

"May I ask why? After all, he is a stranger to both of us."

"Indeed. He is also a man who does a lot of traveling because of his business. I thought we could ask him about your uncle."

Nash stopped against the railing and leaned his back against the long, sturdy piece of wood as he folded his arms over his broad chest. Still, he had yet to crack a smile. Clearly, her suggestion didn't amuse him.

"And why would we do that?"

She shrugged. "Didn't you tell me that your uncle is very powerful?"

"I did."

"If he is so powerful, wouldn't many people know about him?"

Nash nodded. "You forget one thing, Maxey: if people knew my uncle, they would be fearful of talking about him behind his back."

She hadn't realized it until now, but Nash didn't refer to her as his *sweet Maxey* any longer. She wished her chest didn't ache from the loss of his endearment. "I don't see why."

"No, I suppose you do not. It is hard to know what my uncle would do to a person if they betrayed him unless you have seen it yourself."

Maxey held her tongue. It seemed Nash didn't want her to ask Raúl questions, and she couldn't help but wonder if Nash was again lying to her. Perhaps she was on the right track after all. Talking to Raúl was a clever idea.

"Nash, we don't have to come right out and tell Raúl everything. We can just say you're related to Matthew, and you're looking for him."

"Sorry, but that will not work either."

Silently, she growled. No, *he* did not want it to work, which was why he kept discouraging her. The true story lay underneath all of this—the story she would eventually uncover. The sooner, the better.

"Regardless, Raúl has asked us to take supper with him tomorrow, so I think we should be hospitable and join him. Even if you don't think it's a good idea to ask him questions, I certainly do. After all, I'm trying to think like an investigator, and they generally follow their instincts. Right now, my instincts are telling me to ask Raúl about your uncle."

Nash's chest rose and fell with apparent difficulty. His jaw was hard, his lips pursed, and those hypnotic eyes glared at her. She wouldn't allow him to frighten her. Raúl would be able to help them one way or another—she felt it.

"Besides, we're on a ship, are we not? What could happen to us amongst all these passengers?" She gave a light chuckle and laid her hand on his arm still folded across his chest.

His gaze dropped to her fingers before jumping up to meet

her eyes. Within seconds, a different emotion filled his eyes, making her heart beat a different rhythm. His brown stare softened considerably the longer he looked at her. Strange how quickly his moods changed.

Maybe she shouldn't have touched him. He had told her what happened. But now, she couldn't pull her hand away. His melting eyes left her immobile. Then he placed his hand over hers to hold it there.

A knot tightened in her chest, and her throat turned dry. Curse her reaction. Why did he always have to affect her in such a manner? Why did he make her body tingle and cry out to be held by his strong arms?

She swallowed, trying to add moisture to her cotton-filled throat. Clearing her improper thoughts, she scrambled to remember what they'd been discussing.

As she opened her mouth to speak, Nash placed his finger over her lips. Heated sparks spread through her body. The words stopped in her throat, and her mind turned blank.

"Maxey, you forget one thing."

"Wh—what?" Her voice quivered.

"I know my uncle better than you. I know what he can do. If he knew I sailed on this ship, his men would be here with us, also."

Was he trying to frighten her again? Or perhaps he was trying to steer her away from the truth.

Her fuzzy mind waged a battle with her emotions over what she should feel. As soon as she broke contact with him, her brain would function again. But as she gently tugged her hand away, he tightened his grip and wouldn't allow her to budge.

"Maxey, you must believe me."

She nodded slowly, keeping her stare on his remarkable chocolate eyes. "Of course I believe you, Nash. I merely suggested we get to know Raúl a little better. If the worst-case scenario happened, and your uncle's men are on this ship, we may need Raúl's help."

Nash's hold on her loosened, and she pulled her hand away.

He shrugged. "What if Raúl *is* one of my uncle's men? Then what?"

Breathing easier, she took a step back, inhaling the deep salt air, hoping it would clear her mind and cool her heated body. "I don't believe that, Nash."

His long, lean fingers caressed her cheek, and she realized she hadn't stepped back far enough. Her skin burned beneath his touch.

"This is also an instinctual feeling?" he asked.

"Indeed it is."

"And you expect me to trust your feelings?"

"But of course. Just as you expect me to believe in you." She smiled, trying her best to make it genuine. What she said wasn't a lie. Not really. She merely told him what he wanted to hear.

The warmth from his stare caressed her face before he offered her his arm. "Then, by all means, take me to your new friend and introduce us."

Her breath caught in her throat. He couldn't possibly be serious. Why did he change his mind so quickly? It didn't matter. She wouldn't allow his doubtful nature to dissuade her from her goal, any more than she would let his touch distract her from her mission to prove his guilt.

"Promise me one thing, Maxey."

"What is that?"

"When you ask Raúl questions about my uncle, please do not hint of my relation to Matthew. Also, do not let Raúl think you are an investigator. Although you want to pretend to be one, you are not. Servants don't have the same training as investigators, which I'm sure you know."

She hated how Nash constantly reminded her that her station in life was far beneath his. "Why would I hint to being an investigator?"

"Because I know you, Maxey. But remember that if he thinks you are, he will not trust you, and he will not freely give away his answers."

"Then what shall I tell him?"

"I do not know. However, I am certain your clever mind will think of something."

Biting the inside of her lip, she stewed. Her suspicions about him grew deeper by the minute. Well, she would prove to Nash she could pull this off and that Raúl would open up and tell her what he knew.

CHAPTER TEN

THE INTRODUCTIONS BETWEEN Nash and Raúl proceeded smoother than Maxey had expected. Nash acted as her protective uncle, asking Raúl far too many personal questions about his life, finances, and intentions. Like a gentleman, Raúl gave precise answers and never indicated he wanted more than her friendship.

Supper passed easily. Not once did Maxey worry about either man. It was as if everyone had a role to play tonight. She certainly had a part to perform, and within moments, she needed to step into her investigator role. She wrestled with whether to inform Nash of her plan. Knowing that hardheaded man, he would try to stop her, since he assumed she constantly needed protection.

Nash pushed away his empty plate and rose from the table. They ate in the lovely dining area, and thankfully well enough away from everyone so they could carry on a decent conversation.

"That was filling, do you not agree?" Nash asked Maxey.

"Indeed it was."

"Might I suggest a walk on deck to enjoy the evening?"

She switched her focus to Raúl. "What do you say? Would you like to join us?"

He rose and offered his arm. "Only if you will allow me to be your escort."

Maxey remained seated, readying herself for Nash's reaction. Tiny lines of tension pulled at the corners of his mouth. His eyes darkened, but not in the same manner or shade she saw when he held her in his arms and peered into her eyes with so much tenderness. Instead, it almost appeared as if jealousy became the root of his attitude.

A nerve in his neck jumped. "As her guardian, I think you should have directed that question to me first, Raúl."

Panic surged through her, and she lost her breath. It appeared her first order of business would be calming Nash's anger. She needed to stand near Raúl if she planned on lifting his room key from his pocket.

She stood and walked to Nash. Patting his arm, she stared into his eyes. "Come now, Uncle Nash. Don't worry so." She winked. "All will be fine, since you will be joining us."

"I suppose." He arched an eyebrow.

Maxey gave him a quick, platonic hug, whispering in his ear, "I'm going to sneak away in a minute. Keep him entertained so he doesn't follow me."

Nash's forehead creased and his eyes narrowed. She didn't have time to explain. Not now, while they stood with Raúl.

She turned back to their new friend and slipped her hand around his arm. "Shall we proceed?"

Raúl gave Nash an assessing stare. Maxey held her breath, waiting for approval, and after a couple of silent—and very unnerving—seconds, Nash nodded.

Topside, without her cloak, the cool wind played across her skin, sending a shiver through her. She had left her wrap in her room on purpose.

Raúl frowned. "Where is your cape? You will catch your death out here if you do not keep yourself covered."

"I shall be all right. You can keep me warm." She snuggled against his arm, slyly maneuvering a hand into his coat pocket. When her fingers grazed the metallic key, she held her breath. Carefully, she pinched the key between two fingers, slowly slid it out, then grasped it in her palm.

Nash cleared his throat. Anger darkened his face. "Maxey, I am still your guardian, and you must maintain proper decorum. You do not know Raúl well enough to be so open with him. And I insist you hurry back to the room and fetch your cloak this instant."

She held herself from laughing. Although Nash gave a splendid performance as her uncle, he was still very humorous.

"Raúl, please forgive me for—"

"No need to apologize." Raúl threw a glare at Nash. "Unlike most men, I do understand the needs of a woman." Smiling at Maxey, he caressed the hand still hooked over his arm. "But your uncle is correct. You need to have some protection from the cold."

She stepped back and nodded. "If you will excuse me, then. I shall return momentarily."

Nash pulled himself straighter. "Hurry, my dear. In your absence, I shall get to know Raúl a little better."

She held in her sigh of relief until she hurried down the stairs and stood in front of Raúl's room. As she slid the key into the slot, her hand shook. She didn't know why nerves had suddenly made their debut. She really wasn't tense, just excited.

Inside, the room was very dim. Only small slivers of moonlight filtered through the window, but not enough to conduct a thorough search. She found a lamp on the table, and after lighting it and turning it low, she started her search in a corner. Just as in her cabin, there wasn't much space to hide things, which meant everything was probably stored in his trunks. To her dismay, they were locked.

Growling, she fished through her hair for one of her pins, hoping it didn't pull apart her bun in the process. Carefully and steadily, she positioned the pin over the bolt on the first trunk and slid it in. It had been a while since she had to pick a lock.

At a young age, her brother Thomas learned the talent and tried to teach it to her. She hadn't quite polished the skill before her father discovered what his children were doing and took a willow branch to their backsides. Now, when she needed the knowledge the most, she couldn't quite remember how.

Where was Thomas Littleton when she needed him?

Finally, the lock clicked and opened. With shaky hands, she lifted the trunk's lid. Shiny steel gleamed from within, and she blinked to adjust her vision. Several swords lay in a bed of red silk, along with knives and pistols.

Her chest clenched. Why did Raúl have so many weapons? Did this have something to do with his trade business?

The floorboards outside the bedroom creaked, and Maxey froze, straining to listen. Footsteps clicked nearby, making her heart jump to her throat.

Quickly, she closed the lid and snapped on the lock. Not knowing who was in the hall, she turned off the lamp. Taking precautions to be as quiet as possible, she tiptoed to the door and pressed her ear against the wood. A rattle of coins came from nearby as the footsteps neared.

She backed against the wall, hoping it would swallow her. Even if Raúl walked inside, the door would hide her only until he closed it.

A soft rap sounded, and she jumped.

"Maxey? Are you in there?"

She placed her hand on her bosom as she regulated her out-of-control breathing. "Yes, Nash." She opened the door and peeked out.

"Come quickly. We have no time to waste. Raúl is on his way."

Nash grasped her wrist and pulled her out. She didn't have time to analyze his stern expression, or how he knew where she was in the first place.

"What should I do with the key?" She held out her hand; the key lay flat on her palm.

Nash glanced around the area, then snatched the key and laid it beside the door. "It will have to stay there."

He led them from one corridor to the next until they hurried inside their room. She sank on the bed and breathed slower while he paced the floor in front of her. His angry eyes stayed on her the whole time.

"Maxey, will you kindly explain what you were doing inside his room?"

Sheepishly, she grinned and shrugged. "Looking for my cloak?"

The corner of his lip twitched upward. "Try again."

"How did you know I was there in the first place?"

"You have proven time and time again that you are a woman of adventure. You also believe yourself to be an investigator, which you are not. Need I say more?"

It looked as if he was getting to know her habits just as she knew most of his. Holding back a grin, she stood and faced him, planting her hands on her hips. "Exactly. But what excuse did you use to leave Raúl to come find me?"

"I told him I worried about your welfare, since you'd been sick of late, and I needed to find you." Raking his fingers through his hair, he sighed deeply. "Did you discover anything of importance? Should we trust him?"

"I'm not certain. I needed more time to look. Before your interruption, I had barely opened the first trunk. He had two others that I didn't have time to search."

"What did you find in the first trunk? Anything noteworthy?"

"Actually," she said, stepping closer to him and laying her hand on his arm, "many different weapons filled the trunk."

Nash's eyes grew wide.

"I don't know if that is a good thing or not. After all, he is in the trading business, so perhaps he sells weapons."

Nash clutched her shoulders and pulled her close. His soft gaze bored into hers, making her limbs melt and her heart pitter-patter.

"Maxey, be very careful. If Raúl is one of my uncle's men, he is trained to be dangerous. He would not think twice before breaking your neck with his hands." Nash touched her cheek, letting his fingers trail down the column of her throat. "I do not know what I would do if that happened to you, especially when I have promised to protect you."

Her mouth grew dry from his sweetness. "Nash, you forget, I can take care of myself."

He shook his head. "No, you cannot. You are not as strong as you want to believe. I also know this is your first time being an investigator, and you will make mistakes along the way—just as you have done since our first meeting."

She grumbled and pulled away from him. How dare he mention her faults? She would show him that she could be more than a mere servant. Perhaps her calling should have been as an investigator and not a governess.

Chuckling, he pulled her back into his arms. "Do you know what your problem is?"

"*My* problem? I didn't realize *I* had the problem. I believe you are the one with issues."

"Maxey, you are so stubborn and cannot see past the end of your cute little nose." He touched his finger to the tip. "We are going to have many conflicts, and until you realize I am your trusted protector, I will always keep my eyes on you to make certain you do not get yourself in trouble."

"But—"

His lips swooped down and landed on hers. Gently, he kissed her, pulling her closer. Heat spread through her, just as it always did while she was in his arms.

Lifting her hands to link them around his neck, she melted against him, but just as she relaxed, he pulled away. His eyes twinkled as a grin touched his mouth.

"Maxey, you are nearly ready to accept me. If only you can learn to trust what your heart is telling you." He turned and walked out the door.

Her shoulders sagged, and she chided herself for the weakness he held over her. The man could play her like a harp, because every time he caressed her, she sang for him.

Breathing deeply, she sat on the edge of the bed and pulled the pins from her hair. Her hands froze. *Oh no!* She had left one in Raúl's room. Now she prayed he didn't discover it…or she would be in a lot of trouble.

MAXEY STOOD AT the helm of the ship. The smooth wood of the wheel rubbed against her palms as she stared straight ahead. Warm wind blew in her hair, and a stray lock brushed her cheek. Once in a while water from the ocean splashed against the side of the ship and touched her skin, making her blink.

Her thoughts were not on the tour Captain Bushwell gave, and she couldn't stop thinking about last night with Nash and Raúl. She wanted desperately to find something. To prove to Nash—and herself—she had an investigator's natural instincts. She didn't dare tell Nash about her hairpin, though.

The idea of creeping into Raúl's room had surprised her. She really hadn't known if she was brave enough. Thankfully, she had started to think like an investigator and take chances.

Nash was a great performer and had played the role of an older, overprotective relative perfectly. Sometimes his eyes smoldered when he looked upon her, and his touch was like a whispered caress. Since she had instructed him to stop seducing her, she should be very upset over this, but instead, she found her heart softening the longer she watched him.

She hadn't had the opportunity to ask Raúl if he knew Matthew so far today. She couldn't even begin her questions because Nash controlled the conversation the whole time. Thankfully, Raúl hadn't said anything about her hairpin, either. She prayed he hadn't found it.

As she rubbed her palm against the wheel, she barely registered that Raúl and Captain Bushwell stood not far off to her side.

Not when Nash's aura overpowered every other sensation on today's tour given by the good captain.

Directly behind her, Nash explained certain navigation laws. His knowledge on the subject impressed her, and it seemed as though he had become the tour guide. Maxey waited for Captain Bushwell to intercede, but his silence indicated that he, too, was amazed at the vast information Nash shared.

"Leeway is measured by the angle of the course steered and the direction through the water," Nash said.

His breath teased her ear, his deep voice stirring tingles on her skin.

"If the wind hits from the left," he continued, "the ship will move to the right of the course and vice versa. Understand?"

Trying to focus on the ocean, she shivered from his closeness. His baritone voice mesmerized her, and she couldn't resist turning to look over her shoulder, lifting her face to his. "Yes."

"You are an apt student." He smiled.

"How do you know so much?" she asked.

He chuckled. "While at war, I made friends with some sailors. They shared many adventures with me."

His body was so close that she wanted to lean against him. But propriety stopped her. If she maintained the appearance of his niece, she couldn't act like a love-struck girl.

While he rambled on about navigation and the sea, she listened, but the words didn't register in her mind. His hypnotic voice had her under his spell. Training her eyes on his lips, she fought the feelings her body had experienced during those times they had kissed.

"The drift of any current is uncertain, at best," he said. "A navigator must take special precautions to prevent any accidents. First and foremost, he must protect his passengers." Nash looked at Captain Bushwell. "Is that not correct, captain?"

The portly older fellow chuckled. "You are doing just fine, Mr. Black. I couldn't have said it better myself."

She wanted to ignore everyone else and drift into Nash's arms and let the current of love wash her away. Nash looked into Maxey's eyes, and her knees wilted from his intoxicating chocolate gaze. His assured grin even made her heart skip. Of course, she should be used to this by now, but today it seemed that she couldn't control her thoughts or her reactions. Perhaps she had grown weary of fighting her feelings.

After Nash's speech, Raúl walked up beside her. "Miss Littleton?" He held out his elbow for her to take. "May I escort you back to the main deck?" He glanced at Nash. "As long as your uncle approves, of course."

Nash didn't speak, just nodded.

She smiled for Raúl's benefit, hoping he didn't notice her distraction with Nash. "That would be wonderful, thank you." Slipping her gloved hand along the gray material of his suit, she hooked it around his elbow.

Maxey didn't need to look over her shoulder to see if Nash followed. She knew he did. Her traitorous body still tingled for his caress whenever he came near. Trying to keep her mind focused on other things, she glanced across the beautiful Celtic Sea and caught sight of something in the distance.

"Captain?" She pointed at the object. "What is that?"

The captain fumbled with his pocket telescope and peered through it. "It looks like another ship."

"A passenger ship?"

"I assume so, since it doesn't look like a privateer vessel."

"Pirates?" She gasped, releasing her escort's arm and walking to the railing.

Moving beside her, Nash rested his hand on the small of her back. "No, Maxey. Pirates are not the same as a privateer. A privateer ship is a privately owned vessel commissioned in war to capture enemy ships. A pirate captures ships for a greedier and more ruthless purpose."

She smiled as a warm, protective blanket wrapped around her from his nearness. "So, the vessel is neither a privateer nor a pirate ship?"

"No, I do not believe so." The captain shifted nervously as he continued to peer through the telescope. "I shall keep an eye on it, though, Miss Littleton."

"Well, if you assure me it's not a threat, then I'll certainly sleep more peacefully tonight."

Captain Bushwell lowered the telescope. "No, it's not a threat, I'm certain of it. Many ships travel this sea, so it is probably just a private vessel heading in the same direction." He cleared his throat and turned. "Shall we proceed on our tour?"

Raúl quickly stepped beside her, offering his arm again. She nodded, moving away from Nash and toward the other man.

During the remainder of the tour, Nash stayed a short distance behind. Once the tour had concluded, Captain Bushwell stopped, turned toward the small group, and bowed. "Miss Littleton, gentlemen, if you will excuse me, I have duties that need to be finished before this evening."

She nodded. "Of course. I thank you for taking the time to give us a tour."

"Mr. Black?" Raúl asked after the captain had left. "Will you allow Miss Littleton to have the evening meal with me tonight?"

A nervous twinge caught in her stomach as she studied Nash's expression. She detected a spark of anger in his wary eyes. Could it be jealousy? Would he stay in character in front of Raúl and continue to act the outlandish lie of being her uncle?

Nash tilted his head, his arms crossed over his muscular chest. "I assume you are not planning on dining with her alone."

"Of course not. I expect you will join us."

Nash nodded.

Raúl turned his attention to Maxey. "Will it be permissible to pick you and your uncle up at your cabin at seven o'clock?"

She smiled. "That is fine."

"Until then." He bowed and placed a small kiss on her knuckles before leaving.

As she watched Raúl depart, a woman caught Maxey's eye. She recalled seeing the cloaked figure staring at her on a previous occasion, but today the older female wore a shawl gathered around her shoulders. The gown she wore was nicer than the ones some of the other passengers had on. Once again, the woman stood alone, which made Maxey curious as to her identity. Did the stranger have something to do with Nash's uncle? If so, then why did the lady stare at Maxey so often? And why did she find Maxey so interesting?

Maxey wanted to go to the woman and say something, but once again, the mysterious person turned sharply and hurried away.

Very strange.

"Maxey," Nash said, disturbing her thoughts. "Have you discovered any more hidden secrets with our new friend?"

She tried forgetting the confusing woman as she focused on Nash. "No. I haven't had the time."

"I know how intelligent you are, so you must expect he is only after you for one thing."

She scowled. "Pray, what in heaven's name are you talking about?"

Nash's lips tightened and his jaw hardened. "You know what I am referring to, Maxey. Raúl's only purpose is to bed you."

Maxey laughed heartily. "Oh, you are being humorous again, Nash."

"It is true."

"Yes, I'm certain it is, but isn't that the same reason you haven't given up on me? Don't you want to bed me as well?"

His dark brows pulled together. "Our situation is different."

"No, it's not. The only difference is that you have known me longer than he has, but your goal is the same. I think if I had given myself to you that first night, you wouldn't have me coming with you to Devonshire right now."

"Maxey." His voice lowered as he grasped her elbow. "That is not true, and you know it. I have told you the reasons for bringing you with me, and having my way with you has nothing to do with it."

She laughed. "Then why wouldn't you make that promise to me last night? Why did you refuse?"

"Because I am attracted to you."

"Yes, because you want to have your *wicked* way with me. Admit it."

His eyes widened, and his jaw dropped. She held her breath for his reply.

CHAPTER ELEVEN

NASH GROWLED UNDER his breath as his attention darted around the crowded deck. A few people stopped meandering, throwing glares his way. Inwardly, he groaned, knowing they had overheard the conversation.

"Maxey, please lower your voice. Either that or let us return to our cabin to finish our debate."

"No, Nash. I would rather stay out here. Then I'm assured you won't force your lusty attention on me."

"Force?" He looked at her. "I did not force you. I have never forced you. If you recall, your body responds willingly to my touch."

"Don't remind me." She scowled and folded her arms. "I hate that you have that kind of control over me."

"The fact still remains, our relationship is not based entirely on satisfying our desires."

She threw him a glare. "That's because we haven't satisfied them at all."

His heartbeat thudded in his chest. What made her speak of this? She knew how he felt. It sounded as if she *wanted* him to satisfy her. Well, there was only one way to find out.

"Then let us end the argument right now." He took hold of her arm again, turning them toward the stairs, and led her below deck.

She stiffened but didn't struggle. He assumed it was to keep the other passengers from watching them too closely.

"What are you doing?" she snapped.

"I am proving to you that having my *wicked* way with you is not the only reason I like you."

"And how are you going to do that?"

"I am going to make love to you."

"What? You contradict yourself, *Mr. Black*."

"No, because after I make love to you, you will see that I will remain by your side, protecting you until we prove my uncle guilty of killing William. I will show you I do not just want you for your sweet, luscious body, whereas if Raúl would bed you, he would ignore you for the rest of the voyage."

"Nash, please." She squirmed, trying to extricate herself from his grip. But he wouldn't let her go. He hurried below deck and to their room, closing the door behind them.

"Stop this insanity at once," she hissed, pulling away. "I will not let you do this."

Nash stalked toward her, and she retreated. He must be insane, because all he wanted to do was take her in his arms and drug her with passionate kisses. But he also knew that if she told him no, he would stop. He had never forced a woman to love him.

"Maxey," he whispered. "Do not think of it merely as a physical encounter, but as making love instead. We will be sharing not only our bodies, but our souls."

The wall stopped her from retreating further, and she gasped, searching for escape, but he closed in on her. He pinned her against the wall and stared into her wide eyes.

He stroked her chin, then brushed his fingers over her hair, pulling out the blue ribbon holding the bulk of her blondish-brown mass together. Waves cascaded over her shoulder, and he threaded his fingers through her glorious tresses.

"Oh, Maxey," he said, huskier this time. A different kind of craving took over his body, and he gave it free rein. "You are so beautiful, so desirable."

She pressed her hands against his chest. "Nash, please."

Her breaths came quickly, just as his. The fast rise and fall of her chest showed her excitement. He took one of her hands and brought it to his mouth.

"I think of nothing else during the day but taking you in my arms and loving you."

"Nash." Her voice softened.

She was on the verge of giving in, he could tell.

Nash turned her hand over and kissed her palm, slowly and tenderly. When he looked into her eyes, those grayish-blue flecks blazed with passion's fire. He took her hands and placed them back on his chest.

"Tell me, my sweet Maxey." Over the erratic beat of his heart, he flattened her hand. "Do you feel that? Can you tell what your nearness does to me?"

"Nash—" she said, her lids lowered to half-mast, focusing on his lips.

This woman excited him more than any other, and once again, he couldn't resist her. He placed his mouth over hers, and she opened for him. A sigh released from her throat before she returned the kiss. Although anxiety rushed through him, he also wanted to take it slow. If things happened the way he wanted, he didn't want to rush anything. Instead, he would let her take the lead.

Keeping his mouth pressed to hers, he shrugged out of his jacket, hurriedly removed his neckcloth, and loosened his shirt. He broke the kiss, but only to remove his shirt. Her attention dipped to his chest. Excitement surged through him.

He took her hands and placed them back on his chest before he kissed her. Soft, delicate hands moved slowly over his muscles, and it was all he could do to stay in control. Her innocent touch created havoc to his mind. This had never happened to him before.

Soon, her palms slid up as she linked her arms around his

neck. He tightened her in his embrace, pulling her closer. He kissed her in ways that he had wanted to for so long, and so far, she had yet to stop him.

That was encouraging.

Maxey's body had weakened, which allowed him to lift her and carry her to the bed, ensuring not to break the kiss in the process. As she gently laid her on the mattress, he followed her down and nestled beside her.

She threaded her fingers through his hair, and he sighed headily. He couldn't recall when he had enjoyed a woman's touch so much. He also couldn't remember when he loved kissing a woman as much as he did this one.

Just as he allowed his heart to sing with victory, she broke the kiss. Passion played on her expression as she moved her hand down his face to his goatee.

"Nash, you've been very gentle and attentive since we have first met, making me feel things I've never experienced before. But..." She rolled her head to the side, staring at the wall.

"What is it, my sweet?" He cupped her face and brought her beautiful gaze back to him.

"I'm still afraid."

"Of what?"

"That I'll...fall in love with you."

He chuckled. "What is wrong with that?"

She licked her lips. "After this is all over, you will leave me. You are the son of a nobleman, and I am a servant. Our worlds do not mix."

"Have you forgotten that I've been disowned from my family?"

"No, but that doesn't change the fact that you have noble blood, and I do not." She sighed, frowning. "And I'm a governess. I cannot be with you in the Lake District and attend all of your operas because my place is with the children at the estate."

He shook his head. "That doesn't mean—"

"Yes, it does." Tears glistened in her eyes. "Once this is over, I will never see you again."

His chest tightened, and he squeezed his eyes closed. "What do you want, Maxey? What are you trying to say?"

She brushed her lips across his cheek. When she pulled back, he looked into her sad eyes.

"Nash, if I can't have all of you, I don't want any part of you. It's all or nothing."

With a groan of frustration, he rolled to the side of her, raking his fingers through his hair. He stared at the ceiling, silently cursing that she had voiced her thoughts—those he didn't want to know. He wasn't ready to settle down. At least she was honest with him. When she told him she had never been with a man, she had said she wouldn't be with anyone *that* way unless it was with her husband.

Could Nash give her that kind of commitment? Not now he couldn't, but what about after this mess with his uncle was over? Could he commit to her then?

With a sinking heart, he realized he wasn't certain. He enjoyed his freedom as a bachelor. He was pleased with doing as he wished and living the life of a performer in an operatic group, knowing he didn't have a care in the world.

Maxey lifted a hand and wiped away a tear rolling down her face. She stared at him as her lips quivered.

"You don't have to answer," she said. "Your expression tells me all I need to know."

She pushed past him and climbed off the bed, before rushing out the door. He cursed fate for messing up his life again, especially the bad timing it dealt. But then, she had given him a lot to think about. Unfortunately, she already knew his feelings.

Strange, but she was correct after all. The only reason he wanted her was to bed her, but the deep ache inside her argued the point. He didn't want to think about what the crushing pain meant. With so much danger in his life, the best thing for Maxey would be to go back to the Lake District, collect her friend, and return to the Wentworth estate. But could he release her when the time came?

FOR RAÚL'S SAKE, Maxey pasted on a smile and forced herself to eat that evening. She tried to ignore Nash's presence at the table, noting that he acted as if nothing earth-shattering had transpired between them earlier that day.

The way he relaxed in his chair, sipping his wine and conversing with Raúl, irked her. She tightened her fingers around her fork and seethed, fighting the growing urge to claw at Nash's face and ruin his beautiful appearance. No use showing her temper now. It wouldn't make him love her.

She held her breath, wondering why she couldn't control her emotions. Why did she even care? After all, she didn't love him.

Or did she?

Mindlessly, she placed a forkful of food in her mouth, annoyed that Raúl continued to pour on his sweetness, even when she neglected him to stare at the elaborate lobster dish on her plate. His charm had no effect on her tonight. Then again, it never had.

Bits and pieces of the conversation between the two men penetrated her senses, but for the most part, they spoke in Spanish. It impressed her that Nash was so fluent in the language, then she silently scolded herself for being captivated. Was it his deep voice that interested her or the exotic language? Either way, it shouldn't matter. If she didn't straighten up soon and get over this infatuation with him, he would surely crush her soul. She prayed it wasn't too late.

Yet she feared it was.

During the men's conversation, she analyzed her feelings. Although she'd doubted Nash this whole time, she had become close to him. She enjoyed the time they spent together and their talks, as improper as they were. It wasn't just his kisses that had set her on fire—it was his charm and how he made her laugh. It was the way he called her *my sweet*. He was a scoundrel, but his gentlemanly qualities were noticeable, too. He was raised well, and she admired that trait in him.

Swallowing a mouthful of food with a dry throat, she came to terms with her emotions. Despite all the time she spent trying to convince herself to avoid Nash's advances, she had allowed herself to fall in love with him. Strange to think it happened so quickly. It was too late to turn back now. She had made a fool of herself and had no choice but to spend her remaining days on this voyage longing for a man she could never have, hoping for a man Nash could never be.

Raúl's suggestion for a stroll on the upper deck interrupted her depressing thoughts. She blinked and met his eyes, accepting his offered arm. Nash trailed behind as they walked out of the cabin. Maxey wrapped her shawl around her shoulders, trying hard to avert her eyes from him.

Letting her thoughts wander, she looked across the dusk-shadowed sea. The ship she'd noticed earlier today was closer than before. It still worried her that the other vessel had come upon them so quickly, yet if Captain Bushwell wasn't concerned, why should she be?

"Mr. Black, tell me what parts of Spain you have visited," Raúl said.

"I have been all over, really. In my career in the military and my acting career, I have traveled the world." Nash shrugged and chuckled. "I suppose it is the Gypsy blood in me from my mother's side."

"I have heard gossip from some of the other passengers," Raúl continued, "that you are an opera singer."

"I am."

"How long have you been performing?"

"Considering I was always pretending in my youth, as my mother told me many times, and I have been singing since I turned eight, I suppose it is correct to say I have been performing most of my life."

Maxey held in a snicker. Nash was definitely an actor, trying to fool as many people as he could.

"I find that fascinating," Raúl replied. "I, myself, wanted to go into *mí padre*'s business, because he was the greatest matador of all, but I find my love lies in the trading business."

"You must go where your heart leads." Nash nodded.

Too bad *she* hadn't listened to her heart. Maxey's chest ached. If she had kept her mind in the right direction, Nash wouldn't have been able to crush her so deeply. Why didn't she have better control? When had she stopped thinking about being a governess and returning to the Wentworth estate, and instead started thinking about being a desirable woman?

Another gust of wind whipped around her, teasing the tendrils of hair by her ears and cooling the skin at her neck exposed by her fancy upswept hairstyle. This would be a good opportunity to leave. She couldn't stand to be in either man's presence any longer. A shiver passed through her, and she gathered her shawl tighter.

Raúl turned his head toward her. "Miss Littleton? Are you warm enough?"

She chuckled. "Actually, no. I haven't been feeling well all evening, and the breeze is chilling me to the point of distraction. If you don't mind, could we continue this stroll at another time? I would really like to retire to my cabin."

"Why, certainly." Raúl patted her hand, and then draped it over his elbow. "Will you permit me to escort you back?"

"Don't be silly. That is not necessary." She withdrew her hand. "You and my uncle are having such a lovely conversation about Spain, and I would hate to ruin it. So please excuse me." She quickly backed away and nodded to Raúl, ignoring Nash. "Have a pleasant evening, and I shall see you on the morrow."

"Maxey?" The concern in Nash's soft voice nearly shattered her defenses. "I think I should take you back to the cabin."

"Nonsense," she replied without meeting his stare. "I'm perfectly capable of making it by myself."

Without waiting for his reply, she hurried across the deck and down the stairs, only breathing a sigh of relief when she reached her cabin and was safely behind the closed door. She shivered again, but this time, Nash's manly scent lingering thick in the air was the cause. It stirred memories of weak moments she had hoped to forget.

After lighting the lamp, she flung her shawl on the chair and marched to her trunk to pull out her nightdress. Angrily, she removed each article of clothing, taking her frustrations out on the material instead of the man who deserved her temper.

Finally, she left her clothes in a heap on the floor and crawled into bed. Anger still surged through her, hotter now than before. Why had she allowed him to charm her so? And to think, because of this confused emotion, she had pushed aside her main goal—to prove Nash's innocence or his guilt.

She looked at one of his trunks in the corner of the room. This one had always been locked. Hmm... If she could unlock one of Raúl's trunks, she could certainly open Nash's.

Without any further hesitation, she dashed out of bed and knelt in front of his trunk. Since she hadn't taken out the coil from her hair, she fished through her locks to find a hairpin. She slipped the pin into the lock and moved it around until it clicked.

She paused, listening for any signs that Nash was returning. Thankfully, she didn't hear his boots creaking on the floor outside their room in the hall.

Cautiously, she lifted the lid to the trunk and peered inside. Books and a few newspapers lay scattered on top. Then, from beneath a book, something sparkled against the lamplight.

Her heart stilled as she moved the book. A gasp caught in her throat and her eyes fixed on the item. A ring sprinkled with rubies, encased with the Wentworth family crest, winked at her.

No! This can't be right...

She moved a few more books around, to discover a pearl necklace and a man's silver cuff links with a ruby centered in the middle. Lying next to that was a gold pocket watch.

She slapped a hand to her mouth to keep from crying out. Was this William's ring? With a tightening gut, she knew the answer. Indeed, her first instincts had been correct.

Nash was the murderer.

Tears welled in her eyes, and she quickly closed the trunk and locked it. She hurried to her bed and buried her face in her pillow, silently crying out her anguish. Pain like no other stabbed through her heart and caused it to crumble even more.

She prayed for a release from her agony. Never again would she allow Nash's intimate kisses or his charm to woo her in *any* way. Her emotions just couldn't handle it. Rather than go through this much heartache again, she should toss him over-board. Although this would be the best course of action, she still needed to follow Carolyn's instructions and bring Nash back to the Wentworth estate.

Curling in a ball, she gave her sorrow a voice, not caring that her cries echoed in the small cabin.

NASH STOOD BY the railing and stared across the sea. Although relieved to be free from that Spaniard Maxey thought so highly of, Nash still wished for some company to settle his thoughts. Since things had ended so badly with Maxey, his mind continued to toss on turbulent waves.

He had made the right decision, though. He wasn't ready for commitment and didn't want to lead Maxey into believing something that wasn't true. He had hurt her, but it would have been worse had he made love to her and then crushed her dreams.

The ship's gentle sway lured him into relaxation, and he seriously considered retiring to his room for some sleep. But he didn't want to speak to Maxey about what happened earlier. If he waited a couple more hours before going downstairs, she would probably be asleep. So he lurked at the railing, praying for time to pass.

The quarter moon cast spooky shadows on the water, and when he thought the ship jarred a different way, his cautious nature perked up a notch. The water even splashed in an altered rhythm. Peering through the night, he tried to focus on the sea, but didn't see anything out of the ordinary.

Shrugging off the prickly sensations jumping over his skin, he turned away from the railing and walked toward the other side of the ship. He nodded greetings to a few female passengers with whom he had become acquainted on the trip, and considered himself lucky that their husbands accompanied them. He didn't need them trying to steal his attention right now.

He stopped, leaned his back against the railing, and looked at the dwindling group remaining on deck. The brisk sea air had no doubt sent the rest of the passengers scurrying to their cabins. At the far end, he spied Raúl standing with eight strange men. Nash didn't recognize them from those he had seen on the ship.

Since setting sail, Nash had cautiously made note of each face, wary of everything and everyone. What were the odds so many men had kept to their cabins since the first day?

When Raúl's attention skimmed across the deck and rested on Nash, the other eight men whipped their heads around to look at him too. Tightness consumed his chest. This was not some coincidental meeting. Somehow, someway, his uncle was behind this.

On this, Nash would bet his life—which was what he might have to give up soon.

Panic gripped him, making it painful to breathe. He was unarmed. It was quite a while since he'd used his fists to protect himself. He needed to retrieve the revolver from his room, yet he didn't want to lure the men to Maxey.

"Good evening, Mr. Black." A feminine voice pulled his attention to his left as Mr. and Mrs. Summers stopped beside him.

He bowed slightly. "And it is a good evening, is it not?" He glanced over the water. "I have not seen a more calming sight in my life." Despite his words, his mind spun, trying to find a way to retrieve his weapon.

Mr. Summers, probably in his fiftieth year, chuckled, his double chin shaking in the same rhythm as his overlarge belly. "Yes, it's a perfect evening for romance." He squeezed his wife's arm.

Mrs. Summers, who looked to be younger than her husband by at least twenty years, blushed. "Mr. Black? Why are you not sharing the evening with someone?" She glanced around the deck. "Where is Miss Littleton?"

"She has taken to her room. The cooler weather has made her irritable."

Mrs. Summers shook her head. "I hope she has overcome her bout with seasickness."

"She has, thankfully."

Mr. Summers turned away to leave, but Nash touched his arm. "Mr. Summers? Could I have a private word with you?" Nash looked at the man's beautiful wife. "It will only take a moment, I assure you."

Pink stained her face again, and she nodded.

After they had taken a few steps away from the woman, Nash said in a low voice, "I need your help."

The older man's eyebrows arched. "For what?"

"I need you to go to my cabin and get my revolver from Miss Littleton, then bring it to me as quickly as possible."

Mr. Summers' forehead creased. "Whatever for?"

"I think I am about to be attacked."

The other man's fast intake of breath made him choke slightly.

Nash continued, "Please be discreet. I do not want these men to know that I suspect their plans."

"Who—" Mr. Summers started to look around, but Nash tugged on his arm again.

"Please do not look now." He waited for Mr. Summers' attention before continuing. "A group of nine men are gathered over on your right. I do not think they will make a scene with this many people on deck, which is why I will remain up here for as long as I can. I need you to go to my room and get my revolver. Will you do this for me?"

Mr. Summers nodded.

"Take your wife back to your cabin first. She should not be involved."

"Do you want me to inform the captain?"

"Only if you meet him along the way. If you do not see him, wait until after you have brought me my weapon."

He nodded again. "I shall be quick about it."

Nash managed a smile. "I thank you. I will be forever in your debt, Mr. Summers."

Mr. Summers looked calm as he walked to his wife and took her arm, then rushed her to the stairs leading down to the cabins. Nash's worry lessened, and he hoped his instincts were correct. If these men worked for his uncle, they wouldn't cause a scene. Instead, they would wait to grab Nash someplace private. When that time came, he hoped his pistol was with him. Either that, or he prayed God would help him.

CHAPTER TWELVE

A LOUD KNOCK boomed on Maxey's door, bringing her out of a fitful sleep. She jumped to a sitting position. Her body shook. Taking a deep breath, she calmed herself and crawled out of bed, slipping a wrap over her nightdress.

The loud knock came again.

"Who is it?" she called.

"It's Mr. Summers. Mr. Black sent me to get something from his room."

Curiosity led her to open the door. The bright light from the hallway made her squint when she looked upon her late-night visitor. "Why would he send you when he can come himself?"

He shook his head and stepped closer. The terror on the man's face let her know he was certainly not being forward with his actions.

"Mr. Black is up on deck and sent me to get his revolver. He thinks he is in danger."

Although Nash had talked about this subject quite a bit, he had now involved another person. Perhaps Nash had good reason to fear this time, since he was indeed the murderer—but then, why was his uncle searching for him? And why would Nash be in danger? Still, curiosity niggled her, and the investigator she tried to become wanted to solve tonight's mystery.

"Why does my uncle believe that?"

"There are several men up on deck, and he thinks they are waiting for the chance to attack him. He doesn't think they will approach him while there are still people milling about, so he is remaining there until I return with his weapon."

Nothing made sense. In all this time aboard ship, Nash had only suspected one person, and that was Raúl. She knew the reason for Nash's reaction was because of jealousy. As much as she wanted to argue with Mr. Summers, going back to sleep was more important.

She turned and hurried to the trunk that wasn't locked. Underneath Nash's top shirt, she located the pistol.

"Here it is." She gave it to Mr. Summers.

"Oh, thank you, Miss Littleton. I suggest you stay here and keep your door locked until everything has settled."

"I certainly will."

Mr. Summers hurried out of the room, his chubby backside rolling with each movement. She shook her head and closed the door. It wasn't like Nash to involve another person, so he must know something he hadn't shared with her yet. Could his uncle's men indeed be aboard? Why hadn't Nash discovered this before now?

Then again, apparently Nash hadn't been fully honest with her since they met. So perhaps something was going on this evening that might prove he killed his brother—other than the ring, of course.

She stepped to the bed and sat as her heart hammered against her ribs. Her brief nap left her wide awake, but it was the panic in Mr. Summers that worried her. Perhaps she should sneak up on deck to see what act Nash was performing this time.

A grin tugged at her lips. Yes. A good investigator would do that very thing.

Excitement bubbled up in her chest. She would prove to Nash how well she could handle danger, since he didn't think she could. Not only that, but she would show that good-for-nothing man that she *was* a fine investigator, since she *had* caught her suspect!

She rushed to her trunk, pulled out a dress, and quickly changed before going up on deck. She pulled the brush through her sleep-tangled hair in a hurry. As she walked through the door, her smile widened because of what she hoped to accomplish.

She rushed up the stairs, relieved at finding none of the other passengers up and about this late in the evening. Trying to make as little noise as possible, she climbed to the top deck, and then quickly darted behind a water barrel.

In the still night, she strained to hear any sounds. Scanning the area, she decided Nash must be on the other side of the deck, so she scrambled to another water barrel, then on to the next, and next, until she finally spotted him.

A group of several men stood around him, but Nash's masculine frame towered over them all. Although she couldn't hear their exact words, they were very upset. The tone of Nash's voice was strong, yet calm, while the other men seemed belligerent and forceful.

The men's actions set off an alarm in her head, which kept her spying behind the barrel. What exactly were they up to? And why did none of these men look familiar? In all this time on the ship, wouldn't she have seen one of them at least once?

One of the men grabbed Nash from behind and held him in a viselike grip. She gasped, her eyes locked on the tableau unwinding before her. The man who seemed to be the ringleader stood so close to Nash that their noses were inches apart. But Nash didn't move. He seemed to have no reaction at all. Even from where she hid, Maxey saw his creased forehead and tight lips.

She hitched another breath. This was indeed very real. How could she help him if she didn't have a weapon? Perhaps she could find a board or rope, or something else that might assist him. But she couldn't tear herself away from the scene to go look.

She shook her head. Why did she even want to help a murder suspect in the first place? Her heart told her she must.

The harsh expressions on the other men's faces weren't

feigned. Nash might be in serious trouble. The man in front of Nash shouted angrily, then stepped back and ran his fingers through his red hair, appearing greatly irritated. Another man walked up and slammed his fist into Nash's jaw.

Maxey jumped and covered her mouth to keep the scream of fright from carrying through the air. She remained behind the barrel as panic raced up her spine. What could she do? She could not fight off a half-dozen men even if she wanted to.

Her mind churned in agitation. Obviously, these men planned to do Nash serious harm. His stance did not waver, which seemed to make the man who had hit him angrier. Both of his hands formed into fists, and he hit Nash again, then again, striking his stomach. Nash gasped and doubled over. The man holding Nash from behind did not let him drop.

Pain gathered in Maxey's chest. She couldn't stay here and watch Nash get beaten, but what could she do?

Had his story been true after all? Was he *not* the murderer, as he had been telling her? Why was the family's ring in his trunk? She felt confused, and tears slid down her face. Obviously, she had not been a good investigator at all. Perhaps she shouldn't have believed that she could do anything else of importance. She was a governess first and foremost.

A trickle of blood spilled from Nash's mouth. Maxey held her breath. He proudly rose to his full height again, meeting his opponent with a fierce gleam in his eyes. Fear clutched at her chest. Curse his pride. It was going to get him killed.

The man laughed over Nash's stubbornness and punched him again in the stomach. Nash doubled over and coughed, then righted himself, slower this time.

Where was his revolver? Had Mr. Summers not been able to arrive in time to give it to Nash?

He spoke in bold tones to the man, which caused the other men to chuckle. Whatever he said made the man behind him release his hold and step away. The others circled Nash, leaving him and the first man alone to fight.

Perhaps Nash had attacked their sense of honor. From what she had seen, men seemed to hold their honor high. Would it be enough? She had to do something to help.

Nash raised his fists, and Maxey's fear raced out of control. When the fight began, it surprised her to see how well he defended himself. Although he had gone to war, she didn't figure him to be a fighter. Just a lover who broke women's hearts.

Nash connected with his opponent's face, while dodging the blows being thrown at him. He had skills she'd not yet been privileged to see. Nash was beating the other man to a bloody pulp. She doubted the man's friends would accept this outcome and let Nash leave unharmed. He needed help. She must go fetch the captain immediately.

She prepared to leave, but halted as Nash's opponent fell to the ground. Suddenly the other men surrounded Nash and jumped on him. A cry of alarm escaped her, and she quickly covered her mouth again. Luckily, nobody heard.

Again, she prepared to leave her hiding spot to search for help as the men beat upon Nash, punching and kicking him merciless-ly. Would his uncle allow this? What kind of uncle wanted his nephew dead, even if a title and lands were involved?

From behind her, a group of heavy footsteps clamored on the deck, and she glanced over her shoulder to see Mr. Summers and Captain Bushwell lead a group of men. Someone had come to Nash's rescue after all. Surely the captain would stop the fight.

Captain Bushwell aimed his revolver in the air and shot. The pile of men on top of Nash quickly stood and withdrew their weapons, backing away from him. Within seconds, the two groups faced off until fighting ensued between them both. Knives flashed, adding a more dangerous element to the brawl.

Maxey wrung her hands. Fear gnawed at the pit of her stom-ach. Bleeding from his nose and mouth, Nash fought with the man who had held him prisoner before. The stockiness of his opponent prevented Nash from knocking the man down, yet Nash struck him over and over, not allowing the man to get in a punch. Finally, the large man wrapped his hands around Nash's throat. Maxey let out a scream, ignored by the fighting men.

Nash struggled, trying to peel the man's hands away. Failing at that, he dragged the man down with him as he reached for his boot, withdrawing his revolver. Nash aimed into the man's belly and fired.

This was no game.

Men were dying now.

Maxey screamed again and stood. She was uncertain whether to flee back to her room or stay and watch this horror unfold. Nash and the captain would settle this. At least, she hoped they would. She was certain Nash would live. She could berate him later for frightening her so.

As she turned, she ran into a human form. The small light from the moon barely registered on the man's face.

"Raúl." She clung to his arm. "Thank the Lord you are here. You must help Nash."

"Yes, *señorita*, I am helping." He took her arms and pinned them behind her, making her cry out in pain.

"What are you doing?"

"I am helping my men, Maxey."

"Your men? Who are your men?"

"My main purpose is to dispose of your lover." Raúl's lips quirked. "Yes, I befriended you to remain close to my target and only waited for the right moment to strike."

Her chest tightened. He *was* one of Matthew's men, just as Nash suspected. Why hadn't she realized that? Although he'd tried to convince her, she wouldn't listen.

Inwardly, she groaned. Too late to revisit her past mistakes now.

Raúl tightened his hold as he dragged her backward with him to the stairs. She struggled, but his painful grip was immovable. Releasing a scream, she hoped to draw someone's attention, but Raúl quickly slapped his hand over her mouth.

"I would not do that if I were you."

She lifted her foot and brought it down hard on his instep. He howled, but did not let her go, though his hand loosened. Before she could scream Nash's name, Raúl had covered her mouth again.

"If you are smart, you will be quiet and not cause problems."

Not heeding his suggestion, Maxey kicked him again, which made him trip. Since he refused to release her, they both tumbled to the deck. As he tried to right himself, his arm loosened again. Maxey took the opportunity to push away.

Unsteady from the fall, Raúl couldn't grab her gown, and she scrambled away from him on her hands and knees. It was a short-lived victory, as he soon had her pinned. She sincerely wished she had listened to Mr. Summers' warning about staying in her cabin.

Angrily, Raúl yanked her long hair. She cried out, feeling as if he wanted to rip her head from her shoulders. He stood and pulled her with him. They were very close to the railing. The bottomless ocean terrified her, and she didn't want to end up in the icy water by acting foolishly. Nash would save her from this madman as soon as he was free, she was certain.

"Are you going to be a good girl?" Raúl asked, his teeth clenched and his face a purple mask of fury. He yanked her hair again.

A strangled sob escaped Maxey's throat. "Yes."

"Splendid. Now, I am going to take you with me. You see, my ship has been following us, and it is time I boarded the right vessel."

"No, please, leave me here." Would Nash know where Raúl had taken her? She was a fool not to believe Nash before. She would not make this mistake again, but first, she must escape.

"Leave you? I do not think so." He glanced at the group of men still fighting. "It looks as if your lover and his friends will prevail this time, so I need you as bait. Nash will come to save the women he loves, I assure you. Or at least he will try." He snickered and turned, but another man stepped up behind him unnoticed.

Nash! She sighed and relaxed. Raúl's brows drew together as he frowned.

"You are wrong," Nash growled. "I *will* succeed in rescuing her." He pulled back his fist and punched Raúl in the face.

Raúl stumbled and shoved Maxey ahead of him. The blow sent her reeling to the edge of the deck. Unable to regain her balance, she teetered overboard, but caught hold of the railing. The slivered wood bit into her hands as she tightened her grasp, but she continued to slide. Terror choked her scream as she dropped into the deep, dark abyss.

The frigid water sucked the air from her lungs, shrouding her body in darkness. Her heavy skirts weighed her down, and did nothing to shield her from the piercing cold. She waved her arms, kicked her feet, and did all she could to rise to the top. Nothing worked. Quickly, numbness took over her body as she sank deeper and deeper into a dark grave.

⫸⫷

MAXEY'S SCREAM PIERCED the chilly night air. Pain consumed Nash, like his heart was ripped open. Then came the terrifying splash that seemed to drown out all other sounds.

He broke away from Raúl. Fear suffocated Nash as he gripped the railing and stared into the murky depths of the ocean.

Praying for strength and guidance, he hastily shrugged out of his coat and yanked off his boots before bounding over the rail and into the water. Surrounded by nothing but darkness, he flailed wildly, trying to find her...to feel her. He cursed the dead night that made it impossible to see anything, but he searched frantically, praying for God's assistance the whole time.

After what seemed like forever, his hand finally grazed her body. After securing his arm around her, he swam back toward the ship. Shouts from the deck led him to the rope they had thrown down for him.

"Someone bring a lamp over here," one man shouted.

"Just a little closer, Mr. Black," another passenger said.

With their guidance, Nash grabbed hold of the rope. Finding strength he did not know he possessed, he flung an unmoving Maxey over his shoulder and pulled them both up. His arms ached, and his gut twisted from the blows he'd received in the fight, but he forced himself to climb until several others assisted him and Maxey aboard.

The men grabbed Maxey first, but once Nash had his feet planted on the deck, he pushed past them to kneel by her side. Her face was pale, her chest unmoving.

"Oh God. Please do not take her away." He rolled her to her side and tried to push the water out of her lungs. She fell to her back, still not breathing.

He had to get air into her lungs. She needed to breathe and couldn't do it herself. Without another thought, he bent over her and pried her mouth open, then tried to breathe life back into her.

Finally, her body moved. Her racking cough brought up a stream of liquid. Nash praised the Almighty. With a lump in his throat, he gathered her against his chest.

"You will be fine," he whispered. "I will not leave you again."

Captain Bushwell pushed through the men and knelt beside Nash. "We have apprehended the men, but a few escaped onto their ship. We couldn't stop them because of trying to assist you and Miss Littleton."

"What about Raúl?"

"He is tied up and being taken below as we speak."

"That is music to my ears."

The captain scratched his chin. "Will you please tell me what's going on?"

Nash nodded. "Yes, but first, we need to get Maxey into some warm clothes and into her bed."

"I'll fetch the doctor." Captain Bushwell rose.

Nash lifted Maxey and pushed his way through the concerned and curious people on his way to their room. Mrs. Summers waited there, ready to assist. She ushered Nash and the others out of the room to undress Maxey.

Nash paced in front of the door, praying Mrs. Summers would hurry. He didn't like that the rose color had vanished from Maxey's face, leaving dull, pale skin. He wanted her back in his arms so he could bring warmth to her body again. When he held her moments ago, she had shivered so hard that it wrenched his soul.

Finally, Mrs. Summers opened the door, and Nash rushed in. Maxey lay in bed with blankets piled on top of her. Her trembling had decreased ever so slightly, but the bluish color of her lips worried him.

"She will be all right," Mrs. Summers said softly.

Without taking his eyes off Maxey, he replied, "How can you be so certain?"

"Because she has a strong will."

"Indeed she does."

"I think you need to change out of your wet clothes as well."

"I will." He finally looked at the other woman. "I don't know how to thank you, Mrs. Summers. I am most grateful for your assistance."

"Please send for me if you need more help."

"I shall."

Once she left and closed the door, Nash turned his focus back to Maxey, who lay shivering. She hadn't opened her eyes, so he quickly stripped off his own wet clothes and replaced them with something dry. He sat on the bed and rubbed his hands over her arms, which were still under the blankets, but it wasn't controlling her shivering. Not knowing what else to do to keep her warm, he climbed into bed beside her to share his body heat. Slowly, her shaking subsided, and unconsciously, she snuggled against him.

Once he relaxed, he gave a silent prayer of thanks. The strange pain in his heart meant he couldn't contemplate what life would be like without her. She had become so important to him in such a short time. Never before had he felt this close to a woman.

He kissed her forehead, wishing her temperature would return to normal, and snuggled her closer against his chest.

Someone knocked on the door. "Mr. Black? I'm Doctor Lewis, and I'm here with Captain Bushwell."

Grudgingly, Nash tore himself away from Maxey and climbed out of bed, keeping the blankets wrapped tightly around her. "Enter," he called.

Nash stood back as the doctor checked Maxey's breathing, and then did a series of tests to judge her reflexes and body's temperature. Not for one second did Nash take his eyes off her.

"Do you know those men, Mr. Black?" the captain asked.

"No."

"Can you tell me what exactly happened, then? How did they board my ship, and why would they do that?"

Nash shrugged. "I suppose they were in the ship Miss Littleton spotted earlier and used rowboats to get nearer so they could climb aboard, but I do not know why they are here."

"But they singled you out amongst all the other passengers."

"They did."

"Can you explain?"

Nash turned his attention to the captain. "Not at this time."

Captain Bushwell exhaled in exasperation and ran his fingers through his hair. "Mr. Black, you are not making any sense."

"I know. That is because I am just as confused as you." Nash looked back at Maxey.

"Do you know of any reason they had for finding you?"

Nash remained silent for a few moments, then nodded. "I think my uncle sent them to kill me."

"Why would he do that?"

Nash tore his focus off Maxey for a moment when he looked at the captain again. "Because I am the heir to a large inheritance, and my uncle wants it."

Captain Bushwell sucked in a breath. "But I don't understand—"

"Captain," Nash said, his attention back on Maxey. "Can we discuss this at another time?"

"Yes, of course. I need to question my crew to find out why nobody saw those other men climb aboard my ship." The captain turned and left the cabin grumbling.

"Well," the doctor said as he stood, facing Nash. "I think she is going to be fine. We shall keep a close eye on her in case she catches pneumonia, but if you remain by her side and take care of her—"

"I plan on it," Nash interrupted.

"Splendid." The doctor placed his instruments back into his little black bag. "Keep me informed on her progress."

Nash nodded to the doctor as he left.

Breathing a sigh of relief, Nash sat on the bed beside Maxey. Her lips had more color, but she still looked more like a corpse than the exuberant woman he knew.

The strenuous activities of the evening wore on his exhausted body, so he turned down the lamp and crawled into bed, taking Maxey back in his arms. Once he rested her head on his chest, her ragged breathing turned soft.

With a smile, he realized how well she fit next to him. He had always enjoyed the way she felt in his arms, but now, as he lay beside her, he knew their bodies molded perfectly together.

He kissed her forehead. "Sleep well, my sweet Maxey. No need to fear any longer."

And he would make certain of that.

MAXEY'S WEAK BODY lay still as death, but her chest rose and fell with life. Nash remained by her side and nursed her, but a feeling of uselessness grew inside him. She had gained consciousness a few times, but she mostly slept. On a few occasions, her eyes drifted open and he cajoled her into eating a mouthful of hot soup or sipping water from a cup.

Soon, fever consumed her body as coughing racked her, and Nash summoned the physician. Doctor Lewis diagnosed her with pneumonia.

Fighting for control over his own panic, Nash kept his words calm. "Are you saying she is going to die?"

The doctor shook his head. "On the contrary. I know many people who have lived."

"And I, Doctor Lewis, have known people who died from pneumonia."

The doctor patted his shoulder. "She will live, because you won't let her die."

Emotion welled in Nash's chest. His eyes stung with unshed tears, so he quickly turned away and hurried back to Maxey's side. He took hold of her hot, weak hand and gently stroked her skin.

"You are correct, Doctor Lewis. I will not let her die."

"Make certain she drinks plenty of fluids, and keep her as warm as possible. If her temperature rises, we shall have to place cold rags around her body to bring it down."

Nash nodded and returned his attention to Maxey.

The physician left the room. Sighing, Nash ran his fingers through his hair. Death was not an option, yet what could he do to stop it from happening? So far, nothing he had done had helped.

A light knock came upon the door before it opened. He looked back to see who had entered. Mrs. Summers smiled as she brought in a tray of food.

"The cook fixed some special broth for Maxey." She set the tray on the table. "And I brought you some food, as well."

"Thank you, Mrs. Summers, but I am not hungry." He turned back to Maxey.

Mrs. Summers touched his arm. "But you need to keep up your strength if you expect to help her."

He glanced at the lovely brunette and smiled. "You are correct. It is hard to think about myself when I am so worried about her."

"Yes, I can see how concerned you are. It's evident in your eyes." A blush stained her face. "But can I ask you a question?"

"Of course."

"You give the impression you and Maxey are relatives, but I think she means more to you than that. I have noticed the way she looks at you, and she is not looking at you like a woman who looks upon her uncle."

He chuckled. "She doesn't?"

Her cheeks grew darker. "No, and you don't look upon her as a niece, either. You are not really related, are you?"

He smiled. "No."

"Do you love her?"

He glanced at Maxey on the bed, and the unknown emotion twisted inside him again. *Is it love?*

He quickly dismissed the notion. Although he cared deeply about Maxey, he wasn't in love with her. "I do care about her very much."

Mrs. Summers dropped her hand and stepped away. "You men are all alike," she muttered as she turned.

Nash reached out and grasped her wrist. Her pleasant smile was replaced with a scowl.

"Why do you say that, and in a sarcastic tone?" he asked, releasing her.

"Because men like you ignore your true feelings. You would rather follow your head than your heart." She looked as though she fought an inner battle. "At one time I loved a man, but he didn't return my feelings—at least, he wouldn't allow himself to return those emotions. So, when Mr. Summers offered for my hand in marriage, I accepted. I could tell George loved me, but because I still harbored feelings for my young gentleman friend, I couldn't let myself love George the way he needed. Three months after I married George, my secret love finally admitted he loved me, but it was too late."

With the back of her hand, she wiped away a tear before straightening her shoulders. When she looked back at Nash, her smile wavered.

"All I'm saying is: don't hide your feelings. If you love her, let her know or it will be too late. Good day, Mr. Black." She turned and left the room.

Nash blinked in a daze. Did he really feel that way about Maxey? His heart ached with that unfamiliar emotion he was experiencing lately.

Could it be love?

CHAPTER THIRTEEN

WHEN MAXEY STIRRED on the bed, Nash momentarily put aside Mrs. Summers' words. Maxey's eyelids fluttered, and she focused on him. Her pretty grayish-blue eyes darkened with fever, and his gut twisted.

"You're here," she rasped.

"You doubt I would stay with you? I am wounded, my sweet." He smiled, hoping to give her the impression he was emotionally strong. "Are you hungry?"

She nodded. "Just a little."

He quickly moved to retrieve the broth Mrs. Summers had brought, then came back to sit beside Maxey. He propped a few pillows behind her before feeding her. While he carefully placed the spoonful of broth in her mouth, she kept her eyes on him. She offered a weak smile, and his chest ached from the tenderness displayed.

"How do you feel today?" he asked.

She gave him a one-shoulder shrug. "My chest feels like a horse is sitting on it, and my whole body hurts when I cough."

"This broth will help you become well."

"You are so kind," she whispered.

He shook his head. "You forget. If not for me, you would not be in this condition."

"No, you mustn't blame yourself." She coughed, and her

chest rattled. "It was my choice to leave the room and wander on deck to find you, even though Mr. Summers gave me your instructions to stay in the cabin."

He fed her another spoonful. "Why did you come up on deck?"

Her smile widened slightly. "To catch you in a lie."

"What lie?"

"The one I thought you had told Mr. Summers when he came to fetch your revolver."

He fed her again. "Why did you think I was being untruthful?"

She shrugged. "Because I have thought that since we met. I know I told you I trusted you, and I apologize for that. But the truth is, I doubted your story."

It pained him to hear those words. "What about now? Do you still doubt me?"

Her smile disappeared. "No." She opened her mouth and leaned forward for more, so he fed her. She relaxed back on the pillows. "I would still like to know how you came to obtain the family ring Carolyn thinks the murderer has. However, I now believe that men were indeed trying to kill you for one reason or another."

Inwardly, he groaned. He would explain the ring. Just not now. "They were trying to kill me."

She coughed again. "Did you kill them all last night?"

"A few. Captain Bushwell tied up Raúl and took him away, but some of his friends were fortunate enough to escape to their ship. Sadly, the captain was too busy tying up those wounded and trying to help the ones who fell overboard at the same time."

She lowered her eyes. "I'm sorry about Raúl. I should have known he had secrets. I should have not tried to be an investigator."

"But, my sweet, you did know." He touched her cheek. "You were wary about him, which is why you searched his room. That tells me you are very skilled in more than just being a governess. I am just saddened because I know you wanted to be his friend."

She met his stare and gave him a weak smile. "I never thought I would hear you say that. I thank you for having faith in me." She took a deep breath seconds before she had another coughing fit. When she regained control, she shook her head. "As for wanting to be his friend, you are wrong. I used Raúl to distract me, that is all."

"Distract you from what?" He offered a glass of water, and she sipped.

"From you."

He grinned and brought another spoonful of broth to her mouth. "Did it work?"

"No."

He laughed, and his heart skipped a beat. He had suspected she was falling in love with him. She had practically confessed to him yesterday.

She finished eating the broth then weakly sank into the bed. "I don't know why I feel so very tired."

"You are sick, my sweet Maxey. As soon as the illness passes, you will return to your perfect self."

"What does the doctor say I have?"

"Pneumonia."

She nodded. "As a young girl, my father became ill with that. It was a rocky two weeks, but he eventually recovered."

"My maternal grandmother became sick with it, and after a week, it took her life." He reached out and stroked Maxey's hair.

"Don't worry, Nash. That won't happen to me. I'm strong."

"No, you are not, but you are stubborn."

Snuggling into the blankets, she closed her eyes. "I'm so tired, and I ache all over."

"Then sleep." He leaned over and kissed her forehead.

Fevered eyes opened and met his gaze, then she smiled. The impulsive sensation to kiss her lips became strong, but he resisted. She was still too ill, plus he couldn't break her heart again.

"I thank you for helping me," she whispered, closing her eyes.

He waited until her breathing became even and her lips fluttered with each exhalation before he moved to the table and ate his meal. He really wasn't hungry, but he needed to keep up his strength, especially for the days ahead. This illness would get worse before getting better, and he wasn't looking forward to that.

⊱⋆⊰

MAXEY AWOKE IN the middle of the night, heated moisture sopping her gown. At the same time, an icy coldness penetrated every bone in her body. Nash lay beside her with his back turned, so she curled up behind him to feel his warmth. The moment she wrapped her arms around his middle, he jumped and turned.

"Maxey?" he said groggily.

"Nash, I'm—I'm—so cold."

He gathered her in his arms, and she pressed her face against his bare chest.

"Oh God, no! Maxey, you are as hot as fire."

"I'm not hot. Just cold." Her body shook.

He mumbled a few words as he moved off the bed.

"Nash?" She reached for him.

"Maxey, I have to fetch the doctor. Your fever is out of control, and we need to bring it down."

"No, Nash."

After pulling on his shirt, he knelt on the bed and took her in his arms. "I will be right back," he told her in a tight voice, then kissed her forehead.

Maxey curled in her blankets but remained still. Invisible knives stabbed her everywhere, and her body ached. She sobbed from the sheer torture it brought. It even hurt to breathe.

Slowly, a cloud filled her mind, and she saw a peaceful place, a place where no pain could reach her. Emotionally, she grasped for that haven, hoping to escape her sickness.

NASH RUSHED THROUGH the hallways and found the doctor's door. He pounded frantically until the older man opened it.

"Doctor." Nash breathed heavily. "Her fever is very high."

The doctor quickly slipped on his robe and ran with Nash back to the room. When they entered, Nash noticed something different. Maxey lay still as death. He inhaled sharply and ran to her.

"Maxey?" he shouted, shaking her. "*Maxey!*"

The doctor pushed him aside. "Let me look at her. Go fetch a porter and have him bring buckets of cold water."

"Tell me she is alive," Nash demanded, his voice as shaky as his heart.

"She is, but barely. Now go."

Nash would have awakened the whole ship if he had to, but he found people who would help. Captain Bushwell even offered his services, and soon the room was filled with buckets of water.

The physician moved off the bed and soaked a towel. "Nash, please help me. We should lay as many wet rags over her body as we can."

Between Nash and the physician, they covered every inch of her with cool cloths. On her forehead and around her face, they laid a few more.

The doctor cursed. "Well, this is better than nothing, but it doesn't seem to be working." He swiped the moisture off his temples with his forearm.

"I am wondering if that is not the proper procedure," Nash said.

The doctor gave him a quizzical look. "Explain yourself."

"I remember when I was young and had a high fever, my governess placed rags filled with ice in my armpits and between my legs. These are the hottest spots on your body, and so with the ice packed there, it cools the body quicker."

The doctor scratched his head, his focus jumping between Nash, the captain, and Maxey. He heaved a sigh and nodded. "Although we don't have ice, I think we should try it with the cold rags."

Putting aside his own panic, Nash forged ahead with his work until the wet cloths were placed against certain parts of her body, and a whole sheet was soaked in cold water and placed over her. She shook violently. Her lips faded to that terrifying blue color again, as her breathing became shallow and her chest rattled.

Nash swallowed the lump of fear lodged in his throat and wiped at the tears that had crept upon him. He had to stay strong for her.

After a few minutes had passed with no change, Nash shook his head. "What else can we do?"

"We will keep her covered until her temperature drops."

"But she is unconscious. That cannot be good."

"No. I think it's better that she is unaware of her condition right now."

"Will she…die?"

"Not if we are lucky."

Nash groaned and bunched his hands into fists. "And what if we are not?"

The doctor hung his head without answering.

Nash paced the small room, wanting to release his frustration in some way, but not knowing how. Maxey looked white as death. Her uneven breathing frightened him, and he wished he could take on the fever for her. She was too frail to suffer this way. And to think, it was all because of him.

Beside her bed, he touched her burning cheek.

Within time, the cloths dried and needed to be replaced. Tears Nash refused to spill stung his eyes. He fought to keep the turmoil building inside him in check, looking for another way to express his frustrations.

Taking a deep breath, he turned his thoughts to performing at the opera—songs that Maxey loved. He cleared his throat and began humming, creating a theatrical stage in his mind. Not bothered by what those in the room thought, he burst into song. Each lyrical stanza released pent-up emotions, until at the end, he felt totally drained.

He slumped next to Maxey's bed and took her hand in his. Her skin didn't feel like fire to the touch. Her chest didn't rise and fall as rapidly as before. When he touched her again, coolness met his skin.

The doctor rushed to her side, inspected her eyes, and listened to her chest. "I don't know what you have done, my good man, but keep it up. It's making her better."

Driven by the doctor's prognosis, Nash garnered strength for another song. He sang until his voice turned hoarse while the doctor and Captain Bushwell continued replacing dry cloths with ones soaked in cool water from the buckets. It wasn't long before the doctor announced Maxey's fever had broken.

Cheers echoed from the hallway. Nash turned to see it filled with spectators. Unfazed, he brought his attention back to the patient, wanting to be alone with her.

The captain quickly ushered the crowd away, urging them to return to their rooms—all except for Mrs. Summers.

The captain shook his head. "You shall need a different bed. This one is soaked."

"What do you suggest?"

"I will have Mrs. Summers dress Maxey in drier clothes, then you can take her to my room and finish caring for her there."

"Are you certain?"

"Yes. I'll inform my cabin boy to make it ready as soon as possible." He left the room and closed the door.

The doctor stayed to help clean up, then he took the buckets and left. Mrs. Summers had Nash leave the room again so she could dress Maxey. Within a few minutes, she opened the door for him. He lifted Maxey against his chest. Her body hung weakly in his arms, and he treated her as if he held a precious crystal that could break at any moment.

He thanked Mrs. Summers for her assistance, and then she left. After draping several blankets around Maxey, Nash carried her to the captain's quarters. The cabin boy had the room ready and the bed turned down. Gently, Nash laid her down and covered her with clean, dry sheets and blankets.

The captain came up behind him and placed his hand on Nash's shoulder. "I think you should get some sleep yourself."

"No, I cannot rest. Not yet."

"She is going to be fine. She will sleep peacefully, so I suggest you do the same."

Nash smiled. "I thank you."

The captain nodded, left the room, and closed the door.

Exhaustion consumed Nash, and his limbs felt like great weights. But he mustered the strength to change his own clothes before climbing in beside Maxey. He took her in his arms and held her tight.

Sleep beckoned. After kissing her forehead, he closed his eyes. Unbidden tears drizzled down his face. He turned his face into the pillow and sobbed out his relief, thanking the Almighty for sparing Maxey's life once again.

"MAXEY, YOU ARE looking healthier and seem so much stronger today," Katherine Summers commented as she helped Maxey dress. "I hardly helped you with your bath this time."

Maxey chuckled as she crawled into bed. She wished she felt as strong as she led people to believe. Strange how being ill with a high temperature had taken so much out of her.

"I may look healthier, but I'm not making as much progress as I would like. I'm still very tired."

"Your strength will soon return."

"It's been two days since my fever broke. Shouldn't my strength have returned by now?" She sighed dejectedly.

"But the point is, you are getting better by the day."

"Katherine, I want to thank you for helping me. I don't know what I would have done without you."

Mrs. Summers smiled. "All I have done is to help you with womanly things. Nash should be the person you thank. He has done everything else."

Maxey glanced down at her hands folded on her lap. "So I've been told by almost everyone who has come to see me." She met her new friend's stare. "But for some reason, I don't believe it. I'm not saying everybody is lying, but Nash doesn't seem like the kind of man who would do something so selfless unless there was an ulterior motive."

Katherine laughed, moved to the bed, and patted Maxey's leg. "I know he is not your uncle. I also know he has changed, because the man I saw taking care of you worried less about himself and concentrated on you. Isn't his love for you obvious?"

The comment brought a burst of laughter from Maxey. "Love? That's an emotion he will never feel for me."

"You are wrong. I can see it in his eyes when he looks at you. He loves you, but refuses to admit it to himself."

"No, he doesn't love me, and even if he did, he cherishes his freedom more."

Katherine shrugged. "Perhaps he has changed his mind since he thought he lost you."

"I seriously doubt it."

A light knock interrupted their conversation. Both women looked up as Nash stepped into the room. When Maxey beheld his magnificence, she couldn't halt the sigh escaping her throat. In his casual shirt and trousers, he radiated masculinity. His long sideburns and trimmed goatee made him look more sensual, which caused her heart to skip in double time.

Realizing her thoughts had strayed, she shook herself free of the trance his presence caused. She had to control her desires. No, she had to make them disappear forever.

"How is my patient today?" he asked cheerfully as he sauntered toward the bed.

"I think she looks healthier," Katherine replied. "What do you think?"

When Nash stroked Maxey's chin, her stomach flipped with excitement. She mentally cursed her weakness.

He nodded. "Yes, her complexion is back to its normal beauty." Then his thumb dropped to her lips and caressed them lightly. "And the raspberry color on her lips nearly tempts me."

Maxey smiled and noticed Katherine's face darken with embarrassment over Nash's very intimate comment. Turning her head, Maxey pulled away from his touch.

"But I do have good news," he continued.

"What is that?"

"The physician says you can start eating solid foods."

She sighed. "That is excellent news. I'm getting rather bored of broth."

Katherine stood. "Well, I should return to my husband now."

Nash faced her. "I thank you again for your help, Mrs. Summers."

"Please call me Katherine."

He nodded, and then, like a gentleman, showed her to the door. Rather than coming directly to Maxey, he lingered picking up the articles of clothing and towels she and Katherine had left on the floor. It surprised her to see Nash doing such a task, but she quickly squashed the hope rising inside of her. She had to remember he would not become the man she wanted.

"It was very thoughtful of the captain to let us use his cabin until our mattress dried. But now we can move back into our room," Nash mentioned casually.

"Yes, I appreciate his kindness very much."

He dropped the clothes in a pile by the door for the cabin boy to take care of, then walked to the bed and sat by her side.

"You worried the captain," he said.

"That is what people tell me."

"And the physician mentioned you have made a quick recovery."

She smiled. "Thanks to a certain man's singing talent, I was told."

He held her hand. "You do not remember?"

"No. I only remember being cold and that my body ached, but that is all." She paused. "But I do recall dreaming I attended your opera, watching you sing."

"I was extremely worried about you." He rubbed her knuckles. "A lot of people were."

Shyly, she glanced at their joined hands resting in her lap. "It pleases me to have so many people concerned on my behalf. But I fear I don't deserve it."

"You definitely made an impression on most. Many people have asked about your welfare. One woman in particular."

Her gaze bounced up and met his. "Indeed? Who?"

He shrugged. "I don't know, my sweet. But she says she must speak with you posthaste."

"Did she give her name?"

"No, but she hinted that you two know each other."

Unease washed over her. "Then perhaps I should see her and discover what is so important that she needs to meet with me."

"She is here now. Are you up for company?"

She shrugged. "I suppose."

"Do you wish me to stay?"

Maxey had mixed emotions. How dangerous could the woman be? Maxey needed to rely on her instincts, but they had steered her wrong on previous occasions. Did she dare risk being alone with a stranger, especially when just getting over pneumonia?

"Perhaps you should be right outside the door, just in case."

Nash leaned forward and kissed her on the nose. "I will not be far, my sweet Maxey."

Maxey scooted up straighter, fluffing the pillows behind her then making certain the sheet and blankets covered her. Nash left, and after a few minutes, the door opened again and in stepped a woman—the same woman from up on deck that had stared so boldly at Maxey those few times.

Except now, she saw the stranger better. Silver strands heavily streaked her once-golden hair, and age lines wrinkled her face. Maxey felt certain this woman would have been very beautiful at one time in her life, but her sad eyes and tight lips told a different story, one that most certainly held a lot of pain.

The woman closed the door and stood silent. Her piercing stare made Maxey uncomfortable, and she fidgeted beneath the covers. The woman scrutinized her in an unnerving way.

The longer the woman stared, the more her eyes filled with liquid. Emotion tugged at Maxey's heartstrings, yet the woman hadn't even said a word. Curiosity nearly killed Maxey, so it appeared she would have to make the first move.

She cleared her throat and smiled the best she could under the circumstances. "I recognize you."

The woman's gasp surprised Maxey. "You do?"

"Yes. From up on deck. I noticed you staring at me a few times during the journey."

The stranger's shoulders relaxed. "Yes. Up on deck."

Maxey motioned her hand to the empty chair beside the bed. "Would you care to sit?"

The woman's eyes bounced back and forth between the chair and Maxey a few times before she shook her head.

"What is it that you need?" Maxey asked.

From the stranger's tight expression, Maxey knew something heavy weighed on the woman's mind. Her bottom lip quivered slightly.

Finally, the stranger pulled herself straight and lifted her chin. "You don't remember me, do you?"

Hadn't they just covered this? "Yes. From up on deck."

The woman shook her head. "I'm not talking about that. I mean in your life, while you were growing up."

Maxey narrowed her eyes, wariness filling her. "You know me from my childhood?"

"Yes, Maxey." The woman's voice softened. "I was the woman in labor with you for twenty-seven hours. You were a difficult birth, since you had turned slightly in my womb, so the midwife said."

Memories Maxey wanted to keep buried resurfaced. Images of her childhood floated through her mind, and the woman standing beside her resembled her mother perfectly. Reality crashed in around her, making her body cold and numb again.

What was her mother doing here? And pray, why did she have to interrupt Maxey's life now, after all these years of silence?

CHAPTER FOURTEEN

MAXEY BLINKED, STUNNED completely. Suddenly, the woman's eyes seemed familiar, as well as the tilt of her nose and her pointy chin. Memories resurfaced, and she could imagine this woman in her home sitting on the couch reading a book, in the kitchen cooking, then at night tucking Maxey into bed. All the pain and suffering she had experienced those days, months, and even years after her mother left crept into Maxey's chest and weighed it with emotion.

Her mind flooded with the wrenching memories of her father pacing the floor in their house and staring out the window for days on end. Many nights Maxey had stayed awake listening to her father's sobs, and most of those nights she had also cried herself to sleep.

She had waited every day, every month, every year for the moment her mother would come back into her life. As each year passed, Maxey had hardened her heart against the woman who loved her family so little that she abandoned them.

Back then, Maxey had the perfect words to tell her mother if the chance ever presented itself. Now the woman stood before her, and Maxey drew a blank. Shock held her tongue prisoner.

Scrunching the blankets with tight fingers, she kept her gaze on the woman who proclaimed to be her mother—a title she didn't deserve now.

Maxey cleared her throat, forcing herself to speak. "How do you know I'm your daughter?"

"Over the years, I have hired detectives to search you out and inform me of my family. Then, not too long ago, I decided to see you for myself—to finally talk to you. That is how I knew when you and Mr. Burke were going to sail to Devonshire. I overheard Nash's name at the ticket booth."

Maxey swallowed the lump of emotion caught in her throat. "Then it's very unfortunate that you had so many hours of labor with me. Could that be when you decided you were not fit to be my mother? Or did that time come before I was born, when you gave birth to Thomas?"

Nora Littleton brought her hand to her mouth and covered the gasp that sprang forward.

"You...misunderstood. That's not—"

"Please don't." Maxey held up her hand. "I don't want to hear your excuses." A sob rose to her throat, but she willed it away, refusing to show any outward emotion. "I recall the day you left. I remember it as if it was yesterday. I remember every tear, every heartache, and every sleepless night. Those terrible memories will be implanted in my mind forever, and there is nothing you can do to change it."

Nora shook her head as tears streamed down her face. "Please allow me to explain."

"No. You will be wasting your breath. Besides, I don't have the patience right now to hear it." Maxey flipped her hand in the air. "I would like you to leave. Now."

Her mother remained standing and staring for a few moments longer. Sorrow filled Maxey for the obvious grief her mother experienced right now, but it didn't come close to the grief their family had suffered.

Finally, Nora spun around and walked out the door. Maxey's chest tightened. It wasn't until Nash stepped inside that she released her pent-up sobs.

He rushed to her side and took her in his arms. "Maxey?

What is wrong? Who was that lady and why did she leave crying?"

"Oh, Nash." She buried her face in his neck, clinging to his silk shirt. "You won't believe it. I still can't."

"Tell me," he said as he stroked her hair.

"She…she is…my mother."

He hitched a breath and pulled back, meeting her stare. "Your mother?"

"Yes. After all these years." She sniffed and wiped the back of her hand across her nose. "She was watching me, even before we boarded the ship. She knew I was her daughter."

"Did she tell you why she left her family?"

Maxey shook her head. "I don't want to know, Nash. It won't change a thing, anyway. She has been dead to me for years."

He gathered her in his arms once more and rocked her gently. Her heart swelled with love for this man. She wondered if she should allow these feelings for him at all, especially when he didn't return them. Was she just setting herself up for more heartache?

She pulled away and swiped the moisture from her cheeks. "Forgive me, Nash. I shouldn't have broken down like that. I suppose the shock of seeing her was just too great for me to bear." She held her breath before the tears returned.

Nash cupped her chin. "You do not need to apologize. I understand perfectly. Thank you for being open with me and letting me share in your grief."

She shook her head. "It's just that I have been a burden to you of late, and I don't want you to take that responsibility any longer."

"It is my own fault, my sweet Maxey. I should not have brought you with me."

She shrugged. "It's too late to look back. We have to move forward with no regrets."

"But I should not have brought you." He dropped his hand. "Because of my own selfishness, you could have died. Twice."

Anticipation bloomed in her chest, yet she dared not become too excited and read too much into his words. Could Mrs. Summers have been telling her the truth? Could Nash really love Maxey? She dared not hope for fear she would be crushed again.

"Actually," she said, "it has been three times."

"Three times? When was the third?"

"At my house, when that stranger followed us home." She softened her words with a smile.

He grinned widely. He was absolutely adorable this way.

"Will you ever forgive me?" he asked.

"I don't know. I haven't decided." Her answer was playful, even though she still wondered if she would stop blaming him for bringing her along. Perhaps eventually.

"I have something to show you." He stood, walked to his trunk—the one that didn't have the jewels—and dug deep inside. Pushing his clothes aside, he showed her a secret opening in the lining. She sat forward and narrowed her eyes. He withdrew an object, then came back to the bed and sat.

"I want to show you something, even though you have already seen it. This was given to me by my father a year before we parted ways." His hand opened to display a man's large ring, a heavy band of gold with the Wentworth crest encircled by diamonds and rubies.

The ring! Was he going to confess now? She now didn't believe he was the one who killed his brother. Instead of jumping to conclusions, she must have patience and wait for his explanation.

"It's very lovely, Nash."

"There are actually two rings. These rings have been handed down from generation to generation, from father to son. My father and Uncle Matthew each had one, until their father took back the ring and disinherited Matthew. Both William and I received a ring. William's ring has a ruby in the middle, which proves he is the rightful heir to the title. My ring doesn't have a large ruby in the middle. Instead, it's sprinkled with rubies and diamonds. Both rings have the family crest."

She took the ring and studied the crest. Indeed, this belonged to the Wentworth family. "Does Carolyn know you have a ring too?"

"I thought she knew. But even if she doesn't, she will attest to the fact that this ring is different than the one given to her husband."

Sighing, he rested his hand on her leg. Immediately, her body warmed. She couldn't fight her feelings, especially when his touch made her feel so special.

"So, you think your uncle killed William for the ring?"

Nash nodded. "I know he did. I also know that he wants me dead because I have the second ring." He slowly moved his palm over her leg in a gentle caress. "You see, if he has both rings, then neither Joshua nor I can gain William's title."

Maxey scowled. "That is not right. Can he really do that?"

Nash shrugged. "I know Matthew wants me dead. One of the men I was fighting the other night kept telling me to give him my ring. The only reason the man would ask for it is because he is on Matthew's payroll."

"That does make sense. However, your uncle just cannot step in and assume the title."

"Not while Joshua and I are still alive, no. Matthew plans to get my ring first, then he will kill me and my nephew."

She flexed her hands into fists, not understanding the injustice of it all. "How can we stop him, Nash? Men like that should be locked away in prison for the rest of their life."

"I couldn't agree more." He gave her an empathetic smile. "Unfortunately, the only way to stop him is to find the ring he stole from my brother after Matthew killed him. With the proof in hand, we can turn him over to the police."

"Then I suppose you have good reason to want to confront your uncle."

"Indeed I do. I'm not only fighting for my life, but for my nephew's life."

She took Nash's long finger and slipped on the ring. Softly, she rubbed his knuckle. "It's a perfect fit."

"Although I cherish this ring, it sickens me to think it once belonged to my uncle."

"It looks good on you."

He cupped her face. "My sweet Maxey, do you believe me now? Do you know beyond a doubt that I am telling you the whole truth?"

Her chest squeezed with emotion. She should have believed him all this time. Why had she wasted such precious moments with him arguing and doubting him when they could have been working together to stop Matthew?

"I do." Her voice broke. "And I only beg your forgiveness for being so foolish. I should have trusted you."

"Why didn't you fully trust me before?"

He moved his hand down her neck slowly as the pad of his thumb slid over her skin. Tingles grew inside her, and although she tried not to melt from his touch, she also couldn't deny the sensations that made her buzz from awareness.

"Since my mother left, I have had trust problems. Not just with you, but with most people I have met. Even when I first started working for Carolyn, it was difficult to trust her. But now, she is my best friend."

He smiled. "Carolyn is a wonderful woman with a kind heart."

"Indeed she is." She touched his chest before she realized that was a mistake. Underneath her palm, his muscles flexed. "But so are you. I have never known a kinder man."

Taking her hand in his, he lifted it to his lips and turned it over to kiss her palm. Warmth spread through her, and she treasured the feeling, if only for a moment.

"Maxey, there isn't anything I wouldn't do for you. I would fight dragons for you, if only you would trust me."

She studied the bruises still fading on his handsome face. "I know. I saw."

He kissed her fingertips. "It was then when I realized what

kind of danger I have put you in. Which is why I am sending you back to the Lake District once we dock in Devonshire. I have already talked to the captain, and he will set sail as soon as he can. He will protect you. I have also written to Carolyn and explained everything that has happened to let her know you are safe."

Her heart sank in a sea of confusion and sadness, and at the same time, anger filled her soul. He wanted to send her home? Without him? Helpless frustration built inside her, making her chest ache.

Strange, because this was what she had wanted all along, wasn't it? Finally, Nash could free himself of her.

She swallowed the lump of emotion lodged in her throat and pulled her hand out of his grasp. "Are you certain I'll be safe?"

"I have devised a plan in case somebody is waiting on shore and watching us. After we dock, I will take you with me to the nearest inn. The captain will have his cabin boy come later and meet us in the room. The boy is about your height and coloring, so you can dress in his clothes to leave, and our watchers will think you are the servant."

She shrugged. "It sounds plausible, but how are *you* going to remain safe?"

"I have not figured that out, but I will be extremely cautious. I will not let my uncle win."

"So, you think if I am by your side then, it will make your mission more difficult to complete?"

"No, but I will be putting you in danger. If you met with another accident or illness, my heart would not be able to take it."

How could she understand this man? Did he really want to be rid of her? Was he saying these words just to alleviate her worry?

"Oh, Nash, you do care," she said sarcastically.

He gathered her in his arms and kissed her forehead. "Yes, my sweet Maxey, I do. More than you will ever know."

She fought for control. But there was a different tone in his voice that made her pause, one she hadn't heard before. She pulled away and stared up at him. "I don't understand."

"When I thought I had lost you in the sea, heaviness grew in my chest so much I could have suffocated. Then, when your fever spiked so very high, and the physician's methods were not working, I could not stand the massive pain of losing you." He pressed the side of his face against hers. "I would have died for you. If God would have let me, I would have taken your place."

His confession tugged at her heart, weakening her resistance against him. Dare she believe he held some feelings?

Ridiculous.

Cursing her premature enthusiasm, she found her anger again and pulled back. "Thank you for your concern, but once I leave with the captain, I will not be your problem any longer, and there will be no reason to worry about me."

His forehead crinkled. "Maxey, I have never thought of you as my problem."

With a shrug, she turned away from him and snuggled into the bed. "I'm tired now, Nash. I would like to sleep."

Gathering the blankets around her, she turned to her side and fought the feelings welling inside her. She didn't know what bothered her most, his evident change of guilty emotion toward her, or his readiness to dispose of her the first chance he got.

THE SUN HAD set into a tranquil sea, and a soft dusk slowly captured the day as Nash stood at the rail of the ship and gazed out on the water. Darkness intruded upon the blue-green depths of the sea, splaying a million stars overhead on the dark velvet backdrop of a clear night sky. His thoughts carried him back to a time when he was a different man.

Until recently, he was satisfied with his life, not bothering to question fate. His childhood had been happy, until his sixteenth year. Nash wasn't certain the root cause of the constant bickering between him and his father, but animosity only grew from there.

Then the fateful night came when Nash returned home after

spending a pleasurable evening with a woman of ill repute—which, of course, wasn't his first time, but his father would have no more of Nash's wicked lifestyle. He was given the ultimatum of straightening up or leaving the family. Nash was stubborn and wanted to live his own life, so he left.

He had enlisted to join his fellow countrymen in fighting for what he believed in, and he hadn't regretted any decision made during those seven years. Even when he left his home and inheritance, he hadn't looked back—rather, he had anticipated the adventures in his new life.

Sighing, Nash shifted his stance as he leaned against the ship's railing. Actually, there was one thing he regretted: he should have made amends with his brother. Of course, Nash had thought he still had several years to do that. If he had only known his merciless uncle was set on revenge, Nash would have done anything to help save William's life.

Now, things were changing again, and he was helpless to stop fate. His twenty-seventh year approached fast, and for the first time, he thought about settling down and starting a family.

The idea scared him to death.

When he imagined spending his days with Maxey, holding her in his arms, his fear eased. From the very first time he spotted her sitting in her balcony box, watching him with great interest, he hadn't been able to think straight. Like a moth to flame, her beauty lured him, and he couldn't find the strength to pull away. He had no other choice but to let her go. She would be much safer with Carolyn at the estate, living as her governess.

Agonizing pain twisted inside him. It would be extremely hard to watch her sail away without him.

He released a deep sigh and scrubbed his face. He must not falter in his determination. Thankfully, the end of the voyage was near, and although he had mixed emotions, he looked forward to ending this ordeal with his uncle once and for all.

Heavy footsteps creaked on the deck behind him, tearing him from his dismal thoughts. He swung around to see who ventured his way. Captain Bushwell sported a full uniform, looking very commanding in his sailor's attire.

The older man smiled. "It's a pleasant evening, is it not?"

"Indeed. The warmer climate is most welcoming."

"The voyage has passed quicker than I expected. We will reach land first thing in the morning."

"Splendid."

"Are you still planning on sending Miss Littleton back with me?"

"I have not changed my mind. I want to follow through with the plans we made earlier. I would feel much safer with her away from my uncle. I also need you to have someone deliver that letter to the telegraph office."

He nodded. "I'll prepare for a quick departure tomorrow."

"May I ask what will be done with Raúl? What kind of trial will he get?"

"Unfortunately, I will have to turn him over to a local magistrate in Spain, since Raúl is one of their citizens, unless of course they allow me to take him back to the Lake District for the trial he deserves."

"I want justice to prevail, but I suspect Spain will protect the traitor."

"I agree."

Nash bunched his hands into fists and slammed them hard on the railing, holding back the vile words ready to spring from his mouth. "Then the sooner we get Miss Littleton home, the better."

"Very true."

Taking a calming breath, Nash feigned a smile. "I thank you, captain. I will be forever in your debt for all you have done to help me and Miss Littleton."

Captain Bushwell leaned against the railing, took a cheroot from the inside of his jacket, and lit it. The scent from the rolled leaves drifted in the air around Nash.

"Nash? How does Miss Littleton feel about your arrangement?"

Nash drew his brows together. "Why do you ask?"

The captain kept his focus on the sea. "Since her miraculous recovery, I have not seen a smile grace her lovely face, especially around you." He looked over his shoulder and met Nash's stare. "Every time I have seen her, I get the impression she is vexed with you."

Nash sighed with defeat. "Indeed, the little vixen was not pleased with my plans. She refuses to believe I don't need her assistance in stopping my ruthless uncle." His frown deepened. "I fear for her safety, and she doesn't understand."

Captain Bushwell chuckled. "I've seen her temper a time or two on the voyage. She is certainly a stubborn woman."

Nash also chuckled. "Yes, she is stubborn, but I would not change that for anything. Her stubbornness defines who she is, and I admire her for that."

"You are going to miss her, I can tell."

Nash's smile quickly faded. "Again, you are correct."

"She will miss you, as well."

"No. I think she will be happy to be away from me. The few times we have talked since her accident, we have done nothing but argue."

"Perhaps she doesn't want to go back?"

Nash laughed again. "Oh no. She wants to return to her position with my sister-in-law, I assure you."

"How do you know?"

"She never wanted to come with me in the first place."

Captain Bushwell straightened and clapped his hand on Nash's shoulder. "Nash, I must say you don't read women very well. The way I see it, her stubborn streak intensified when she found out she was being sent back. The girl wants to stay. It's obvious."

The captain's opinion bothered Nash, only because he hesitated to believe it. Just thinking about the possibility that Maxey might want to stay with him sent his heart into a frenzied beat.

But he quickly stopped his whirlwind of emotions. It didn't matter what he wanted. Maxey would be safer going home.

"No, captain. Maxey has to go. I don't know what I would do if my uncle got hold of her. He wouldn't think twice about torturing her."

Captain Bushwell nodded and stepped away. "I understand. But will you do me a favor before you say your last goodbyes?"

"What is that?"

"I have known since the accident that she is not your niece. Tell the poor girl you love her. Don't send her back with a broken heart."

Silence ripped through the air as the captain walked away. Nash scratched his chin. Strange, but two people had made the same comment about this very thing. Katherine Summers had also mentioned the word *love*.

Did he love Maxey? Perhaps that was the gripping ache inside his chest that wouldn't leave. How could it be so obvious to others but not to him?

The tightness in his chest grew as he gave in to his emotions. *I love her!*

Finally, there was an answer for his glorious emotion. He loved her more than life itself. But he couldn't confess his feelings to her. His life was too complicated for love and marriage right now.

He turned and walked back toward the cabin, struggling with his thoughts. If he told Maxey he loved her, would it make her happy? She had told him once that she was falling in love with him, so could her feelings be as strong, especially now? If she did return his love, she would not want to return home.

No, he couldn't allow that. She was safer at the Wentworth estate.

Quietly, he turned the doorknob and entered the room. Maxey wasn't asleep, as he had expected, but sitting in bed reading. She lifted her gaze for a moment when he entered, but then her attention went back to the book.

He closed the door and walked to the spot on the floor where he had slept. Without a word, he pulled off his shirt in front of her. She raised the book to block her view, and he couldn't stop his smile from widening.

He decided not to retire to bed and left his trousers on. He dug through one of his trunks to find a book to read that would settle his turbulent thoughts, but nothing looked interesting—nothing except the beautiful young lady sitting in bed.

He studied the woman who confused him. With Maxey's knees pulled to her chest, her cute toes peeked out from underneath the nightdress she wore. Her hair was just how he liked it, unbound and cascading over her shoulders in beautiful waves.

Sighing deeply, he walked back to his corner of the room and plopped on the floor.

Finally, she met his stare. "Is something amiss?"

"No."

"That irritable grunt you just made sounded like something troubles your mind."

He grinned. "All right, then, there is something on my mind, but I do not think you would like to know."

She laid the book on her lap, but kept her knees hiding her chest. "Tell me anyway."

"The captain talked to me a few minutes ago and said that we will be docking in Devonshire tomorrow."

A grimace tugged at her delicate lips, turning her expression sour. "I bet that bit of information had you dancing with delight."

"Actually, no." He shrugged. "I will admit I am looking forward to seeing my uncle in prison, but..." He hesitated in telling her the truth.

"But what?"

"But I shall miss you when you leave."

She lowered her head to her knees in contemplative silence, with her arms wrapped around her legs. Patiently, he waited for her response, wondering if she would verbally lash out at him again.

"Stop saying things you don't mean," she whispered.

He moved to the bed and sat beside her. "I do mean it, Maxey." He stroked her shoulder. "I will miss you terribly."

She sucked in a ragged breath before raising her head. The tears swimming in her eyes stabbed at his heart like a knife.

"Nash, I will miss you too. We have been through so much together."

"I will never forget those times."

Her slender throat contracted in a swallow before she nodded. "I shall not forget them either."

He slid a lock of her hair between his fingers, but his eyes stayed on hers. "I would still like to keep in touch. Perhaps we could write to each other."

She shrugged. "Perhaps."

"Or maybe Carolyn will allow me to finally meet my niece and nephew."

"Yes, I'm certain Lady Wentworth will let you visit."

"And I shall inform my sister-in-law that I kidnapped you."

She snorted a laugh and rolled her eyes. "Oh, so now you are admitting to that."

"Yes, it was all my fault. But what was I to do when you mesmerized me so much? Even your investigative skills captured my interest."

She gave a weak chuckle. "Thank you. However, we both know I was never a good investigator. I'm a better governess."

He grinned and caressed her chin. "I think you can be extraordinary in whatever you decide to do. Maxey, you are an amazing woman."

"Please don't lie. My actions during this voyage have proven otherwise."

"Oh, my sweet Maxey. I see more than you think I do. You are indeed an accomplished woman."

Satisfied with gazing into her eyes, he remained beside her, but the ache in his chest kept urging him to say more, to confess his love. He wouldn't. Maybe he would send her a letter in a few weeks and tell her his feelings, but now was not the time.

Reluctantly, he dropped his hand and moved off the bed. "I better get some rest tonight. Tomorrow will be a busy day for both of us."

Her mouth trembled when she nodded.

"Good night, my sweet Maxey," he said as he lay on his makeshift cot.

When she didn't respond, he turned on his side, away from her. The bed creaked as she moved, and the lamplight turned very low. In the stillness, her muffled sobs floated in through the air.

He ached terribly for causing her pain, but he remained on the floor. Going to her now would only cause more damage, because he would certainly take her in his arms and comfort her with tender kisses, which he was certain would turn into more.

And in the end, he would still send her home.

CHAPTER FIFTEEN

MAXEY WALKED OFF the ship with her arm hooked through Nash's like a grand lady. The rich silk of her black and white dress made her feel like royalty. She sauntered proudly, knowing the square neck of the bodice gently enhanced her bosom. Feeling very feminine, she lifted her bonneted head as the wind blew the few carefully coiffed ringlets she left hanging by her ears.

Through the crowded docks at the port, she held herself erect as she glided beside the most perfect-looking man she had ever met. She glanced at Nash and studied him closely. For somebody who wasn't trying to be noticed, he didn't accomplish that feat very well. He was more handsome than anyone man she had met, and judging from the way he turned heads, other ladies agreed with Maxey. Clean-shaven now, he emanated more magnetism than she had seen before.

Black trousers hugged his legs, outlining their muscular build. The dark fabric of his coat pulled tightly across his broad chest, and the crisp white linen of his shirt made him as regal as a prince. His hair had grown slightly longer, and now fell to his collar in beautiful black waves. But this only enhanced his glory and made her proud to be the woman on his arm. Unfortunately, she would lose that privilege by this afternoon.

Nash hailed a fancy carriage to take them and their trunks to the nearest inn. As Maxey sat waiting inside the vehicle, she looked out the window and admired the scenery. The land was greener than she remembered from childhood. Tall, full trees and shrubbery decorated almost every building. Ancient-looking structures made her gasp, and she yearned to take a stroll through each and every building, walk on every cobbled path, and lift up her skirts and race through the distant forest that stretched for miles. Immediately, she fell in love with the town of her birth.

The carriage shifted as Nash climbed inside, and once the door closed, the vehicle lunged forward into a steady ride. Nash looked at her and smiled. Immediately, her heart ached with sorrow. Would she ever feel happy about their parting and knowing she would return home soon?

"Well? What do you think of Devonshire?" he asked. "You told me you haven't been here for quite some time."

"It's lovelier than I remember. There are so many more houses and buildings. It's unfortunate you won't be able to take me on a tour. I would really like to see more."

He patted her gloved hands folded on her lap. "Perhaps another time."

"If I'm ever back in Devonshire, I will call upon you," she snapped, turning her attention out the window, determined to remain quiet for the short ride to the inn.

When Nash registered them under Mr. and Mrs. Black, she tried not to appear shocked. Why hadn't he used a different name instead of the one people called him on the ship?

Nash was friendly to the porters who helped carry their trunks to their room, and he tipped the servants very well. One porter spoke only Spanish and was quite surprised when Nash answered him in his native tongue. The porter sneaked a peek her way and said something she couldn't understand. Nash chuckled and replied with a touch of humor in his voice.

Maxey arched a brow. What were they talking about, and why did Nash laugh when he looked at her?

After the door closed and they were alone, Nash sighed heavily and sank against the wall. His gaze moved to her, and he smiled.

"What was that all about?" she asked.

"What do you mean?"

"The conversation you had with the porter."

He grinned, making her stomach do flip-flops. "He said that your hair resembles wheat fields at harvest time on a bright, sunny morning."

"I suppose, from being in the sun, my hair is lighter than before."

"It is. The porter also said it is a rare pleasure to see such beauty. I agreed, since I think you are the loveliest woman I have ever met."

She shrugged. "Then he needs to get out more. So do you."

"Here at the docks, it is rare to see a woman whose beauty outshines the sun. Perhaps it is a good thing you are leaving. My uncle would be able to spot you immediately, and I would definitely have to keep my eyes on you every second of the day."

"Thank heavens I'm leaving this afternoon, then," she mumbled.

He took a deep breath and released it slowly then slipped off his overcoat and draped it on the back of a chair. "I think we managed to leave the ship without any problems. You definitely make a beautifully regal lady."

"I thank you for purchasing this gown. I have never owned anything so fancy," she said without feeling as she yanked off her bonnet. "And as always, you turned out an excellent performance of a gentleman of nobility. Many women turned to watch you as you passed by."

She sat at the small vanity and peered into the mirror. Her lips were pulled tight, and sadness had taken the spark out of her eyes. It hurt to know Nash insisted on sending her home, and she wanted to lash out at him and make him feel her pain.

She yanked out the pins holding her hair in place. As each one clinked on the table, her rage intensified. Once they were all out, her hair plummeted down her back and shoulders. She plucked at the styled curls around her face, loosening them in the process.

Nash walked behind her and stopped. Meeting her eyes in the mirror, he removed his cravat and laid it on the top of the table. "Why are you straightening your hair?"

"Since I need to look like a boy soon, I need to prepare for that role. Of course, without donning the cabin boy's clothes, I will always look like a woman."

Nodding, he touched one of the curls by her ear. "When I first saw you sitting in the balcony box at the opera, I thought you were the most beautiful woman I had ever beheld." His hand dropped to her shoulder and caressed the small amount of skin exposed around her neck. "Then, when you reappeared night after night for seven days, I could not wait to meet you. During the scenes, I peered through the stage curtains at you. I could not get enough of your beauty." He stroked her cheek. "I still cannot get enough."

She wished he would quit making her ache with his tender words. "Yes, I can tell." She laced her words with ice. "That's why you're sending me back to where I belong at Wentworth Manor."

He knelt by her side, taking her hands in his. "I am sending you home for your own safety. Believe me when I say that deep inside my heart, I really do not want to let you go, but I worry about my uncle harming you. I shudder to think what kind of torture he would put you through if he was able to take you away from me."

"I thank you for caring about my welfare, but I think you are using your uncle as an excuse." She yanked her hands away and stood. Pushing past him, she marched to the window. She parted the curtains slightly and peered out onto the street.

He sighed heavily and stood. "You still do not believe me?"

She shrugged. "Not about this."

"But I suppose it does not matter now. You will be leaving later today, anyway." He stepped up behind her and stroked her hair. "I just want you to know how much I will miss you."

She remained silent as she fought the tears threatening to come forth.

"My sweet Maxey, I don't quite understand why you are so angry. If you recall, you didn't want to come with me in the first place. Now I am sending you home, and you are still not happy."

Huffing, she spun around and faced him, crossing her arms over her chest. "Yes, I'm still not happy. I'm beginning to think this was all planned."

He shook his head. "Planned? What exactly do you mean?"

"I think you go around the world setting out to break women's hearts. I think it satisfies your male pride. You planned to make me fall in love with you, didn't you? And yet you are going to send me back home anyway. You don't care about my feelings, so quit pretending like you do."

Large but tender hands cupped her face as a smile touched his mouth. "You...really love me?"

Another wave of pain yanked at her from the softness in his chocolate eyes. "Not anymore."

He tilted his head and narrowed his eyes. "When did you lose this feeling?"

"During the carriage ride from the ship. As I looked out the vehicle's window and realized you are truly sending me away. I lost all emotion where you are concerned."

A twitch in his lip lifted to a grin. "Ah, but, my sweet, you cannot turn loving feelings into hate that fast."

"What's the use of loving you?" Her voice trembled. "I tried, heaven knows I tried not to give my heart to you, but you purposely teased me with your sultry kisses and made me develop strong feelings for you. I'm innocent, and you know it, but you still played out your gentle seduction. Couldn't you tell how you affected me?"

"Maxey," he whispered, leaning forward as he brushed his lips over her cheek. "I wanted to affect you. I wanted you to love me." He pressed his mouth over hers, but she turned her head and broke the contact.

"Why?" A sob tore from her throat. "So you can send me home? If you wanted me to love you, why are you being so merciless? Can't you tell I want to be with you? Can't you see I want to help? And can't you see that leaving you will rip the heart from my chest and leave me lonely for the rest of my life?"

Nash groaned, buried his face into the curve of her neck, and wound his arms around her. Heat surged through her body, and she trembled with desire.

"Oh, Maxey, you don't know what your words are doing to me." He lifted his head and gazed into her eyes. "As much as I want to keep you near me and love you like you deserve, I'm still fearful my uncle will find and kill you."

"But Nash…" She threaded her fingers through the hair on his nape as she held on to him. "You have guarded me so far this trip, and when I'm in your arms, I feel so protected. How can your uncle get to me when you have been my hero since our first meeting?"

He groaned and covered her mouth with his, silencing her words. With a sob of pleasure, she clung to him and returned his kiss with urgency. Although her mind told her to stop, she didn't. She couldn't. This was her last chance to show him just how much she loved him.

The tightness in her throat made her realize he must have also been struggling with an intense desire he couldn't control. She could think of nothing else, for she burned with yearning beyond description.

As he kissed the pulse of her neck, he murmured tender endearments. Smiling, she tilted her head, enjoying the sensations running amuck through her. While she listened to his deep voice, chills raced over her arms. She loved this man, and nothing would change her mind about him now. If only she could change his mind about returning her love.

The mere thought of leaving his side and never seeing his handsome face or feeling his intoxicating touch again caused tears to gather in her eyes once more. She tightened her arms around him, pressing herself closer, hoping to show him how she felt through her kiss.

How she wished he would confess his love. But therein lay the problem. Did he love her as much as she loved him? Dare she say it aloud again, in hopes that he would repeat those words? The way he kissed her made her think he did have those feelings for her after all.

He flicked his tongue possessively inside her mouth, and she tingled with rapturous pleasure. Her limbs grew weak, leaving her trembling as her breaths became more ragged.

A moan ripped through her throat, and she thought he replied with the same passionate sigh. She couldn't let him leave her. She must convince him that they had to be together. Forever.

He broke the kiss, but only to slide his lips over her chin and down to her neck, kissing the pulse of her throat. She moved her hands to his shoulders, then to his chest. The rhythm of his heartbeat hammered against her palm.

"Oh, Nash." She sighed heavily as her mind repeated the words *I love you.*

She should tell him again and again. In doing so, he would have to repeat the words, since she knew they were what he felt. Why else would he say these things to her and kiss her with wild abandonment? Why would he care about her so much to want to protect her? Indeed, he would tell her how much he loved her.

"Nash…" Her heartbeat grew faster, and the words were on the tip of her tongue. She had been hurt by him so many times. If he didn't return her love, it would shatter her.

He lifted his head, looking into her eyes. Passion was written all over his face, and she smiled.

"Please, Nash…"

"Please what?"

"Don't stop. Ever."

As he captured her mouth again, she realized the words weren't exactly what she had wanted to say. Close, but not good enough. All she knew was that kissing this man made her mind turn to mush, and her limbs feel like cooked noodles. Thankfully, his strong arms held her up, or she would have melted to the floor by now.

He tilted his head, and the kiss turned wild and passionate. His hands wandered over her back, not seeming satisfied to rest in one spot. Although she loved touching his chest, she found that wrapping her arms around his neck pulled them closer, and that was just as exciting.

But as much as she didn't want to stop their exquisite moment, she must tell him again. She must make him confess his feelings.

Reluctantly, she broke the kiss and looked up into his beautiful chocolate eyes, mentally preparing the words she would say.

Smiling, he gently rubbed her cheek. "You have made me very happy."

"Are you as happy as I am?"

His smile stretched. "Perhaps more so." He kissed her nose. "Kissing you fulfills me more than I could ever imagine."

He was almost ready to confess. She just knew it. "I feel the same."

He brushed his mouth against hers, but briefly this time. "I promise, my sweet Maxey, that we *will* see each other again after all of this is over. I will move heaven and earth to hold you again." He stepped back and pointed to her satchel. "But I fear the captain's cabin boy will be here shortly. You must get in your disguise."

She lost her breath. They had shared something so passionate, only to have it shatter all around her.

Grumbling under her breath, she wanted to hit him, or scream at him, or...just cry. Perhaps telling him she loved him again wasn't the best thing to do. Obviously, he still planned on sending her home no matter what.

➤➤➤✜◄◄◄

"I LOOK ABSOLUTELY ridiculous," Maxey growled as she stared at herself in the vanity mirror. Her hair was pulled tight against her scalp and stuffed in a man's sea cap. The baggy gray coat hid her womanly figure, but she still didn't think she resembled a cabin boy. Nash finished lacing up her heavy boots, another unflattering item she had to wear to hide her identity.

He stood and smiled. "You will pass. If my uncle's men are watching, all they will see is a small lad."

She glanced at Captain Bushwell's cabin boy, who stood against the wall, waiting for her. "I thank you for giving me these clothes," she told him.

He nodded.

"How are you going to get back to the cabin?"

"I'll sneak in the back way. The captain will be here in a moment to come walk you to the ship."

She nodded too, then turned her attention to Nash. Emotion had been lodged in her throat since their heady kiss not too long ago. Nash hadn't said any words of love, and he still acted as if he couldn't wait for her to leave. Apparently, her confession hadn't stirred anything within him. She had once thought him to be a caring man, but now she realized he was as cold as ice.

"Well, I suppose this is it," she said in a near-whisper.

Nash frowned. "It is."

"Will we ever see each other again?" she asked with a catch in her throat.

"I will live through this, and after it is over, I will come to Wentworth Manor to find you." He drew her into his embrace and kissed her forehead. "After all of what we have shared, do you think I will let you out of my life so easily, my sweet?" His voice was rough with emotion.

Her heart hammered as she clung to him. "Nash," she said softly, tears brimming in her eyes, "you had better not be lying to me."

He kissed her forehead again then looked into her eyes. "I am not lying. I have *never* lied to you."

"I shall miss you terribly," she said, her voice breaking.

"And I shall miss you just as much."

She rose on her tiptoes and pressed her mouth to his. Nash tightened his arms around her and kissed her with great urgency. As quickly as he began, he stopped and rested his forehead against hers, his breath ragged with pent-up emotion.

"My sweet Maxey," he said, "before you leave, I must tell you something."

"What?"

"It is something I have been withholding from you for a couple of weeks."

Her hopes sank. She didn't want to hear bad news now. Not before she left him forever. "What is it?"

He looked into her eyes and smiled. "Strange, how others have noticed the way I feel before I realized it myself, but it seems you are not the one who has fallen in love."

She held her breath, and her heart picked up rhythm. Happiness filled every inch of her soul, making her want to sing—and cry at the same time. "You love me?"

He nodded. "Yes. I think I fell in love with you that very first night we met."

"Nash." She sobbed and buried her face into his chest and relished the few earth-shattering moments before they were torn apart.

"Please forgive me for not saying it sooner." He chuckled lightly. "I, too, am very stubborn."

She lifted her face and smiled. "I love you, Nash."

He crushed his mouth over hers for a kiss so wonderful that it made her want to stay in his arms forever. She had almost forgotten about the other person in the room until a loud knock sounded at the door. She jumped, and Nash's arms tightened around her.

"Who is it?" Nash called out.

"It's Captain Bushwell."

Nash sighed, placed another sweet kiss on her lips, and pulled away. "It is time for you to go."

She nodded, tears slipping from her eyes again. Using the back of her hand, she wiped them away.

The cabin boy opened the door. When the captain looked at Maxey, he nodded. "Your disguise will work, but you better splash water on your face to get rid of your swollen eyes...and lips."

Maxey hurried to the washbasin and did as she was told. When she turned back to the men, she squared her shoulders and held herself strong. "I'm ready."

Nash came to her and held her hands. Smooth skin rubbed against hers, causing warmth to spread through her.

"I will return for you. I promise," he said.

She gave him a weak smile. "Now that I know how you feel, I will wait forever if I have to."

He kissed her again, then let her go. On stiff legs, she made herself move beside the captain. As they walked out of the room, she forced herself not to look back. If she did, she would run into Nash's arms. She took deep breaths to keep her emotions from showing.

"I must admit," the captain said after about five minutes, "you could pass for my cabin boy. If you would like to stay in disguise until we are halfway through our voyage, I'll let you. It's just a precaution, of course."

She chuckled and swung her attention to him. "And will you expect me to clean your room, bathe, and dress you, too?"

"No, of course not. I'm thinking about protecting you, Miss Littleton."

"I shall definitely consider your most tempting offer."

He scratched his chin as he slowly inspected her. "You know, if you kept your hair covered and wear those clothes, you could go unnoticed for a very long time."

Suddenly, an idea jumped into her mind. "Indeed?"

He shrugged. "Possibly. I'm certain that if you keep a boy's identity, nobody will know you are a woman, unless they are up close to you, of course."

Slowly a smile spread across her lips. Whether the captain knew it or not, he had just given her a way to stay and continue to help Nash. He might not like it at first, but after the ship sailed without her, he would have no other choice but to allow her to remain to help him.

Two people working together were better than just one person. Hadn't she taught the children that as their governess? Now was the time to prove her theory.

CHAPTER SIXTEEN

NASH STAYED IN his room until the early-morning hours. The sun had not yet made its debut, and this time of the day gave him a great head start over his uncle's men. The first thing on Nash's agenda was to search for his governess. Mrs. Jackson's knowledge of Matthew's estate would assist Nash greatly.

He dressed all in black, knowing this would help him move freely through town without being noticed much. In haste, he removed his clothes from the trunk and stuffed them in a small satchel with a long leather strap, perfect for carrying. If, by chance, his uncle's men searched this room, they would find an empty trunk.

As he made a last inspection, a garment hanging over a chair caught his eye. The cloak belonged to Maxey. Her sweet jasmine scent drifted from the material to his nose. He inhaled deeply, sparking memories of their time together. Her love for him showed in every touch, every kiss, and every caress.

His heart twisted, and a knot formed in his throat. He missed her already, and it hadn't even been eight hours. Then again, this was the longest they had been apart since they first met, and his arms ached to hold her. Holding her one more time would make him want to keep her there, where she belonged.

Cursing his weakened state, he folded the garment and gently placed it in his satchel on top of his clothes. First, he would get the information needed from Mrs. Jackson. Second, he would search through Matthew's manor and find the ring. Third, he would do everything in his power to get the ruthless man arrested. And last, he would hurry to his dead brother's estate and take the woman he loved in his arms, never to let her go.

He smiled.

And then he would ask her to marry him.

Instead of using the room's door to leave, he opened the window and climbed out. The peaceful predawn morning made him hesitate; he did not want to disturb the chirping crickets or belching frogs near the seaside.

As his feet hit the ground, he stilled, listening for anything out of the ordinary. Once the early-morning sounds picked up again, he crept along the shadows, glancing over his shoulder to see if anyone followed. After about a mile, he relaxed, knowing his uncle's men had not been hiding near the inn. And if they had been, they were most likely still there.

Cautiously, he walked along the road, watching closely so he didn't step on anything that made a noise or kick a rock by accident. Out of the corner of his eye, he spotted an old farmer's hat lying on the side of the road. He stopped, glanced both ways to see if anyone watched, then bent and picked it up. After close inspection, he dusted it and placed it on his head. This would help to shield the glare when the sun rose higher in the sky.

As he passed an orchard, he spied fresh red apples dangling from the trees. His mouth watered and his stomach growled. He had skipped breakfast, and the last meal he ate was with Maxey.

He jumped the fence, hurried to the nearest tree, and snatched the fruit. Sinking his teeth into it, he sighed while the sweet juice trickled down his chin.

It was a long time since he'd resorted to fence-hopping in orchards to steal food. As a boy, he and his brother would sneak away from the estate and rob their neighbors of whatever fruits were in season. For some reason, their fruit tasted better than what was growing in the family's orchard.

He chuckled softly from the memory and picked a few more apples for later, stuffing them into the pockets of his jacket before he continued on his way.

The farther he walked, the greener the land became. A rush of contentment overwhelmed him, and he smiled. He had some pleasant memories of living in Devonshire after parting ways with his family. Of course, he hadn't really known how terrible his uncle was at that time, and Nash found friends easily. No matter where he traveled, Devonshire would always feel like his second home.

From his calculations, the next town was a few miles away. If his former governess lived in the same place he remembered, he was within hours of finding her. He yearned to see her once again.

The sounds from farm animals in the pasture he passed intensified as the sun hovered in the sky, announcing its awakening. It had seemed a lifetime since he enjoyed the refreshing sounds of farm life. He observed the large barn, the owner and his two young sons wearily moving about the yard, throwing feed to the animals as they hid yawns behind their hands. They glanced at him as he passed. Nash acknowledged them with a wave.

It seemed strange when one of the boys kept moving his attention to something behind Nash. The little boy stretched his neck to get a better look. Curious, Nash glanced over his shoulder in hopes of seeing what caught the boy's interest. At first, he didn't detect anything out of the ordinary, but soon he noticed the shadowy figure hiding behind a tree.

Nash's gut clenched, and he balled his hands into fists. Had someone been following him since he left the hotel? If so, why hadn't he noticed it before now? Prickles danced over his skin, making the hairs on the back of his neck rise in alarm.

Acting as if he didn't see, he continued walking but took a different path, where there were more trees. This time, his ears alerted him to the different sounds surrounding him.

Once he passed the farm, he slowed his pace, hoping to give

the stranger enough time to catch up. The loaded pistol anchored in the waistband of his trousers eased him slightly. He patted the weapon for reassurance. He would not hesitate to kill any man that stepped in his way.

His uncle would pay dearly. Nash would see to that.

The clump of trees to his left was the perfect place to hide. Without hesitation, he quickened his step and crept through the thicket, searching for a tree large enough to hide behind. When he found one, he flattened himself against it, listened, and waited.

Leaves rustled on the ground, teased by the light wind that had picked up since this morning. It was more difficult to hear footsteps now. Even the birds' singing gnawed at his nerves. Couldn't they keep quiet for five minutes?

A twig snapped, alerting Nash to the intruder. Slowly, Nash drew his pistol. Unease washed over him, but he kept calm, ready to pounce at the first chance. When the crunch of leaves disturbed the field, his scalp tingled with fear. The sound grew closer.

Nash held his breath until he spotted the figure not more than ten feet away. The sun glared in his eyes, not allowing him to see very well. But from what he could observe, the stranger, a lad, perhaps fifteen or sixteen, crept past, darting behind trees.

Without revealing himself, Nash studied the boy. His black clothes practically hung on his slender frame, and his hair and face were concealed by the wide-brim farmer's hat, similar to the one on Nash's head.

He breathed easier knowing this mere boy would be easy to deal with. He placed the pistol back in his trousers.

Should he let the boy wander through the trees until he disappeared, or should Nash pounce on him and force some response from the lad? Nash knew that answer. He had to know why the boy followed. Did he work for Uncle Matthew?

Once the boy turned his back, Nash jumped and wrapped his arms around the slender frame like bands of steel as he pushed both of them to the ground. The moment they hit the earth, a pained, high-pitched cry came from the young boy. Beneath Nash's hands, the softly curved body became noticeable.

A woman?

Quickly turning the stranger over on her back, Nash pinned her to the ground, holding the thin shoulders down.

When the hat rolled off her head, cascades of black hair fanned over the ground. Wide eyes surrounded by dark lashes blinked at him. He sucked in a breath and cursed.

A sheepish grin appeared on her face. "Good morning, Nash."

It took a full minute for it to register, and when he finally realized Maxey was really lying beneath him, his anger kindled. He rolled off and jerked up to a sitting position.

"What are you doing?" he practically yelled. "You are supposed to be on the ship."

She gave a half-shoulder shrug as she sat next to him. "I changed my mind."

Cursing again, he squeezed his eyes closed, quickly thinking of how he could get her back on the ship. Impossible. The ship was probably four or five hours away already.

The touch of her hand on his face made him look at her. A soft smile graced her pretty face as she caressed his cheek.

"Nash? Are you not even a little bit pleased to see me?"

Try as he might, he couldn't stop the happiness from expanding in his chest. He grinned. "I ought to be very annoyed with you for deceiving me. I may never forgive you."

She wound her arms around his neck and pulled his face to hers. "But you will kiss me, instead, won't you?" she asked before touching her mouth to his.

Immediately, the kiss turned wild as he pushed her back to the ground. He slid his fingers through her silky hair as he met her demanding mouth. When he had released her into the captain's care yesterday, Nash never thought he would see her again. And now that she was here, he wanted to hold her, kiss her as long as he wanted, and love her with his heart, mind, and soul.

Unfortunately, this was not the place to become intimate,

even though his arms didn't want to let her go.

With a growl, he broke the kiss. "Maxey, we cannot do this here." He breathed slower, trying to regulate his heartbeat.

She kissed his jaw. "I missed you too," she said with a light laugh.

He smiled. "I really ought to reprimand you for what you did."

"I would rather be here with you than on the ship with the captain. I figured you needed me more than he did."

He glanced at her hair and groaned, rubbing her locks between his fingers. "What have you done to your beautiful hair?"

"I colored it. Do you like it?"

"I prefer the other color, my sweet."

"So do I, but this color doesn't stand out. And with my hair like this and wearing boys' clothes, I won't be spotted so easily."

He shook his head. "What am I going to do with you?"

"Love me."

He brushed tender kisses over her mouth. "You know I do."

"Let me be with you."

"You know I cannot."

"No, you just won't relent. You are too stubborn to admit you need my help."

His chest clenched. "And you know why."

"Because of your uncle."

"Yes."

"But Nash, I'm safer with you. I trust you will not let anything happen to me."

He nuzzled his face against her neck. "I will kill anybody who tries to hurt you."

She played with his hair, and heated tingles shot through his body from her gentle touch.

"We make a great pair, I think," she said.

He pulled back and stared into her shadowed eyes, which were warm with desire. "We make the perfect pair."

"So, can I come with you? Please?"

He chuckled. "It would be foolish of me to turn you away now."

She laughed and kissed him again, this time keeping it tender and passionate. His body relaxed, and it satisfied him to just savor her taste, the feel of her, and those caressing fingers moving over his neck and around to cup his face.

They really shouldn't do this here, his mind reasoned. Then again, they were alone in the group of trees, out of sight from anyone who happened to pass by, and far enough away from the main road to not be noticed.

He kissed her harder, enjoying the closeness they shared, but behind him came quick footsteps crunching in the leaves and breaking twigs along the path. Fast as lightning, he jumped to his feet. Clumsily, he drew his pistol, wishing Maxey's drugging kisses hadn't affected him so.

He aimed the revolver toward the sound and tightened his hand on the butt, praying to the Almighty it wasn't one of his uncle's men.

WHEN THE STRANGER made an appearance, confusion washed over Maxey, and she blinked. A woman stood in the sunlight, wearing a plain brown gown with her hair pulled back in a knot. Familiar eyes gazed at Maxey as she lay on the ground. She gasped loudly as shock shook through her.

"Mother?"

The older woman's eyes widened, but she rushed to Maxey and grabbed her arm. "You and Nash must hurry. Matthew Burke's men are not far behind me."

Maxey's heart hammered in a different rhythm. Panic surged through her as she stood, embarrassment burning through her. What could her mother be thinking right now? Then again, did it really matter? From what her father had told Maxey, Nora

Littleton knew more about passion than most women.

Nash picked up the farmer's hat and stuffed it on Maxey's head. "Tuck your hair inside," he commanded before grabbing her elbow, leading them through the thicket of trees.

"I apologize for interrupting your…um, private moment," Nora stammered, "but when I recognized two of your uncle's men, I knew I must warn you."

Nash stopped, bringing Maxey to a jerking halt as she stumbled into him. She steadied herself and held on to his arm.

He threw a glare at Nora. "How do you know my uncle?"

"I have lived in Devonshire for many years. I know a lot about your powerful uncle and his control over people." She glanced behind them before meeting Maxey's stare. "Now are you going to believe me and let me help you?"

Maxey swallowed the lump of doubt in her throat. She searched for the investigative skills she had once tried to develop, especially for her ability to read people, but strangely enough, they had disappeared. Perhaps she was too emotionally involved this time.

"Why should we believe you?" Nash snapped.

The thin woman stood tall, placing her hands on her hips and lifting her chin in defiance. "Because I love my daughter—no matter what she believes—and I want to prove my devotion to her." Her bottom lip quivered. "I want a second chance, and I pray she will give it to me."

Maxey's hands moistened. Her first reaction was to bluntly tell Nora that it was long past the time of getting a second chance. Maxey didn't want to allow her mother back into her life. Not now. Not ever. But now was not the time to argue. They needed to hide themselves from Matthew's men.

"Fine," Maxey said. "I will put my trust in you right now because I have no other choice."

Nora's smile made her blue eyes twinkle. "I know the perfect place to take you."

"Where is that?" Maxey asked.

"To my home." Nora glanced behind her again then motioned for them to follow. "Come quickly."

Nash grasped Maxey's hand as they hurried along. "Mrs. Littleton, I will be truly in your debt if you can get us out of here alive."

Not another word was spoken as Nash held Maxey's hand and they ran through the woods, dodging the trees and bushes and jumping over fallen branches. Maxey's mind spun in a whirlwind of confusion. Was her mother truly helping them, not leading them into a trap? After their time with Raúl, Maxey was leery of trusting anyone. Nash had taught her that *nobody* could be trusted.

Many years ago, Maxey had believed her mother would always be there, and she would be the kind of mother all the other girls in town had. Maxey had trusted Nora to return and reclaim her family one day. At the time, the family had needed Nora so desperately.

But Maxey didn't want Nora back in her life now. The anger and pain she had experienced for years was still so real. She didn't want to relive the heartache. But as hard as it was to trust Nora now, Maxey had to believe her mother was not working with Matthew.

Another thing that baffled Maxey was hearing her mother say she lived in Devonshire. Why would Nora live in the place where she had given birth to both of the children she eventually gave up? Was this all a coincidence, or had fate lent a helping hand?

Nash squeezed her fingers, and she glanced into his soft eyes. His smile warmed her and spread comfort throughout her body. Here was one man she could always trust. A man she would love forever.

They took a path up a knoll, and Maxey tried to keep pace beside Nash, even while wearing men's boots. Tonight, her muscles would scream from exertion, but she would worry about that when it happened. Now, she had to show Nash that she could keep up, since he still thought of her as a woman with tender sensibilities. Inwardly, she chuckled. She was determined to make him proud.

They climbed up and over the knoll, only to find a cliff, which, thankfully, wasn't very high, but it was someplace to hide nonetheless.

Nash stopped. "We shall hide down there." He jumped over the bush and into the small ravine. Maxey stopped suddenly and glanced at him for reassurance.

"It is not far. I will catch you," he said, holding out his hands.

She nodded then hopped over the bush and into his arms. He put her down and helped her mother into the gully.

Nash pressed himself against the earth's wall as he drew his pistol and cocked it. Maxey and Nora stood beside him, waiting and listening.

Maxey shivered. Immediately, Nash wrapped a protective arm around her shoulders and pulled her next to his hard body. She rested her face against his chest.

The wait seemed forever. Of course, trying to keep quiet made the time creep by, but soon came the heavy hooves from the horses. Maxey held her breath and squeezed her eyes closed, praying the riders would look past them.

Nash's arm tightened around her. Standing beside Maxey, Nora clasped Maxey's shoulder. Maxey look at her mother, and wide, frightened eyes met her gaze. Empathy tugged at Maxey. It must be the caregiver inside her that wanted to soothe her mother's fears, so she offered a tentative smile and clutched Nora's hand.

Within minutes, the thunder of galloping horses riding away eased Maxey's fears. Soon, the men were gone, and she quickly released Nora's hand as if it had turned to fire.

Nash exhaled a heavy breath. Releasing his hold on her, he placed his pistol back in the waistband of his trousers. He looked down at her then switched his focus to her mother.

"I think we are safe. For now."

Maxey nodded. "At least for now."

"Yes," Nora agreed. "But let us not stay here any longer. I think you two will be safe at my house."

"Where is that?" Nash asked.

Nora smiled. "Not too far from here. If we hurry, we will be there by the lunch hour, and my cook is the best around."

Maxey scrunched her forehead. Confusion worked its way into her heart again. Her mother had her own servant? After a slow inspection of Nora, Maxey's confusion grew deeper. Why did she not look wealthy now, as she had on the ship?

Giving a nod, Maxey allowed Nora to lead the way. The truth would soon be uncovered, and frankly, Maxey thought it was past due. After all these years, she was ready to know.

CHAPTER SEVENTEEN

MAXEY STARED WIDE-EYED at the three-story red brick building. So far, this was the fanciest establishment she had run across since arriving in port. Green grass surrounded the place, along with a four-foot stone fence.

Nora led the way while Maxey and Nash walked side by side behind her. As they neared, they saw women dressed in beautiful silk dresses on the wraparound porch and scattered around the lawn, all accompanied by a well-dressed man.

Maxey eyed each one carefully. They must have walked into some kind of soirée. But so far, nobody questioned them, or their attire, even though neither she nor Nash were dressed as elegantly. However, the women called out greetings to Nora and appeared genuinely happy to see her, welcoming her back from her trip.

Nora walked up the steps to the front door, then opened it and hurried inside. As soon as Nash walked in, he grabbed Maxey's hand, bringing her to a halt. She looked into his eyes in silent question. His hooded expression didn't tell her anything, just that he needed to observe the people in the room before they proceeded.

She tore her attention away from him and took in everything, from the hard wooden floors, to the beautiful, colorful designs of meadows and the sky painted on the walls, then to the very expensive furniture scattered around the floor. The white lace curtains allowed the afternoon sunlight to pour through, making everything appear shiny and new.

All the people in the room were dressed in silks and satins, but it was the way they paired off that made Maxey curious. Usually at soirées, people stood together in groups. So why had every woman been paired with a man? The ladies giggled as they whispered things in the men's ears, or cuddled next to them in an indecent display.

Nora started up the staircase, then stopped and turned toward Maxey and Nash, who still stood in observation.

"If you would follow me, I will show you to your room."

"Forgive me, Mrs. Littleton, but I must protest," Nash stated loudly.

An uneasy feeling washed over Maxey. Something in the tone of his voice made her alert and suspicious.

Nora squared her shoulders and faced them. "What is it, Nash?"

Gently, he squeezed Maxey's hand. "Please do not think I am a simpleton, Mrs. Littleton. Although your daughter has not been to places like these, I certainly have, and I highly doubt she will feel comfortable here."

Pink highlighted the older woman's face, but she remained standing firm. "My apologies. I do not believe you to be a simpleton at all. I brought you here to hide you. This is the one place your uncle and his men will not look. After all, why would they think my daughter would hide out in this type of environment?"

Pain welled in Maxey's chest. What were they talking about, and why was Nash so leery? Once again, she took a quick look around the hallway, then into the nearest room. The only thing out of the ordinary was the couples who cuddled up to each other in an improper fashion.

Laughter from up the stairs drew her attention. Another woman and man came into view. The man's shirt hung open as he stuffed his shirttails into his trousers, and the woman wore the most indecent nightdress Maxey had ever seen. The very short gown exposed the woman's bare limbs, and the deep cut in the bodice displayed most of her full bosom.

Maxey gasped as her hand flew to her mouth. Heat rushed through her, and finally pieces of her mother and Nash's conversation fit together in her mind.

Jerking her head around to Nash, she blinked. "Is this a…one of those places?"

His lips stayed in a thin line when he nodded. "Indeed it is, my love. This is the type of establishment I had hoped you would never have to go inside."

She hissed and swung her focus toward her mother, who was still on the stairs standing proud and rigid.

"How dare you," Maxey said.

Nora's mouth twitched into a grimace. "Please come with me, and I will explain. We need not air our discussion in front of these people."

Nash leaned down to Maxey's ear. "She is correct, my love," he whispered. "We need to go to a room posthaste. We should not give these people a reason to ask questions."

Stiffly, Maxey nodded. "Then make it quick, because I wish to hear my mother's explanation for this very soon, before I give her a piece of my mind, and before I empty my stomach all over her fancy floors because of the disgust rolling through me."

Grabbing handfuls of her skirt, Nora lifted it to her ankles as she hurried up the stairs. Nash and Maxey were close behind.

Agony wrenched her chest, and disappointment settled in her stomach. Her mother had lowered herself to *this* kind of life? What happened to the wealthy man she had run away with and left her family for? Then again, Maxey's father had mentioned that passion ruled her mother. Did he know she was reduced to living in a prostitutes' house before he died?

Nora led them all the way down the hall then opened a door with a key. Maxey half expected to find a man and woman on the bed. Instead, an empty room greeted her. The furnishings looked to be as expensive as the ones downstairs. Everything was straightened and dusted. The large bed in the far corner against the wall had beautiful covers and matching pillowcases, and red scarves were draped along the posts. Armoires and trunks lined the walls, and nearest to the door sat a mahogany desk with a Chippendale chair.

Obviously, her mother lived in luxury. Why would she regret leaving her poor family when she had all this?

Nora closed the door behind them and leaned against the solid oak. Silence filled the room until Nash cleared his throat and shifted in his stance, obviously uncomfortable.

"Why..." Maxey swallowed hard. "Why did you bring us here? Was it to show your daughter what kind of life you live now that you are no longer her mother?"

Tears filled Nora's eyes. "As I tried to explain a few moments ago, this place was the only place I could hide you."

Maxey glanced around the room again. "Do you actually live here?"

Nora lowered her head. "Yes," she whispered. "I actually *own* this house."

Emotion clogged Maxey's throat, and she dared not speak, but she needed answers. The pain of betrayal cut a hole inside her that had to be fixed.

"Well, I appreciate your help, Nora," Maxey said in a tight voice, "but we won't be staying long. As soon as it gets dark, we will be gone."

Nora's bottom lip trembled, but she didn't lift her head.

Nash rubbed Maxey's arm, and she looked up into the comfort of his eyes. He offered a soft smile. "I think you and your mother need to talk. I shall wait outside."

She grabbed his arm. "No, don't—"

"Not to worry, my love. I will keep a sharp eye for any of my uncle's men. Right now, you and your mother need some privacy."

He kissed her forehead before stepping out. Emptiness filled her from his absence, and worry tried to take over the space. She really didn't want to be alone with her mother, yet how else would she know the reasons Nora had left all those years ago?

Heaving a ragged breath, Maxey turned and walked to the window, looking out into the yard. Green bushes and a rainbow of flowers colored the lovely landscape. She had learned by now that first impressions were always so deceiving.

"I'm sorry I have disappointed you," Nora said brokenly.

Maxey shrugged. "I'm surprised you are not more worried about disappointing yourself." She looked over her shoulder at her mother. "This is not the kind of profession one can be proud of."

"Don't you think I know this?" Nora walked closer, stopping at the foot of the bed. "Do you honestly believe I chose this lifestyle?"

Maxey let out an unladylike snort. "Are you trying to tell me you were forced into it?"

Sighing heavily, Nora sank to the bed and covered her face. "No, I wasn't forced. I just didn't have any choice."

"I beg to differ, Nora. Everybody has a choice."

When Nora lifted her head, her throat contracted. "As a young girl, my family was very poor. My father died, and my mother had a hard time keeping the family fed. She worked as a maid for a wealthy family, but she still struggled."

From her pocket, she withdrew a white handkerchief and wiped underneath her nose, then dabbed her eyes. "One day, the man who my mother worked for approached me. He said he knew a way I could make money. Loads of money. He said I was the perfect age."

"How old were you?"

"Seventeen."

"What happened?"

"He took me to a house of ill repute, grander than this one." She swept her hand through the air. "He introduced me to the madame, who then explained to me that because of my class, I would never make enough money—the kind to help out my family, that is. But if I worked for her, she would dress me in silks and jewels, and men would fall at my feet. I agreed. At the time, my brother was very sick, and we had no money for a doctor."

Nora sniffed and wiped her eyes again, still keeping her focus on the floor. "Little did I know at the time, but the man had *sold* me to this madame. Once I realized what they expected of me, it was too late. I was already one of Madame Patricia's girls."

She waited a few minutes. Silence surrounded them, except for her sniffles. Then she lifted her head and looked directly at Maxey. "I made a living doing that for two years. I hated every minute of it, but I couldn't leave." She shrugged. "I didn't know how. One day while in the marketplace, I met a man passing through town. He didn't know about me, and I wasn't about to divulge the truth, mind you. Immediately, we were attracted to one another. I feared he would find out about my profession, so I met him secretly for two weeks. When he first proclaimed his love, I thought I had died and gone to heaven. Then he proposed, and I was the happiest woman alive. I lied and told him I didn't have a family. I also told him I worked as a maid."

Nora took a deep breath. "So, I married him and left with him that very day, back to where he lived, which was far away from this type of life. I had never been happier, except when I had his children. I loved my family completely."

Maxey's throat tightened with sorrow, so she swallowed, not allowing her emotions to take over.

Turning, she leaned against the wall and folded her arms across her chest. "Then why did you leave us?"

"My world came to an end when one of my former customers recognized me with your father. The man walked up to us on the street and asked where I had been all these years. He asked if I was now giving my favors to your father. I tried to cover it up with lies, but your father's curiosity got the better of him, and he sought answers. It nearly killed me to have your father look at me with accusing eyes. He was ashamed of me. He told me I didn't deserve to be his wife and the mother of his children, so he ordered me to leave."

Maxey's heart slammed in her chest, and she bolted away from the wall. "What? You're telling me Father instructed you to leave your own children?" She shook her head. "I'm sorry, Nora, but that's hard to believe. What father would do that to his children?"

Sobs took over Nora, and she cried into her handkerchief. "It's the truth," she muttered. "I never wanted to leave you." She lifted her head and met Maxey's eyes again. "I wouldn't leave, but your father became very forceful, and his words crushed my soul. He was right. Because of what I had done, I wasn't good enough to be a mother to my children. He feared that you might be with me the next time I crossed another one of my…men."

Maxey's head throbbed as confusion filled her. Whom should she believe? Then again, her mother's story did sound plausible. Maxey never understood why her mother had chosen to leave the family and run off with a wealthy man. Moreover, her father was very angry with his wife at first, and then heartache took over until he died.

Hearing her mother's story now, it started to make sense. No wonder he had referred to Nora as "a harlot."

Maxey covered her ears and closed her eyes. Pain burst in her chest, crumbling her defenses and making her ache even more. She wanted to rush to Nora and allow her mother to hold her as she used to a long time ago. Maxey wanted to return to yester-year before her mother left…before Maxey's life was ripped apart.

"I'll give you some time to think," Nora said. "I need to make certain our lunch is prepared, anyway."

It wasn't until the door shut that Maxey allowed the tears to come forth. She fell on the bed and cried.

Suddenly, two strong hands lifted her and pressed her against his solid chest. She breathed in Nash's masculine scent and wrapped her arms around his waist. Together they lay on the bed. He stroked her hair as she sobbed into his shirt. His soothing touch calmed her, and soon she felt as weak as a newborn lamb.

Heaviness weighed her eyes, and she let sleep consume her.

THE SOFT WOMAN in Nash's arms moved against him, bringing him awake and very alert. He pulled back enough to look at Maxey's face. Her eyelids lazily fluttered open as she met his stare. Thankfully, the puffiness had disappeared. The poor darling had been through so much, and holding her was the way he could think to comfort her.

She smiled and snuggled closer. "Morning."

"Good morning, my sweet." He kissed her forehead. "How do you feel today?"

It obviously took a few moments before her memory returned, because soon her eyes clouded over with hurt and anger. She glanced around the room, and her smile turned into a scowl.

"Where are we?" She pushed away and sat up on her elbows. "We are still in my mother's room?"

"Yes."

"Where is my moth—um, Nora?"

"She slept in another room."

Maxey cringed, and then quickly hopped off the bed. Swiping her hands up and down her arms, she shivered. "I can't believe I slept in *her* bed, knowing she has done *those* things on this very mattress."

Nash rolled to the side of the bed then stood. He stretched his cramped arms and legs before walking toward Maxey. "My sweet, let me tell you something I'm certain you don't understand about this type of establishment."

When he reached her, he cupped her chin, and her eyes met with his.

"Your mother is a madame, which means she does not sleep

with men for money any longer."

Maxey's forehead creased. "Are you certain?"

He shrugged and pulled away. "From what I have seen from other places like this, that is the way it works. By the time a woman makes it to a madame, she doesn't need to make a living in this way. This is now her business, and she runs it like the owner of any establishment would. Most women I have met who are like your mother are very professional."

Maxey grumbled, turned away, and stormed to the window. "It doesn't matter how professional my mother is. The fact remains she is still a woman of ill repute."

Nash released a heavy sigh. Maxey hurt inside, and he didn't know how to help. It was understandable she would be so upset over the news of her mother's profession. He hoped she would soon soften her heart and find room to forgive.

He had known several harlots in the past few years, and they lived a very hard life. Women did not choose this lifestyle—they were forced into it, and once the deed was done, they didn't feel worthy of a normal life. If only he could help Maxey see this. But now was not the time, and he couldn't push her. Maxey's wounds were still too fresh.

Rubbing the sleep out of his eyes, he stepped to the small washbasin on the oak drawers. Water had been added to the pitcher, probably when they were still asleep, so he poured a generous amount in the basin and splashed the cool liquid on his face. Washing his hair was important, but that might have to be put off for a while. He needed a bath, but that, too, would have to wait, at least until after he talked with Nora about their room and board.

He didn't know how staying at a house of prostitution could be that safe. True, most men who came here were not looking for people on the run, so Nash might be safe for a few days, or even a week. Either way, he would keep a sharp eye on the men who frequented this place.

As he scrubbed his hands over his two-day-old beard, he

looked in the mirror. Time to change his appearance again. While they stayed here, he couldn't wear his fancy clothes or dress like he wanted. Instead, looking like a servant might work better. So, as much as Maxey had loved his clean-shaven face the other day, he would have to grow out his beard and have the scruffy look.

He glanced over his shoulder at her. She would have to change, too. He didn't want her in a boy's disguise, nor did he want her dressing like a harlot and having men think she would give them favors. That might cause a brawl, with Nash doing the punching. She would have to be a servant, just as he would.

It was better that way. They would both be able to get out of the house and walk around in peace, as long as he made certain his uncle's men did not spot them. He didn't need others to become curious, either.

In a couple of days, he had to search out his uncle's house-keeper, Mrs. Jackson. Now that he knew Matthew's men were looking for him, he had to stay low and out of sight. Nash prayed they didn't find Mrs. Jackson first.

Soft hands touched his back then caressed his shoulders. Smiling, he turned and looked at Maxey. Sadness still marred her beauty, which made his chest wrench.

"Nash? I would rather not speak to my mother right now, but I fear my stomach is eating a hole through my backbone. Would you be so kind as to get us some breakfast?"

He cupped her face and kissed her sweet lips briefly. "Of course my love. I, too, find myself very hungry. I will wander downstairs to the kitchen to see what I can throw together."

Her eyes grew wider. "You are going to *make* breakfast?"

"I'm not afraid of cooking."

"You continue to amaze me."

"Good. I hope I will never stop."

As he made his way downstairs toward the kitchen, the house remained quiet, as it should be, since everyone would be sleeping off their wild nights of spirits and passion. Not too long ago, he was one of the men who visited these types of houses. Never again. Now he wanted more out of life. He wanted Maxey to be his wife and bear their children. He wanted to share their lives together. Forever.

He entered the kitchen to the heavenly aroma of scones and eggs. Nora stood by the oven stirring a spoon inside a pan. Her shoulders slumped, and the wilted expression on her face tore at his heart. Because he knew how harlots lived, he could sympathize with them. If only Maxey would forgive her mother and mend the ties.

But it wasn't up to him. Although he wanted nothing more than to take the pain away, Maxey had to deal with this on her own.

The floor squeaked, and Nora swung around, her eyes wide. Then she relaxed and smiled.

"Good morning. Are you and Maxey hungry?"

"That is why I am here."

"Let me prepare your plates. I'm afraid my cook has come down with a stomach bug, so I'm helping her."

"No, Mrs. Littleton. You do not have to wait on me."

"Nash," she said as her smile disappeared, "please call me Nora. I haven't been called Mrs. Littleton since—" Her eyes grew misty. "For quite some time."

"As you wish."

She fixed the plates of food. Silence lasted a few minutes, then she cleared her throat. "Did you and Maxey sleep well last night?"

"Yes. Your hospitality has been most generous."

She turned with two plates in her hands. "I'm grateful you think so, although my daughter may have a different opinion."

"True."

Nora handed him the plates, then shrugged. "I'm very happy you let me talk with her, though. Now she knows the truth."

"I am very sorry for what happened. I know Maxey was hurt terribly, and I pray she forgives you soon. I know what it is like to carry a grudge for a long time. I did that with my father, along with my older brother. They are both dead, and I regret not making amends before now. I will forever carry that burden of guilt."

She smiled and touched his arm. "You are good for my daughter. I can tell she loves you very much."

His heart melted. "I love your daughter completely. I will try to make her happy."

"You will." She nodded.

"Nora, we will need clothes for our new disguises. Both Maxey and I should dress as servants. Can you get these clothes for us?"

"Yes. I'll find some right away."

"I thank you."

"Feel free to take a walk around the estate. It is very secluded, and there is a pond out back a ways. I must say, it's very lovely."

He nodded, then turned and carried the plates of food back to the room.

Neither he nor Maxey said anything while they ate, but through her tender smiles and twinkling eyes, he knew she loved him. Before they had finished eating, Nora brought up their clothes. Maxey stared at her plate, refusing to look at her mother, so Nash thanked Nora and closed the door after she left.

He would have to take Maxey with him to find his governess. Matthew knew Nash was close. Soon it would be a battle of wits between them, and Nash prayed he would turn out the winner.

Without exchanging words, they both dressed in their new disguises. Maxey used combs from her mother's vanity table to fix her hair. He shook his head. Maxey was definitely not supposed to be a servant. She was too graceful, and had the natural beauty that spoke of a higher position. She'd look well on his arm as his wife.

As he finished buttoning his shirt, his attention fell on the cupboard where the washbasin sat, and next to it, a bar of soap. He needed a bath, as did Maxey, but he didn't want to stay in this room another minute. Taking a walk would do them both good.

Suddenly, he recalled Nora mentioning the secluded pond out

back. He grinned. *Perfect!*

"Oh no."

Maxey's worried voice had him swinging his gaze to her. She stood with her arms folded across her chest, her head tilted as she studied him through narrowed eyes.

"What is on your mind, Nash?"

"What do you mean?"

"You have a grin stretching across your mouth, which tells me something is cooking in that brain of yours that is not good."

He swaggered to her and gathered her in his arms. "And why would it not be good? What if I tell you it is indeed very good?"

She toyed with the top button of his shirt. "Well, don't keep me in suspense. Tell me what it is."

He shook his head. "I'll do one better."

He stepped back and took her hand, pulling her toward the door. As he passed the basin, he grabbed the bar of soap. She didn't ask what he had in mind, but followed him down the hallway, down the stairs, and outside. It was his goal to take Maxey's mind off her mother, and he would do anything to accomplish that.

Chapter Eighteen

Fter Nash took them to the pond and allowed Maxey to bathe while he gave her some privacy—and she returned the favor for him—he walked with her hand in hand through the glade of trees. Being with him like this filled her with love, and she realized she wanted this always.

"What shall we do now?" she asked.

"We will head out to find my uncle's housekeeper." He squeezed her hand. "Mrs. Jackson worked for Matthew while I lived there. She will be able to tell me where my uncle would keep important documents. She will also know his daily routine and might be able to help me to sneak into his manor. No matter what it takes, I will protect you."

The darkness of his eyes and softness of his expression told her he was telling the truth. "I know you will. I trust you completely."

"You do? When did that change?"

She bumped her arm against his. "I've been utterly foolish since meeting you, and I'm regretting not trusting you from the start. Nash, you have never lied to me, and I see that now. Actually, I have known for a while, but my stubbornness argued with my feelings."

He nodded, bent his head, and kissed her lips briefly. "My heart grows warm from your words. I have never lied to you, and

I never will."

"So, tell me, do you have a title?"

He laughed loudly. "No. I was never given one. Only my brother. Besides, I enjoy the way you say my name. It has always been like music to my ears."

"That is because I say it with love."

He stopped them, took her in his arms, and covered her mouth for a wonderful, passionate kiss, but soon he pulled away and continued on their walk.

"Tell me about your uncle's housekeeper," she said.

When he talked about Mrs. Jackson, he held so much emotion in his voice. Maxey could feel the love he had for the older woman.

Regret for not having a mother figure in her own life stabbed at her chest again.

How long had she waited for her mother to return when she was a child? Too many days to count. Her father had never remarried, and now Maxey wondered why. Could he have longed for his wayward wife as Maxey had longed for her mother?

Life wasn't fair. How could her mother have been so thoughtless? From what Maxey had seen so far, her mother did still love her. Why else would Nora try to protect her daughter and Nash?

"I do not think Mrs. Jackson will remember me," he said.

Nash's voice brought her out of dark and confusing thoughts. She glanced at him. His smile had disappeared.

"It has been many years since we have seen each other," he finished.

Maxey patted his arm. "We shall make her remember. Do you resemble your uncle?"

"My father always told me I did. Perhaps that is why we argued so much while I was growing up."

"Then I'm quite certain the housekeeper will remember."

His jaw hardened. "I pray my uncle has not found her first. If he knew…" He took a deep breath. "She may be dead."

Maxey prayed for the housekeeper's safety. "How much farther?"

"We are nearly there. I think perhaps another ten minutes at the most." He glanced down at her feet. "Why? Are you tired of walking?"

"Don't be silly. I shall be fine as long as I'm by your side."

He grinned and winked. "You still think I am your protector?"

"No, I don't think. I *know*."

⤜⤜⤜✦⤛⤛⤛

SEEING MRS. JACKSON was within minutes, unless she'd moved since Nash last saw her. The town where he'd lived during the stay with his uncle hadn't changed much. The church stood erect, but definitely needed a good painting. The houses appeared as rickety as he remembered—perhaps even more now. And the tavern was still packed.

Many people watched him and Maxey as they walked down the street, but nobody acknowledged with a wave or nod of greeting. This was their way. They had always kept to themselves. Besides, he didn't want to draw any undue attention.

Nash turned down a side street, Maxey following close beside him. Although he wanted to hold her hand to openly proclaim his love, everybody needed to see them as servants to keep suspicion away.

From up the road, a small adobe house grabbed his attention. The familiar fence, the same shutters, and the crooked windows made his chest swell.

On those occasions when Nash had needed someone to talk to about his family situation, and Uncle Matthew didn't care to listen, Mrs. Jackson would bring Nash to this part of town while she shopped for items needed at the manor. A few times she had brought him to the house where her family lived, as well.

Several children played a game in the yard, laughing as they ran after each other. Sweet memories tugged at him. During the times with Mrs. Jackson, he had felt content. She treated him like a son, and he pretended she was his mother.

When Nash reached the gate, the children stopped. He smiled. "Does Mrs. Jackson still live here?" he asked.

A few of the children exchanged glances, then met his eyes again.

"There are two women here with that name," the oldest one said.

"Lucinda."

The child nodded. "She is here."

Nash breathed a deep sigh. *Thank God.* "May I speak with her?"

Another boy stepped forward. "Who are you?"

"I am her friend from long ago. She used to work for my uncle."

All the children's eyes grew wide. One little girl gasped. This was not the reaction Nash had expected. He assumed they knew the merciless man Lucinda had worked for.

The boy stepped closer. "What is your name?"

"Nash Burke."

Gasps circled the group of children, and some lost coloring in their face.

Nash gulped as ice ran through his veins. Obviously, his uncle had visited already. Why else would the children give him this reaction?

"Is she here? It is most important I speak with her."

"She does not want to talk to you," snapped a girl who couldn't have been much younger than the first boy.

Nash scrunched his forehead. "What do you mean? She was my friend. I loved her like a mother."

The boy turned to the children and whispered something, then they scattered, running in all directions. Nash's heart clenched. Something was not right.

He cleared his throat. "May I see her, please? It is most important."

The boy shook his head. "You are not wanted here."

Anger surged through Nash. It wasn't in his nature to hurt a child, but he was most tempted to turn this one over his knee and show him some manners. Squaring his shoulders, Nash walked to the gate and opened it.

"Forgive me, but I insist on speaking with an adult."

The boy ran to him and yanked on his jacket. "Please, Mr. Burke," he whispered. "If she talks to you, she will die."

"Why will she die?" Nash asked.

"Because that mean man will kill her."

Nash didn't need to ask whom the child spoke of. This had Uncle Matthew's signature all over it. Squatting to the boy's level, Nash lowered his voice. "Is that man watching now?"

"No, but he knows everything."

Nash nodded. "What if you give Lucinda a message for me? Tell her I need to speak with her. Tell her I will return after dark and go to the back door."

Tears welled in the boy's eyes. "Will that man kill her?"

Nash tousled the boy's hair as he stood. "No. I will not let her die. I promise."

A weak smile crossed the lad's mouth. "Then I will tell her what you said."

Giving the boy a nod, Nash turned and walked away from the house with Maxey by his side.

Maxey tugged on his sleeve. "Nash? How can you protect her?"

"For those eyes watching, we will leave town, but after dark we will sneak back. I will not let my uncle's men touch her. That kind, selfless woman has done nothing but befriend me and treat me like a son."

He peered at Maxey, whose expression twisted as pain touched her face.

"What worries you?" Nash asked.

Maxey blinked and shook her head. "Nothing."

"Something has."

"I'm worried about all of this. What if you can't find the ring?"

He sighed. "I must believe good will overcome."

"Yes, but what if—"

"Maxey," he said, "we cannot worry about something that hasn't happened. The way to get through this is to take one step at a time and watch our backs the whole way."

She nodded. "I'll never forget the fear in that boy's eyes."

Nash's chest wrenched. He stopped and turned toward Maxey. "Indeed, Matthew is very powerful. But if you fear for your life, then perhaps it is best I leave you with your mother and come back to meet Lucinda by myself."

Maxey clung to his arm. "Don't say such things. We will be stronger if we stay together. One person alone cannot fight your uncle."

Pain weighed on his chest, but he smiled through the confusion. He wanted to be strong for her. But he also knew his uncle wouldn't blink an eye to take Maxey in order to get to Nash. Leaving her behind was the only way.

He lifted his hand to touch her, but, remembering their disguise, he dropped his hand by his side. "Maxey, you are a very stubborn woman. But we are in danger. If you remain by my side, there is that chance—"

"Shh." She stepped closer. "I will not leave you, Nash. Wherever you go, I shall follow. You protect me, and I shall protect you."

His heart warmed. The urge to take her in his arms and kiss those sweet lips was strong, but he fought it. They couldn't be seen embracing. Matthew would certainly see through her disguise.

"Come, my love. Let us leave and return after dark. Perhaps we can compile a plan in the meantime."

Maxey walked close beside him, her arm occasionally bumping into his. He missed breathing in her exhilarating scent of jasmine and burying his face in the tender curve of her neck. Holding her made him feel like a man. She completed him. He would move heaven and earth if he must, but his uncle would not harm a hair on her body.

They walked back to Nora's house to wait. The day would pass by too slowly, and in the meantime, he must not tell Maxey of his plan to go without her. She would never understand. In his mind, it was better to ask forgiveness than permission.

THE HOUSE OF prostitution had not yet started the evening ritual, and Maxey didn't want to be anywhere near the harlots or their guests when that happened. Nash was out back by the fence repairing something her mother had asked him to do, which left Maxey a lot of time on her hands.

Still upset about Nora's way of life, Maxey didn't want to talk to any of the painted ladies, but when she walked into the kitchen, the few women sitting at the servants' table stopped and looked her way. One jumped up and motioned to the chair.

"You may sit here if you wish."

Maxey nodded and sat. One of the women placed a plate of steak and potatoes in front of her. The other women in the room continued to stare, so Maxey proceeded to eat, hoping they would find something else to aim their attention toward. Maxey didn't like feeling as though she had grown two heads.

The harlot across from her leaned back in her chair and folded her arms over her ample bosom. Although the gown she wore displayed a lot of skin at her neck and chest, at least the red silk material covered more than what Maxey had seen last night when she and Nash first entered the house. The color of the woman's dress matched her fiery hair perfectly.

"Miss Maxey, I hope you don't mind me saying, I'm very happy to finally meet Nora's daughter. Your mother has spoken of you quite a bit."

Maxey had lifted a bite of her potatoes to her mouth, but paused as she glanced at the woman. "She has?"

"Oh yes." The brunette who had offered Maxey the chair sat beside the redhead and nudged her friend's elbow. "Nancy here has known Nora longer than the rest of us. But even I have heard your mother speak of you."

Bile rose in Maxey's throat, but she shoved the potatoes in her mouth and forced herself to eat nonetheless.

"Did you know she had a detective to keep track of you for many years?" Nancy asked.

When Maxey swallowed, the potatoes almost stuck. "Yes. Nora mentioned that."

"She wanted to know everything you and your brother were doing, how you were growing up, and what you looked like. Whenever mail arrived from the detective, it brightened her day."

The brunette reached across the table and touched Maxey's hand. "She loves you and your brother very much, and missed you greatly."

Irritation stiffened Maxey's spine, and she arched an eyebrow. "Well, she had a poor way of showing her affection. Both of her children never knew what happened to her, except that she had left them to live with a wealthy man."

Both harlots gasped. Even the cook whirled from the stove with her hand covering her mouth.

"Dearie," the cook said, her double chins wobbling as she shook her head. "You couldn't be more wrong. Your mother loved you unconditionally, and wanted to show her children how much she missed them, but her husband—your father—wouldn't allow it."

Suddenly the food wasn't appealing any longer, and Maxey pushed the plate away. "Yes, my mother told me he was ashamed of her career choice, and rightly so. What decent man would want a harlot for a wife?"

Pink covered the faces of the women across the table. The

cook huffed and shook her head.

"But she wasn't a harlot then, Miss Maxey. She had changed herself and wanted a new life. She married a caring man and had two wonderful children. Changing our life is one thing all of us *harlots* want."

Pain gripped Maxey's chest and made her head throb. She scooted her chair out and stood. "I appreciate your words, but I have had many years of hatred built up in me. I cannot change how I feel." She straightened. "If you'll excuse me, I must leave. I have a terrible headache."

Thankfully, the women didn't try to stop her. She marched out of the kitchen, hurried through the parlor, and darted up the stairs before anyone could see the tears building in her eyes. She refused to cry, although confusion swam in her head, making her want to believe that her mother had cared for her all of these years.

She walked into the room and closed the door behind her. Emotion clogged her throat. She sat at the vanity and looked at herself in the mirror. For so many years, she'd carried the guilt that her mother left because of something she may have done as a child. When Maxey met Nash and realized she also had the passion that her father hated her mother for, it left a sour taste in her mouth. She didn't want to become like her mother.

Of course, back then she hadn't fully understood the type of woman her mother had become. Could her father have been wrong all this time? Nora had loved her children enough to have a detective follow them throughout their years of growing up. Apparently, Nora had wanted her family after all.

Maxey groaned and pressed her palms against her forehead, praying the pain in her skull would leave. She hated feeling this way.

The squeak from the door opening pulled her attention to her visitor. Nora walked in.

"I need to get something." She pointed to her armoire.

"Of course. After all, this is your room."

Her mother smiled, even with pain still in her eyes. Maxey's heart was tugged by confusion again, squeezing her chest tighter.

"I declare if Polly's head wasn't attached, the poor girl would lose that, too." Nora shuffled through her shoes. "I don't understand how that girl can misplace so many things in one day." She pulled out a red pair of satin button-up booted heels. "It's a good thing we have the same size feet."

She gave Maxey a smile, and then turned to leave, but Maxey reached out and grabbed her arm. "Can I ask you a question?"

"Certainly, my dearest."

"Do you know what Thomas did when he was sixteen that put him out of commission for a few months?"

Nora stared at Maxey for the longest time in silence and nodded.

"He broke his arm when he fell out of the tree. Apparently, he was watching a girl in her bedroom window and was discovered when he accidentally fell out, breaking his arm in the process."

Maxey's heart sped up. Nora was correct.

"Do you know what happened when I turned eighteen?"

Nora stepped closer. She shifted the shoes under one arm as she stroked Maxey's cheek with her fingers. "You were offered a teaching position at the school once you graduated, but you turned it down to take care of your sickly father."

A dam of tears leaked through Maxey's eyes. Her lips trembled when she nodded. "You...you really kept track of us?"

The shoes dropped from her mother's arms when she gathered Maxey against her bosom. "Indeed I did. Every day of your lives. Since your father wouldn't let me near, I needed to know how you fared. I missed you so much."

Years of anguish and sadness poured from Maxey as she clung to her mother and cried. How she wanted to change the past and have her mother in her life every day, but it was impossible. For now, she must savor the moment and cherish it.

"Please forgive me, my darling daughter." Nora kissed Maxey's forehead. "I wanted to be with my children, but couldn't. Your father knew how to punish me for lying to him, but I knew my children suffered along with me."

"We did." Maxey raised her head and looked at her mother through teary eyes. "Every day you were gone."

"But I'm here now." Nora smiled with trembling lips and dried the wetness from Maxey's face. "I want to be here from this day forward. I want to be your mother if you'll allow me."

"Oh, Mother." Maxey cried harder and buried her face in her mother's bosom.

Maxey didn't even realize her mother had moved them to the bed until she lay on soft pillows and a blanket was thrown over her. Her mother gathered her in her embrace again and held her until Maxey fell asleep.

CHAPTER NINETEEN

N ASH SLOWED THE horse Nora had given him as he neared the sleeping town he and Maxey visited earlier that day. He'd prayed there would be a good excuse not to take Maxey with him this time, because he didn't want to upset Lucinda or have her worried. Thankfully, when he'd checked on Maxey, she was resting peacefully. Nora told him they had talked, and Maxey forgave her, which brought him relief.

Now, if everything would work out perfectly with Lucinda, his future might be getting better as well.

Clouds covered the moon and didn't give him much light as he crept back to Lucinda's house. Every few feet he stopped and surveyed the area, keeping a sharp eye out for his uncle or the ruthless men who worked for him. A light wind blew against his face, slightly cooling his heated skin. Trying to keep hidden was more work than he had anticipated.

Finally, he made it to the yard, then through the gate. He stopped again and listened. In the distance, the gentle strum of a guitar and a familiar folk song from one of the neighboring homes drifted through the air, bringing a reminder of his time spent with Lucinda. For a brief period, his life was filled with joy and love. Although he'd missed his real family, Lucinda made a great replacement.

Through the kitchen window, a low-burning lamp sat on the

table. Resting his hand on the doorknob, he took a deep breath and prayed all would go his way. He turned the handle, and the door clicked open. With his heart beating in a fierce rhythm, he stepped inside. A cinnamon scent wafted through the air and shook his memory. He grinned. She had made his favorite sticky buns.

"Lucinda? Are you there?" he asked in a low voice.

The rustle of material came from the far corner of the darkened hallway, and he sucked in his breath. From the shadows came a figure of a round, short woman, waddling closer.

"Lucinda? Is that you?"

"Stand by the light," the familiar voice commanded.

Nash smiled and walked to the table to stand next to the lamp.

From the quiet room came her gasp. Through the semidarkness he saw her hand fly to her throat. *"Nash."*

Tears of joy filled his eyes. "Lucinda? Please do not deny my presence. I need you now."

The older woman took another step closer, still not quite into the light. Her hands twisted against her middle as she shook her head. "It is very dangerous, my boy. Men want to kill you, and they will kill me if I say I know you."

"It is my uncle. I believe he is trying to take over the Wentworth title, and he killed my brother for it. He is now hunting me. If he kills me, he will kill my nephew."

"Oh dear." Her hand trembled as she brought it to her throat. "Matthew Burke is a powerful man."

"But he must be stopped. And I am the only man who can stop him."

"Impossible," she mumbled.

"No, Lucinda. All I need is to find my brother's ring in Matthew's possession. That will prove he killed my brother. But I need your help to tell me where I should search."

"Matthew Burke plans on stopping you."

Nash fisted his hands. "I will not allow him that privilege."

She stepped closer, the light barely touching her face. Wrinkles he had never seen before creased the skin around her sad eyes and frown. Pain tugged at his heart.

"I believe you," she whispered.

"Please, help me stop him."

She nodded. "In his bedchamber he has a hidden shelf under the ledge of the hearth. While working for him, I saw him place items in there to hide them."

"I thank you, Lucinda. You may have just saved our lives."

"I shall pray for your safety." She swiped under her moist eyes. "And I shall never forget you."

"I shall cherish our memories as well." He smiled before turning toward the door, but then he stopped and glanced back at her. "Lucinda? What made my uncle come find you this time?"

"I don't know. But he has ways. He sent one of his men to warn me—a slender, young, handsome man that did not appear dangerous when I first talked with him. He was charming when he showed me your miniature and asked questions about your past. I told him I had worked for your uncle and thought of you as my son. He seemed surprised at first, then he became angry. That was when he threatened me."

Confusion swept over Nash, and he shook his head. "There was only one man?"

"Yes."

"Very strange. I thought my uncle sent all of his henchmen to do his dirty deeds. How long ago did this happen?"

"Just the other day."

He nodded. "My uncle knows I'm here looking for him. Nonetheless, I will keep a cautious eye out for a man of this description." He opened the door.

"Nash?"

He looked back at Lucinda.

"Please be careful."

A knot of emotion caught in his throat and made it hard to swallow. "I will."

As he rode back to Nora's place, his mind kept going over what Lucinda had told him. Things just didn't add up. So far, all the men he had run across who worked for his uncle had all been large, powerful, and middle-aged. True, they were all charming, but the physical description Lucinda gave him just didn't fit. Slender? Handsome? And young?

Putting his confusion aside, Nash kicked his heels into the horse's belly, pushing the animal faster. Apparently, his uncle was one step ahead of him. Nash couldn't have that.

As he rounded a hill, a bright orange flaming light appeared above the trees surrounding Nora's home. Smoke hung in the air. His heart dropped, causing his whole body to shake, but he pushed the horse faster. Screams and cries absorbed the air around him as the harlots and the servants rushed from the well to the house, throwing water upon the flames. Most of the fire was out, thank heavens.

He couldn't breathe, and the thick smoke had nothing to do with it.

He jumped off his horse and ran to the nearest harlot. "Nancy? Where is Nora? Where is Maxey?"

She wiped her tear-stained face and pointed toward the tree. Leaning against it was Nora, while the cook tended to her wounds. He rushed to her and knelt by her side. Both eyes were bruised and swollen, and her lip cut and bleeding. The cook wrapped a bandage around her dainty wrist.

"Nora, what happened?"

Maxey's mother cried and shook her head. "I tried to stop them, but they wouldn't believe me."

He knelt beside her and grasped her shoulders. "Where is Maxey?" he demanded in a stronger voice.

"They…took her."

Nausea rose to his throat. "They? Do you mean my uncle's men?"

Nora nodded and cried louder. "They were too strong for me. I couldn't stop them." She lifted her hand and held a folded piece of paper. "This is for you."

With shaky fingers, Nash unfolded the paper and held it up to the light the fire created.

We have Miss Littleton. To get her back, come for her, but bring no one. Bring your ring.

Invisible pain stabbed Nash's chest, bending him over. He clutched the paper to his mouth, holding back the cries straining in his throat. His uncle was using her as bait, and would kill her once Nash was dead.

If Nash handed over the ring, Matthew would kill him and Joshua and take over the title. If Nash didn't give his uncle the ring, Maxey would be tortured.

Rocking back on his heels, Nash reached into his shirt and withdrew the ring hanging on a gold chain around his neck. His chest ached, and he closed his fingers around the jewelry in a tight fist. Curse his uncle for making him choose. Curse his father for not stopping Matthew years ago. And curse Nash's tender emotions for loving Maxey more than life itself.

Wiping the moisture under his eyes, he stood and took a deep breath. Whoever took Maxey couldn't be that far ahead of him.

"I will get her back. I promise." He tenderly touched Nora's arm.

He dashed toward the horse, his heart beating harder with each step. The dark night enveloped him as he rode toward town. Shops had closed. People were nowhere in sight. Matthew had planned this kidnapping perfectly. Nash prayed that his uncle didn't know where he had been tonight, or Lucinda would be next.

As Nash rode, he searched for signs of his uncle's men. His chest twisted from the thought that Maxey's body might be lying somewhere, undiscovered.

He couldn't think this way. His uncle would use her as leverage. And until Nash handed the ring over, Maxey would be safe.

The clouds moved away from the moon, helping him see the road better. Something out of the ordinary captured his attention.

A cloth hung on the limb of a tree, flapping in the breeze. He slowed his steed, snatched the white fabric, and rubbed it between his finger and thumb. It felt like part of a woman's shift. He lifted it to his nose and took in a deep breath. The faint hint of jasmine hung on the cloth.

He smiled. *Maxey.* She must have ripped this off and left it for him as a clue. He would have to remember to tell her she'd thought like a great investigator to help him.

Along the path, she had left other small objects for him to notice. The tie from her bonnet, and closer to the docks, he found her bootlace. The clues were going toward the docks. His uncle had a ship. That must be where they took Maxey.

Nash urged the horse faster. He would find his uncle and personally tear the man's heart out. Matthew had killed too many people, and it was time his power was taken away.

The pink tint on the horizon let him know the sun would make its appearance soon. Nash must sneak on his uncle's ship before that happened. After he had Maxey safe in his arms, then, and only then, would he put a stop to Matthew's tyranny.

Amongst the ships docked, Nash recognized the one that had followed them during their travel to Devonshire. Nash ducked behind a crate. Peering through the slats of wood, he noticed a group of men standing near the gangplank, all dressed in the expensive clothing Matthew insisted his men wear, and all drinking out of their own bottle of whiskey.

Nash gritted his teeth. None had a care in the world. They were all protected by Matthew's powerful hand.

One man clapped another one on the shoulder, and then walked onto the ship. When the second man turned and looked toward town, Nash sucked in a breath. *Please, God, no!* By all that was holy, what was Nash's manservant, Peter, doing with Matthew's men?

Bile rose in Nash's throat, and his heart broke into tiny pieces. Betrayal's ugly claws wrapped around him and squeezed tightly.

Peter was the traitor.

No wonder Nash's uncle was one step behind them the whole time—because Peter knew what Nash was doing.

Fisting his hands, Nash brought them to his pounding head and closed his eyes. How long had his so-called friend been in Matthew's employ? Had Peter been lying to him all this time?

Breathing slowly in through his nose and out his mouth, he tried to calm his anger, but the more he thought about Peter's treachery, the more upset he became. He must use this frustration and let it guide him on the ship. His anger would be his weapon—along with his pistol.

Within minutes, all the men who had gathered by the gangplank walked onto the ship. Nash crept in the shadows until he reached the water then swam toward the ship. Every few strokes, he stopped, looked, and strained to listen for any sign of being discovered. His uncle must know Nash would do all he could to save Maxey. Matthew wasn't the type of man who took chances. But neither was Nash.

This meant he needed to be more cautious.

MAXEY'S HEAD POUNDED so hard it threatened to split her skull apart. *What in the blazes happened?* Since it hurt too much to open her eyes, she tried lifting her hand to her face, but found it useless. Her limbs had become heavy weights.

Through the intense pain throbbing through every inch of her body, she struggled to see. A familiar scent hung in the air and tickled her nose, but she couldn't remember what it could be. Her body rested upon something soft, but for the life of her, she didn't recall her mother's bed being this uncomfortable.

Then her memory cleared, and she remembered being hit over the head. Three men had forced her out of the house of ill repute while two others beat her mother. Before they left, they set fire to Nora's place. In her groggy state, Maxey had still remembered to leave scraps of clothing along the way for Nash to see. She had no doubt he would find her.

The movement of her surroundings rolled like waves, just as it had when she sailed with Nash. Her stomach lurched, and she peeled her eyes open. They were on a ship! How long had they been sailing?

The bright light straining her blurred vision made her squint. She mouthed Nash's name, but her voice croaked. Cotton dryness lodged in her throat, and she swallowed. "Nash?"

A deep, unfamiliar, eerie chuckle came from within the room. She shivered. Blinking, she tried to focus and get her bearings. The light from the lamp fell on the man sitting in front of her a few feet away. He had dark hair like Nash's, but this man's formal attire was far different than his.

He sat as regal as any prince. Ribbons and gold medals were pinned across the dark suit covering his broad chest. His arm rested on the table next to him as he drummed his fingers on the hard wood. Diamonds from his rings glittered in the light.

"Who…" She swallowed again. "Who are you?" She tried to move her hands, but the rope tied around her wrists burned her skin. She tested her feet, and they too were bound. "Why am I tied?"

He chuckled again, and the evil sound grated on her nerves.

"You are very lovely, Miss Littleton. Now I see why Nash is so enamored with you. Not only are you beautiful, but you have a wild spirit most men would love to tame."

She clenched her jaw. This must be Nash's dominant uncle. He even dressed fancier than the King of England, for heaven's sake. "Who are you, and what did you do with Nash?"

He leaned forward, his face coming into view. She sucked in a breath. He did resemble Nash quite a bit. Although Matthew had the same dark, wavy hair, streaks of silver blended with the color around his ears. But he had the same strong jaw, covered by a trimmed goatee that enhanced his powerful appearance.

"Who am I?" he asked. Leaning back, he linked his fingers

across his stomach. "I may be your worst terror if you do not cooperate with me." He narrowed his eyes on her, and chills ran up her spine.

"What do you want?" She tried not to let her voice waver or her body shake. But inside, her nerves rolled quicker than the waves outside the ship.

A low chuckle rumbled through his chest as he shook his head. "For now, I only require your company. Eventually, Nash will come to rescue you, and I will allow it. But in the end, he will give me what I desire most."

If she ever needed investigation skills, it was right now. She had to get out of this, or talk Matthew into letting her go.

She glared. "I take it you don't know your nephew very well. Nash doesn't care about me. He will go about his business now that I am out of the way."

He arched a brow. "Indeed? Then why did he risk his own life to save yours on several occasions?"

"Where have you learned this, may I ask? Because you have been given false information."

"Oh, I think not, my dear. I am well informed in matters of importance."

Inwardly, she cursed. How could she sway him? Obviously, she couldn't. But she couldn't give up, either.

She let out a heavy sigh. "Believe what you will. I just thought to let you know your effort in kidnapping me was a waste."

Chuckling again, he stood and walked closer to her. She withdrew as much as she could against the mattress, but it would not hide her from his touch. Bile rose to her throat.

"Ah, Miss Littleton. The things I do are not a waste of time. And I trust the men in my employ. It might come as a shock to you, but Nash's manservant, Peter, was not whom he appeared to be."

She gasped, her chest clenching. Immediately, she ached for Nash. When he discovered this, he would be livid.

"That is correct, my dear. This is how I know Nash's feelings. I suppose I should also let you know that Carolyn's maid, Sally, was also on my payroll."

"You lie!" Maxey snapped. "Why are you saying such things?"

"You have no idea how many people I can sway with jewels or money. Sally didn't want to be a maid any longer, so I helped her start a new life."

Tears of betrayal burned in Maxey's eyes. "Sally would never do that. She was devoted to Lady Wentworth."

Matthew shrugged. "Perhaps at first, but she changed her mind quickly when I gave her money."

"Forgive me if I don't believe a word you say."

Shaking his head, he moved slowly around the bed. "Think back to whose idea it was to go to the soirée that evening when you first met Nash. Was it not the maid who mentioned she had talked with someone who thought Ignatius Burke was the opera singer?"

Through her pounding head, Maxey recalled the conversation she'd had with the maid. Her throat tightened and she wanted to scream with frustration. How could Sally have done that?

"If Sally was on your payroll, then why did Peter add a sleeping draught to her drink?"

Matthew laughed. "Because Nash instructed him to do that, and Peter follows directions well."

She wanted to cry, but refused. Sally didn't deserve Maxey's sorrow. "Regardless, you shall just have to get accustomed to the idea that Nash is long gone. He left me asleep at my mother's house. He never wanted me to follow him anyway."

Matthew gave her an evil grin as he touched her leg. "Even if my nephew doesn't come for you, I will make use out of you one way or another." His focus slid down her neck to her bosom.

"Over my dead body." She jerked away from him and glared, her heart still breaking from the startling news about two people she'd thought she could trust.

"No, my dear woman. I will kill you after I tire of you. For now, I will enjoy your company and the attributes you were blessed with. I enjoy toying with women before I please them."

She lifted her chin. "I'm quite certain you will be a great disappointment."

He narrowed his eyes and balled his hand into a fist. He raised it to hit her, and she cringed, but he didn't follow through with the threat.

"I *will* get that ring one way or another. Before the month is over, I will be rightful heir to Wentworth Manor. Mark my words, Miss Littleton."

He stormed out of the room, slamming the door behind him. She allowed her tears to break free and run down her face. Sobbing, she turned and buried her head in the dirty mattress. Silently, she prayed Nash would come for her, but as each minute turned into hours, her hope deflated.

Lying on her back, she stared at the shadowed ceiling as the waves slapped against the side of the ship. Her heart still ached from Sally and Peter's deceit, and for the pain Nash would experience when he discovered the horrid news.

Soft footsteps stopped at the door. The knob turned and the door cracked open. A head peeked in, and then out quickly. Seconds later, the head returned, followed by a man's body. Excitement leapt inside her. Even in the shadows, she could see it was Nash.

"Nash," she cried out as she struggled to sit up.

After closing the door, he rushed to her and took her in his arms.

"I can't believe…you are actually here," she said, sobbing.

"Shh, my love," he whispered. "I do not know how or why, but thankfully, nobody has seen me." He fumbled with the ropes at her wrists.

"Nash, your uncle is expecting you. He might even know you're here."

"Then we must leave quickly."

When the ropes came free, she wrapped her arms around his

neck and kissed him. "Thank you for coming."

He smiled. "I love you, Maxey. My life will not be complete unless you are in it."

The tears she'd thought were gone returned. She nodded, too choked up to say anything.

He released her to untie her feet, and then he pulled her off the bed. "We must hurry. I know you do not like the water, but that is our only way of escaping. We will have to swim to shore."

She sniffed. "I shall do it because you're with me."

He pulled the door open slowly, then poked his head out just as he'd done before he entered. He looked back at her and nodded. "I think we can go."

Taking careful steps, she followed Nash, keeping her hand in his. They made it a few feet before loud footsteps pounded on the floor, growing louder by the second. Nash mumbled something, then pulled her back into the storage room, closing the door softly.

"What are we going to do?" she asked.

He glanced around the room before cupping her face in his large hands. "My love, we must stay here a bit longer. Go lie on the bed and pretend to be tied up. I will hide behind one of the barrels."

The footsteps grew louder, and her heart hammered in a faster rhythm. She nodded and hurried to the bed, gathering the ropes to hide them before curling in the same position Matthew had left her.

Nash blew her a kiss before he ducked behind a barrel. She breathed slower, trying to steady herself. She couldn't let their unknown visitor know something was amiss—unless Matthew already knew Nash was here.

CHAPTER TWENTY

NASH KEPT HIMSELF still as he peeked between two barrels. Panic filled him, and he tried to regulate his fast breathing.

His fearsome uncle entered, his large frame filling the doorway. Matthew's eyes moved from Maxey and slowly scanned the room. Nash held his breath, silently praying his uncle would not see him.

When Matthew shut the door and walked toward Maxey, Nash curled his fingers around the butt of his pistol. If Matthew laid one finger on her, Nash wouldn't hesitate to shoot.

"My pretty Miss Littleton," Matthew said as he neared her bed. "I must admit, I'm very disappointed in your lover. For reasons I cannot explain, he has not come to rescue you, and so you must sail with us to an island I own, and we shall wait for him there."

Maxey lifted her chin in defiance. "Didn't I tell you he wouldn't come?"

Matthew chuckled and folded his arms across his middle. "Oh, my nephew will come, but we must sail as soon as possible, and so cannot wait for him to arrive."

She shook her head. "It's a wasted effort, I tell you. His freedom means more to him than I do."

Nash's chest clenched. He hoped Maxey didn't mean that.

Matthew pulled the chair away from the small table, closer to her bed, and sat. Leaning forward, he linked his fingers across his knees. "I would have thought that as well, but Peter has been telling me very interesting facts about the nephew I never really knew. It surprises me that he has a weakness for a certain little governess."

"I still don't understand why you can't accept your fate. The Wentworth title does not belong to you. It never did. Besides, don't you have more power and money now than if you were titled?"

He shook his head. "Indeed, you don't understand at all. You see, the Wentworth estate has secrets even Nash doesn't know about."

Nash narrowed his eyes and strained to hear his uncle's every word. Secrets? Very interesting.

Maxey tilted her head. "And what might those secrets be?"

Matthew's smile widened. "In the mid-fifteen hundreds, a ship wrecked near Whitehaven. The ship carried a treasure that was buried somewhere on the land. Many years later, gold pieces were found on the shoreline, which led people to believe the rest of the gold may be nearby. But nobody has been able to find the treasure."

"And what does this have to do with the title or the rings?"

He laughed. "The rings were part of the treasure. My father's father searched for a treasure map, and before my grandfather died, he hinted that the two rings might be the key to finding the treasure."

Maxey rolled her eyes. "I have heard this fable as well. It was told to me as a child, but even as young as I was, I still knew it to be false. I cannot believe a grown man like yourself would be a treasure seeker."

Matthew's expression turned stern. "My grandfather was not a foolish man, and neither am I. I want those two rings to find where the map was hidden."

Inwardly, Nash groaned. His uncle had indeed lost his mind. Nash's father and even William knew the story of the treasure was made up to stir excitement. Nash couldn't believe his foolish uncle would kill for this.

Maxey chuckled as she squirmed on the bed, keeping her hands behind her back and feet underneath her. With any luck, Matthew wouldn't notice she was untied.

"Mr. Burke, you are very humorous. There's no way that ring hints to a map's location. I have seen the ring, and there's no place for a map."

Matthew arched an eyebrow. "Have you inspected it closely with a jeweler's glass? I assure you, the map is there. Do you think I would go through all this for nothing?"

Nash had to admit, his uncle wouldn't do all of this without a reason. Perhaps Matthew knew something he didn't. Then again, his uncle had always been a little demented in the head.

"Are we sailing toward Whitehaven?" she asked.

"Yes. I gave my crew the orders before coming to see you."

"And now we wait?"

Matthew laughed. "We wait, but we shall entertain ourselves during this time." He scooted closer to Maxey. "And you can be assured, I *will* pleasure you beyond your imagination."

Maxey fell back into the mattress, her eyes wide with fright. When Matthew took a lock of her hair, she whimpered. Anger consumed Nash, and he tightened his hand around the pistol. *God be with me.*

Swift and sure of his movements, Nash darted around the barrels without making any noise. Maxey's sobs rose higher, which ignited his temper. Matthew had his back to him, and Nash raised the butt of the gun as he neared, focusing on his uncle's dark head.

Matthew's large hands cupped Maxey's head. "You, my dearest, will be mine. I will remove Nash from your memory."

She glanced over his uncle's shoulder and met Nash's gaze. Suddenly, her expression hardened, and she yanked her arms from behind her and pushed them against Matthew's chest. He gave a sharp inhale mere seconds before Nash brought the pistol down against his skull.

Matthew jerked around and toward Nash. Confusion and pain marked his expression as he stood and stumbled toward his nephew. Matthew blinked then steadied himself. He touched the blood oozing down the back of his head and looked at his stained fingers. He snickered.

Maxey scrambled off the bed and dashed around Nash, clutching his shirt as she stood behind him. He kept his aim on Matthew, who was still laughing.

"My wayward nephew finally makes an appearance. And to think, I had given up hope of your chivalry."

"If I have to kill you in cold blood, I will," Nash sneered. "I will not let you harm another person as long as I live."

Matthew stumbled a few steps backward before regaining his balance. "Ah, famous last words, Nash. You should know me better than that, dear boy."

Nash glared at him. "I am not the boy you remember, but a man who has vowed to stop you no matter what it takes."

"You underestimate me."

"And you underestimate me." Nash squared his shoulders and stepped closer to his uncle. "I swear on the graves of my father and brother, I will kill you. I will not let people fear you any longer. And I definitely won't let you take control of my family's estate."

"You cannot win." Matthew touched his fingers to his head again as more blood poured from the wound. "I have men out there who I have trained to fill my shoes."

"They are lacking one thing, dear uncle. They are not blood related and will never get those rings."

Matthew's expression hardened, his lips curling in a sneer. "You have crossed paths with the wrong person." Suddenly, he jumped at Nash and knocked the pistol from his hands.

Nash fell to the floor, and his uncle landed on top of him. Strong fingers wrapped around his throat and threatened to choke him. Pain shot through Nash's head from the sudden lack of air. He pulled at his uncle's fingers while kicking his legs. The old man was stronger than he appeared, and for a moment, Nash panicked.

His lungs burned, his head throbbed, but he continued to fight. Using all of his strength, he rolled them both over until he lay on top. Nash slammed a fist into his uncle's face, which broke the hold Matthew had on his throat.

In one swift movement, Matthew reached into his boot and pulled out a knife. The blade swung very close to Nash's neck, and he grabbed the weapon to hold it away.

Maxey screamed and crawled across the floor.

"Maxey…get the pistol," Nash bit out.

She scrambled to her feet, holding the loaded weapon and aiming it at Matthew. "Stop, or I'll shoot!"

Matthew bared his teeth in an evil grin. "Not until I kill you first," he growled at Nash.

Matthew pushed the knife closer to Nash's throat. Nash's hands shook as he struggled to keep the blade from slicing his skin or plunging into his flesh.

Maxey pointed the pistol at Matthew's head. Nash jerked back just as the weapon fired. The wind from the bullet whooshed through the air as it passed near his face and lodged into his uncle's head. Matthew's body jerked then stilled as his hands dropped to his side, knocking over the lamp. Breaking glass echoed in the room. As quick as lightning, fire spread on the floor and up the wall.

Nash swore and jumped to his feet. Maxey stood shaking as she stared at the dead man on the floor.

"I…I cannot believe I killed…" A tear slid from her eye when she finally met Nash's gaze. "He was going to kill you. I couldn't let him do that."

"Oh, my darling." He pulled her trembling body into his arms and kissed her head. "You did the right thing."

The fire was moving fast toward the barrels of gunpowder. He grabbed Maxey's hand. "We must leave. Now!"

He led her out the door and up the hallway. Men shouted on the deck. Nash's breathing quickened. They must not get caught.

Without another thought, he dashed into the nearest room, remembering it had a window. "Maxey, we need to go out that window." He met her wide, frightened eyes. "We will have to jump out the window into the water. I know you fear water, but we must do this. I will not let anything happen to you."

She nodded. "I trust you."

He slammed his elbow into the glass until it shattered. He slipped off his jacket and blanketed the edge of the window.

"You go first. I will be right behind you."

Maxey shook as he lifted her to the window and pushed her through. He crawled up, hefted himself out, and plunged into the water. Maxey had surfaced already, but as soon as he grabbed her hand, he pulled her close.

"Take a deep breath. The gunpowder is going to explode at any moment. We need to be underwater. Do not let go of my hand."

She nodded and sucked in a big gulp of air along with him. He held her tight and took them under the water, diving as deep as he could go. Within seconds, the blast from the ship knocked into them, breaking their hands apart.

Swinging his arms about, he searched for her as his chest burned with the lack of air. When he bumped into her, he grabbed her again and pushed them away from the explosion. He swam to the top, and when they surfaced, each breathed in a lungful of air.

Maxey threw her arms around him and buried her face in his neck. "Oh, Nash. I thought… I thought…"

"I know." He kissed the side of her head. "Nothing will ever tear us apart again."

He maneuvered them in the water to look at the burning ship. A great weight was released from his chest, yet he mourned the loss of everyone who had suffered.

"Do you think they all died?"

"No. I am certain some lived."

He wrapped his arm around her waist and swam back to the shore. As Nash neared the sand, he saw someone struggling to crawl on land, his body burned, his ragged clothes charred from the fire.

Nash's chest clenched. *Peter.*

Keeping Maxey's hand in his, Nash moved to his friend, turning him over on the sand. Weak eyes laced with pain met Nash's stare, and tears filled Peter's eyes.

"I—I did not want to," Peter rasped. "Matthew threatened to kill my family if I didn't."

A tear slipped down Peter's face and tugged at Nash's heart. A knot tightened in his throat as his own eyes misted over. "I understand."

"I am sorry. I did not want to hurt you. I love you like a brother."

Nash gulped back a sob as a tear leaked from his eye. Emotion choked his throat and kept him from saying anything.

"Nash, please forgive me?"

Swallowing hard, Nash nodded and touched his friend's hand. "I forgive you."

The corners of Peter's lips lifted as his eyes drifted shut. His chest stopped moving, and his body lay still.

Maxey sobbed and clung to Nash's arm. He silently cried, mourning his friend's death. He leaned over and kissed his friend's forehead. No more would Peter be in pain.

MAXEY SNUGGLED NEXT to Nash as they sat on the hillside and watched the burning ship sink into the water. Her limbs hurt from everything she had endured, but her heart ached more. Poor Peter. Poor Nash. The Lord may look down on her for this, but happiness burst inside her that Matthew was dead. Peter shouldn't have had to choose between his best friend and his family. Nash shouldn't have had to choose, either.

She studied Nash, whose attention stayed on the ship. A frown marred his handsome face. As she reached up and swiped the wet lock of hair away from his eyes, he met her gaze.

"What are you thinking?"

He managed a small smile. "I'm very relieved this is all over."

"Me too." The image of her mother's beaten face snapped Maxey out of her relief, and she clutched Nash's hands. "My mother. We have to see if she is all right."

"She is." He cupped her face and placed a brief kiss on her lips. "She was being cared for by the cook when I left to find you."

Relief surged through her again, and she smiled. "You are a godsend, Nash."

"I'm happy to know you have forgiven her."

She nodded. "Me too. I will have a mother again. I hope my brother feels the same."

"It will be a shock to him, I'm certain, but if his heart is as loving as yours, he will forgive her too."

She leaned up and kissed his lips.

"So, what are we going to do now?" Nash asked.

She pulled back and cocked her head. "You don't know?"

He shrugged. "I suppose we should return to Whitehaven and let Carolyn know we are all right."

"Yes." Her chest tightened. "I am your witness that you did not kill your brother."

"I know."

"But the question is, what will *you* do once we get there?"

His smile widened. "You don't know?"

"Of course not. Would I have asked otherwise?"

He laughed and cuddled her closer. She slipped her arms around his waist and rested her head on his chest.

"I'm sorry to say, but I don't want you to be my sister-in-law's governess any longer."

She lifted her head enough to see his amazing eyes. "You don't?"

"No. I have a better position for you."

She arched an eyebrow. "Dare I ask what it is?"

"I want you to become my wife."

She relaxed in his arms again. "Ah, marriage." She sighed. "I believe I can accept that position. However, I wonder if *you* can handle that."

He laughed and kissed her forehead. "Keeping up with you will be worth every moment. Waking up next to you each day will make me the happiest man on earth."

Her cheeks hurt from grinning so hard. "Our marriage will certainly be an adventure."

He tilted her face up and brushed his lips across hers. "One I look forward to with every breath I take."

As Maxey kissed him, she was filled with love. Should she tell him how many children she wanted or wait until later? And what about the treasure? Then again, she had already found her heart's treasure.

The End

About the Author

Marie Higgins is a multi-award winning, bestselling author of sweet romance novels, from refined bad-boy heroes who make your heart melt to the feisty heroines who somehow manage to love them regardless of their faults. She has been with a Christian publisher since 2010. Between those and her others, she has published over a hundred heartwarming, on-the-edge-of-your-seat stories and broadened her readership by writing mystery/suspense, humor, time travel, and paranormal, along with her historical romances. Her readers have dubbed her "Queen of Tease" because of all her twists and turns and unexpected endings.

Website – www.authormariehiggins.com
Facebook – facebook.com/marie.higgins.7543
Instagram – instagram.com/author.mariehiggins
Bookbub – bookbub.com/authors/marie-higgins
Twitter – @mariehigginsxox